Tom Benjamin grew up in the suburbs of north London and began his working life as a journalist before becoming a spokesman for Scotland Yard. He later moved into public health, where he developed Britain's first national campaign against alcohol abuse, and led drugs awareness programme FRANK. He now lives in Bologna.

Last Testament in Bologna is the fifth novel in his Daniel Leicester crime series.

Find Tom on Instagram, Twitter and Facebook @tombenjaminsays

T0271645

Also by Tom Benjamin

A Quiet Death in Italy
The Hunting Season
Requiem in La Rossa
Italian Rules

Last Testament in Bologna

Tom Benjamin

CONSTABLE

CONSTABLE

First published in Great Britain in 2023 by Constable

A CIP catalogue record for this book
is available from the British Library.

ISBN: 978-1-40871-555-0

Typeset in Garamond by Initial Typesetting Services, Edinburgh
Printed and bound in Great Britain by Clays Ltd, Elcograf S.p.A.

Papers used by Constable are from well-managed forests
and other responsible sources.

Constable
An imprint of
Little, Brown Book Group
Carmelite House
50 Victoria Embankment
London EC4Y 0DZ

An Hachette UK Company
www.hachette.co.uk

www.littlebrown.co.uk

To my mother

. . . e nonna nonna nonna nunnarella
'O lupo s'ha magnata'a pecurella!
. . . e pecurella mia comme faciste
Quanne mmocc'a lu lupo te vediste?
. . . e pecurella mia comme farraie
Quanne mmocc'a lu lupo te vedarraie?

. . . and nanny nanny nunnarella
The wolf has eaten my sheep!
. . . and my little sheep what did you do
When you found yourself in the mouth of the wolf?
. . . and my little sheep what will you do
When you find yourself in the mouth of the wolf?

Neapolitan lullaby (traditional)

Chapter 1

Once they had realised why we were there, the brother and sister looked dismayed, and who could blame them? A stranger is about as welcome at the reading of a will as a former spouse at a wedding, perhaps less so – there is money involved.

The Comandante and I had received the call from the notary herself, but she could not provide us with any further details, 'according to the law'. Only that the deceased – Giorgio Chiesa – had requested our firm's presence as an 'interested party' at the reading at her office in Osteria Grande, which was on the Via Emilia between Bologna and Imola. We had checked our database, along with the memory of the Comandante, which often proved more reliable than the company's pre-digital files, but Chiesa did not appear to have been a client of Faidate Investigations.

'Maybe you once did him a favour and he never forgot,' I said. 'You'll get a nice cheque, or inherit some property.'

The Comandante gave me a pitying look.

'Favours are easily forgotten,' he said. 'It is grudges that persevere.'

Osteria Grande – the town's name always made me smile.

Literally, Big Pub, albeit that 'osteria' had long-since become synonymous with restaurant in Italy, at least at the reasonable end of the spectrum.

There were no large restaurants in Osteria Grande, let alone pubs, but there was a half-decent, medium-sized place along the main road where we lunched before walking the thirty or so metres to the notary's office in a low-rise, salmon-coloured block.

Across the road, a field of wheat was stirred by the cleansing April breeze, while the few puffy clouds above moved hurriedly along as if they were expected elsewhere – England, perhaps. We were deep in the *Pianura Padana* – the granary of Italy – and the town had spent much of its history as a farming hamlet before expanding in the late twentieth century to accommodate overspill from Bologna. This may have explained the venue for the reading – houses were cheaper the further out you moved and so, presumably, were notaries.

Because of the Comandante's hip (he was due for a partial replacement soon), we took the small lift up a single storey to the notary's office. She answered the door herself. Her assistant could have been away, more likely she didn't have one. The notary was a small, bone-thin woman in her mid-thirties whose lime-green framed glasses lent some levity to an otherwise dissatisfied mien, as if she had once come across a particularly egregious clause in a conveyancing contract and never quite gotten over it.

The family had yet to arrive, she explained, and asked us to wait in the hallway.

Despite the modern building with its low, fluorescent-lit panelled ceiling, tinted windows and cream marble floors, the buzz of the cars and lorries whizzing along Via Emilia, the notary's entrance was as sombre as any venerable Bologna *palazzo*. Heavy, dark wood benches were set on both sides, while yellowed certificates and age-dimmed paintings lined the walls. An ancient grandfather clock ticked imperiously away. Behind the *notaio*'s closed 'studio' door, she might have been labouring beneath the scowls of frescoed deities.

The front door buzzed. The clack of the notary's heels as she emerged from her sanctum and passed without acknowledging us. She opened the door and greeted the couple in low tones before ushering them through to her office. The man appeared to be in his thirties, the woman perhaps a decade older. It was clear they were siblings, albeit the man was puffy faced and unshaven in a dark blue V-necked tunic and matching, loose-fitting cotton trousers beneath a dark grey Ferrari-embossed fleece, while the woman was smartly dressed in a black suit with a white blouse. But they shared the stocky build of provincial Bolognese and a familial aquiline nose. The pair nodded cordially at us before the notary closed the door behind them. I exchanged a glance with the Comandante – I doubted they had as yet been told we would be joining them.

It didn't take long – neither the thin walls or the rumble of trucks managed to muffle the booming lamentations of the man. It took his sister to finally shut him up with a shrill: '*Basta*, Francesco' before we heard those heels again and the door swung open.

It was our turn to nod a greeting. The brother, Francesco, looked stonily ahead, his thick, hairy fists clamped atop the dark oak table. Veins bulged from his smooth skull. He might have seemed threatening if his flushed, over-fed face hadn't given the impression he was on the verge of a stroke, while his sister sat beside him as white as a sheet. She crossed her arms and met my smile with an expression of unabashed anxiety.

Taking her chair at the head of the table, the notary opened the maroon folder. I was vaguely surprised to see it contained just two pages of double-spaced, typed text. I had never attended the reading of a will before – my late wife had not left one, and the subsequent legalities had been handled by her father, the Comandante, as neither my then linguistic or emotional state was up to it – but I had yet to see any official Italian document that could be described as brief or to the point, and certainly no public functionary who would miss an opportunity to cite lengthy legal statutes at even the most joyous occasion. I leaned a little to the side to check if the notary had perhaps a further, bulky file set on the floor beside her.

Apparently not.

She peered at the date. 'Yes,' she said as if in response to a question we had not been privy to. 'This was filed just over four years ago.' She pulled herself up straight and cleared her throat. 'Before myself, Dottoressa Chiara Mignotti, Notary of Osteria Grande, and in the presence of witnesses: Giovanni Buonpresenza . . .'

'Buonpresenza!' said the brother. '*That piece of shit*, I'll—'

'*Francesco.*'

The notary read on: 'Date of birth, third of September, 1947, resident in Bologna, Via Regnoli 17, and Vladimir . . .'

'Of course, of course,' Francesco muttered.

'Bonnacini, date of birth seventh of March, 1952, resident in Via delle Pecore 38, Dozza, and in the presence of Giorgio

Chiesa, date of birth, nineteenth of September, 1942, resident at Via Paolo Fabbri 4B.

'The said signor, Giorgio Chiesa, whose identity has been confirmed by the notary, wishes upon the cessation of his life to have his testimony made public in the presence of his surviving children, and Comandante Giovanni Faidate and/or a representative of Faidate Investigations.' She acknowledged me.

'Signor Chiesa states: "The law requires me to leave two thirds of my estate, which consists of my house in Via Fabbri, to my surviving children, so I express my formal wish to do so in my testament to avoid any additional expenses, along with whatever meagre balance is contained in my bank account, and do so with pleasure – I am only sorry I cannot leave you the substantial inheritance you so richly deserve. I also leave you any heirlooms or furniture contained therein, to be divided between yourselves as you see fit.

'However, I pray you will also understand why I want to commit the discretionary third of my estate that, in truth, I would have left to be divided between yourselves and your late brother, to Comandante Faidate, or his successors in the firm Faidate Investigations. Comandante – you don't know me, but I know your reputation as an honest man. I therefore bequest the legacy that I legally control to you or your heirs in trust – I trust you to find whoever was responsible for the death of my youngest,' Francesco hissed like a fast-puncturing tyre, 'son, Fabrizio, drawing upon the equity as you see fit. Once you have fulfilled this commission to your satisfaction, I respectfully request that you reimburse the outstanding balance to my surviving children."'

'Signed, Giorgio Chiesa.'

'I finally understand,' Francesco said to his sister. 'I wondered why he'd shut up about it.'

His sister shook her head. 'He never "shut up" about it, Fran. He just knew better than to mention it in your presence on the few occasions you could be bothered to visit.'

Francesco looked at the Comandante. 'Did you know about this?'

'As your father stated, Signor Chiesa, we were not acquainted. This comes as much as a surprise to us as it does to you.'

'You're private eyes, the signora says.' His phone, which was set upon the table, began to buzz. 'Excuse me.' He picked it up. 'That's right,' he said. 'Run her through the pre-op. The bloodwork was fine, but there's a family history of malignant hyperthermia, and the anaesthetist has recommended a low dose of Propofol. Okay. Yes, that should be fine.' He put the phone down, transformed in those blue coveralls from seemingly a manual worker, to some kind of surgeon. 'There's nothing in there that actually *obliges* you to take the job,' he continued. 'And who are you, anyway? Dad had clearly heard of you, but I'm afraid your fame has passed me by.'

I looked at the Comandante with curiosity. In all our years together, I had never witnessed him introduce himself further than a curt: *Faidate*.

Giovanni gave the son a fatherly – or perhaps, grandfatherly – smile.

'Comandante Faidate,' cut in the notary, 'was head of the Carabinieri's Special Operations Directorate in Bologna, *dottore*. His agency is the most respected in the city, if not the state.'

The doctor's mouth drew appraisingly downwards. 'In any case,' he said, 'the best connected, no doubt.' He sat back, the status of a former chief of police apparently qualifying Giovanni Faidate for his attention.

The Comandante turned to the notary.

'*Dottoressa*, did Signor Chiesa furnish any further information about the death of Fabrizio?'

'I'm afraid not, Comandante.'

That equanimous smile again. 'Signori?'

'Fabri died in an accident seven years ago,' said Dr Francesco Chiesa. 'Dad never accepted it. The old man was convinced he had been murdered.'

'Was it investigated by the authorities?'

'Of course! They confirmed it was just a terrible accident, but he wouldn't let it go.'

'And the accident itself?'

He looked at us if it was obvious. 'Car crash.'

'Was anyone travelling in the car with him?'

He shook his head. 'He was alone in the hills . . .' He paused as his sister reached around the chair for her handbag. She pulled out a pack of tissues and blew her nose.

'He had popped in to see me,' she said. 'He was going home.' The brother placed a comforting arm around her shoulders.

'But that's not half of it,' he said. 'Not three quarters. *Four fifths.*' He delved into the top of his tunic for an unselfconscious, grizzly-like scratch. 'Look – our youngest brother, the apple of our father's eye, was a racing driver. And not just any boy racer – a test driver for Molinari. He was being groomed for their F1 squad.

'Our Fabri . . .' His voice grew gruff. 'Well, the boy was a wizard behind the wheel. Dad couldn't accept he'd just driven off a cliff.'

A silence settled around the table. We might have been standing around the drop, looking respectfully down.

I asked finally: 'And who did he suspect, your father?' Francesco frowned.

'You're not Italian,' he said.

'English.' He shrugged, apparently unsurprised.

'Molinari. Of course.'

'The company?'

He slapped the table. 'The man! Fucking Massimiliano Molinari! The owner!'

The sister squeezed his hand and he withdrew like a stung bear. 'Daddy blamed him for everything,' she said. 'Ever since he stole his fuel injection system – back when we were kids.'

'Or so he claimed,' mumbled Francesco. 'We were raised on it like our mother's milk, but he couldn't prove a thing.'

'He took him to court,' said the sister. 'Our childhood was dominated by cases. But it was just him against the might of Molinari Automobili SpA.'

The brother looked unconvinced. 'In any case, Dad never got over it – from then on, everything was Molinari's fault. If a bolt of lightning had struck the Holy Father himself, you could guarantee that bastard Massimiliano Molinari would have had something to do with it.'

'And yet,' I said. 'His son went to work for him, or at least the company.'

Francesco smiled. 'He did indeed, indeed he did, Englishman. Darling Fabrizio, Dad's favourite, inculcated even more than the rest of us on the myth, ended up working for Dad's nemesis – who took him on, incidentally, despite my father basically having *stalked* him for a quarter of a century.

'So you see, signori, you're on a fool's errand – Giorgio Chiesa has managed to sustain his ruinous obsession beyond the grave, while our poor brother continues to have his rest disturbed.'

'Thank you, *dottore*,' said the Comandante. 'This is all most helpful.' He turned to the notary. 'However, in the circumstances, I do feel obliged to follow Signor Chiesa's instructions.'

'We will look into the matter as requested,' he turned back to the siblings, 'with the hope of remitting as much of the legacy to your family as possible.'

Francesco raised his hands in mock surrender. 'For myself,' said the brother. 'I couldn't care less about a house in Cirenaica.' He turned to his sister. 'Although I guess you could do with the cash?'

'It was what Dad wanted,' she said glumly. 'We should respect that.'

Francesco turned to us. 'By all means, *Comandante*. Give *Ingegnere* Chiesa the respect he's due. But let's not exaggerate, eh?'

There were some further details to go through with the family, so the notary excused us. We walked back to the Comandante's old but still immaculate black Lancia limo in the restaurant car park. I was about to set the navigator to home when Giovanni said: 'Dozza, if you please, Daniel, Via delle Pecore, 38.'

'Oh?'

'The address of Vladimir Bonnacini,' he said. 'One of Signor Chiesa's witnesses, who *was* a client of mine, in a manner of speaking.'

'A manner of speaking?'

'Yes,' said the Comandante. 'I arrested him.'

Chapter 2

They call Dozza 'the City of Art', and it is pretty enough, a walled town (it's certainly no city) crowning a hill a little further along the Via Emilia, famous for the paintings that line its walls. It's the sort of place you go for Sunday lunch when you fancy a change from Bologna and a short drive. Having said that, as we pulled into the visitor's car park on the fringe of the town, I realised I hadn't been here since Lucia had been alive and we had got up to those kind of family things, inevitably with my father-in-law in tow. Back then, in the absence of her friends, he had cheerfully filled the role of my daughter Rose's chief playmate.

'I can go alone,' I said, eyeing the cobbled slope running up through the blue painted gatehouse.

'I will grit my teeth,' said the Comandante, opening the car door. I walked around to help him out.

'You know, you probably shouldn't aggravate it.' I avoided mentioning the surgery, which I suspected he was dreading.

'Better still, don't aggravate me.' He linked his arm in mine and, leaning surprisingly heavily against me, we made slow but steady progress up the slope.

It was a quiet Tuesday afternoon and Dozza was dozing. There were more cats in the street than people. It really was a pleasant place – venerable buildings clustered around a typical fifteenth-century *rocca*, or fortress, which remained largely intact. Had we been in Tuscany, it might have been thick with tourists and trinket stores, but it was far enough away from Bologna, which fell outside the main tourist circuit, to still have a pulse. Sure, there were a few wine shops (closed) but also the kind people needed to survive – a butcher, iron-monger, Co-op supermarket. When the burghers of Dozza began inviting artists to decorate their walls in the 1960s, it had been to beautify their living space rather than cash in, and out.

The auto repair shop was down a side street, beneath a wide, red brick archway which might once have been the entrance to a tannery or some other large-scale medieval enterprise. The presence of a garage in the heart of the walled city did seem rather anomalous, given that non-residents were banned from entering in their cars, but I didn't let that trouble me – I had been in Italy long enough to know it rhymed, most of all, with anomaly.

The big old wooden doors into the courtyard were open, but a gate with prison-like bars blocked further progress. Above, I noted a CCTV camera and winking alarm box. For good measure, there was also a Beware of the Dog sign. I looked hopefully through the bars – I liked dogs.

The courtyard reminded me of our own – hadn't the Faidate Residence once been its own hive of medieval activity? – but *Carrozzeria* Bonnacini was on an altogether larger and shabbier scale. While *La Residenza* had become precisely that – somewhere to reside – this place still had dirt beneath its fingernails.

The whiff of rubber and metallic paint. A pair of mechanics dressed in black shorts and T-shirts bent under a car on a ramp. The shapes of three more automobiles beneath black covers sheltered by a corrugated iron awning. A radio set to *Nettuno Bologna Uno* – some kind of interminable football chat.

'His daughter,' said the Comandante. A stringy blonde in her forties emerged from the office carrying a clipboard. She lolloped towards us in excessively high heels.

'Can I help?'

'Faidate, dear, for your father.' She blinked, then took a pair of unsteady steps back.

'I'm sorry?'

'Faidate,' he repeated. 'He might know me as "the Comandante".'

'Then it *is* you.' She pressed her clipboard to her chest. 'He's not done anything wrong.'

'It has nothing to do with the law. It concerns another matter. He is probably expecting me.'

She stood staring at him. '*You*. You stole ten years of my life.'

'Your father will be expecting me,' he repeated gently but firmly.

'You . . .' Still clasping the clipboard to her chest, she swivelled around and wobbled back to the office.

'It was six, actually,' said the Comandante. 'He was convicted for eight but released after six, although I suppose to a child it must have seemed like . . . a childhood. He was

almost certainly involved in a couple of jobs after he got out
– which is where I suppose this place comes from – but I
couldn't pin anything on him.' The Comandante stroked his
neatly clipped beard as if still contemplating those missing
leads. 'Ah, here he is.' A man came towards us, stick thin
like the woman, with a grey, closely cropped widow's peak so
severe it might have spelt V for Vladimir.

'What was he?' I asked.

'Getaway driver.'

Vladimir Bonnacini, in black cargo shorts and a T-shirt
like his mechanics, stood as his daughter had, two steps back
from the bars.

'Comandante,' he said. 'Not the first time we've met like
this.'

'But this time you have the key, Speedy.'

'Or at least, the magic button.' He raised his hand and
pressed a fob. There was a mechanical whir as the bolts withdrew and the gates opened inwards.

'An impressive set-up,' said the Comandante.

'Speedy' grinned with teeth as yellow as his nicotine-
stained fingers. 'We're both independent businessmen now,
Comandante. Like you, I'm putting my know-how to good
use.'

'If I'm not mistaken, isn't that a Fiat 124 on the ramp?'

'Bravo, Comandante! You're not mistaken – a 124 Special,
1970.'

'I had one myself, a wonderful vehicle.'

'Franco,' Speedy called to one of the mechanics. 'Come
here *un attimo*.' Wiping his hands on his T-shirt, the younger
of the two men approached. 'This is an old friend of mine.'

The mechanic nodded respectfully. Speedy chuckled. 'Oh yes, me and Comandante Faidate of *Comando Speciale dei Carabinieri* go way back.' He relished the look on the young man's face. 'Don't worry, he's in the private sector now. Let's show the Comandante what we're hiding.'

We followed the two men to the awning. Together, they drew back the cover of the first car. It was a sleek, bronze two-seater Alfa Romeo sports car with a detachable tan roof. It was unarguably a thing of beauty.

'Spider Junior,' sniffed Speedy. '1981. One-point-six litre.' He ran his hand lovingly along the curved ridge that ended with the missile-like headlights. 'Pininfarina did the coach-work. We're polishing the heads.' He moved onto the next one.

They pulled back the covers to reveal some kind of silver sports car, not so different to the Alfa, only with a solid, bulbous roof and softer lines.

'My goodness,' said the Comandante. 'A Zagato.'

'Bravo, Comandante. Is there anything else you can tell us?'

'A partnership between Abarth and Fiat in . . . fifty-seven? Fifty-eight?'

'Fifty-six, although you're right, it was re-launched in Paris in fifty-eight.'

'Single cam,' continued the Comandante. 'Nicknamed "the double bubble" because of its distinctive, supposedly aerodynamic roof.'

'That memory of yours, Comandante. Nothing wrong with the noggin, eh? A collector down Riccione way – likes to check it's running, even though he never runs it.'

'And finally, we have this.' With some difficulty, Speedy and the mechanic rolled back the cover from the wide, low-slung vehicle.

Its brooding dark green came close to black, and seemed to ripple beneath the shadow of the awning, its rear spoiler aloft, like a whale fin before it disappeared beneath the waves or, if you were on the *autostrada*, along the fast lane.

'Molinari Tenebre,' said the Comandante.

'1991. Six litre, V8, 485 horsepower. Zero to hundred in four point two seconds.'

'The first Molinari to break the two hundred miles per hour mark,' the Comandante said to me. 'For the American market.'

'The Comandante here knows a bit about cars,' said Speedy. 'Had his unit set up a fake dealership to nab a gang going up and down the A14 knocking off showrooms.'

'Oh?'

'They would hit at night, break in through the roof, get the cars going, then use a truck to smash through the glass, or at least I heard it was something like that, right, Comandante?'

'Yes,' Giovanni said tartly. 'Something like that.'

'They'd speed off down the *autostrada*. The Comandante's idea was to lure the crooks – mousetrap tactics. They called in a few favours, borrowed a lovely spread of local brands on the quiet – Maserati, Molinari, Lamborghini. Put in a state-of-the-art surveillance system and deactivated the cars so they couldn't be started.

'They didn't have a full squad on the premises of course, we're talking a stake-out of months, so they just had a couple of blokes stationed there overnight.

'Apparently, one of the thieves slipped in during the day, removed the ceiling panels in the bathroom, and waited for the showroom to close. When the time came, he dropped down, crept into the back office and held the officers up. Then they switched off the alarm and got the cars.'

'Didn't you say they were deactivated?' said the mechanic.

'They'd disconnected the ignition fuse, CKP, removed the sparkplugs. Still, easily replaced – those cunning thieves simply wheeled the buggers out, and into the back of a lorry.'

'And this,' I said, 'is how you ended up behind bars?'

'Oh, no,' said Speedy. 'I didn't have anything to do with *that*. First thing I knew was what the Comandante here shared with me when he called me in for a chat.'

'You mean, arrested you.'

A jaundiced grin. 'You never did manage to track those cars down, did you, Comandante?'

'Sadly, no.' The Comandante contemplated the skulking Molinari.

'Of course, it's all water under the bridge now,' said Speedy.

'The haul included a 1991 Tenebre,' said the Comandante, 'although it was red.'

Speedy shook his head. 'Only two registered owners for this one – Count Isolani, who handed it down to his son. I've got all the documentation, naturally.'

'Naturally.'

'No, if I was you, I'd try looking further afield – the desert, perhaps. I hear those Arabs love racing them. They're probably in some Gulf prince's lock-up, in my opinion. *Just* an opinion, mind you.'

'And now even the Italian aristocracy trust you with their

automobiles, Speedy,' the Comandante observed. 'Quite the turnaround.'

'I'll take them up to 2000, but after that, honestly, I wouldn't know where to begin, and wouldn't want to, what with all these computers, electricity . . .'

'He means electrification,' said the mechanic.

'The magic's lost.'

'Like the difference between a battery-powered and mechanical watch,' I said.

'Is it?' Speedy himself was wearing a cheap G-Shock. 'If you say so, young man.'

'My son-in-law,' said the Comandante. 'Daniel.'

'Daniel,' he said solemnly. Of course – he knew about the Comandante's late daughter. The story would have long circulated in the world we inhabited as a kind of coda to Giovanni Faidate's legend. And as if it had reminded Speedy why we were here, he added: 'So, poor Chiesa kicked the bucket.'

The Comandante nodded.

'Come.'

I have yet to see a grease monkey's office that isn't a mess, and *Carrozzeria* Bonnacini was no different. Stacks of folders were piled atop grey carpet tiles filthy with the grime walked through by mechanics. More files were stacked on the two desks, at the furthest of which, Speedy's daughter eyed us insolently through cigarette smoke. The walls were plastered with pages torn out of newspapers or magazines featuring classic cars, along with photos of Speedy beside similar models at shows, stood with elderly sports-car owners who were looking exceedingly pleased with themselves, and with a smattering of Bologna celebrities like singer Gianni Morandi and Bologna FC manager Siniša Mihajlović.

A brown-and-white speckled greyhound bitch looked dolefully up at us from a stretcher-bed set beside what I supposed constituted the reception area – a battered leather sofa and some rickety office chairs. A few tatty car magazines and copies of the *Carlino* were scattered on a coffee table. I took my seat and reached down to give the dog's head a scratch. She closed her eyes appreciatively.

'She's very old,' I said.

'Like everything else here, eh, Comandante?' replied Speedy. Seventy-eight-year old Giovanni Faidate shrugged – like many elderly Italian men, he plainly considered himself still in his prime. 'Then there was one,' added Speedy. 'I heard the other witness, Buonpresenza, kicked the bucket last year . . . That's him.' Speedy got up and plucked a photo from the wall. 'Chiesa, I mean.'

There were three of them around the table. I recognised the trattoria – Da Vito in Cirenaica – raising glasses in a toast.

Giorgio Chiesa was in his mid-sixties. Not looking as miserable as I somehow expected after everything we had heard. Nor did he carry the heft of his offspring, but he had bequeathed them that beaky nose, which elongated his face as if, like a sports car, it had been moulded for aerodynamics. He was wearing the tentative smile of someone taken by surprise.

'Do you mind?' I took a photo with my phone.

'The meal was on me because I owed Giorgio for helping with a Berliner coupé,' said Speedy. 'He wouldn't accept payment, never would, but no one knew Molinari like him.'

'So we've heard,' said the Comandante.

'Oh, Molinari stole his design, don't doubt it. They had an agreement, shook hands, there were witnesses! And the *Cavaliere* might have stuck to his word if it had just been a one off – given the *scuderia* that extra oomf on the track, even used the design in the production models, but the trouble came when its wider applications became apparent – when they patented a slightly modified version which went on to become the industry standard, and it only had one name on it – Massimiliano Molinari!

'Almost every high-performance car – Italian, German, Japanese . . .' his grey eyebrows steepled upwards, 'British – uses a variation or adaption of the Molinari to this day.'

He nodded at his daughter. She flung a pack of cigarettes in his direction. He plucked it out of the air.

'You still have the reflexes, Speedy,' said the Comandante.

'Reflexes were never my problem, Comandante.' He offered the open packet to us. The Comandante took one. 'Daniel doesn't look like he approves.'

'He thinks he's my nurse.'

'He's got an operation in a couple of weeks,' I said. 'On his hip. I'm in no hurry to become *his* heir.'

Speedy chuckled. 'I'm sure if the Comandante thinks you're up to it. And an English detective – well, aren't they the best?'

'They're not all Sherlock Holmes,' said the Comandante.

'Thanks,' I said. 'Well, we can't all be Montalbano.'

'Or Inspector Coliandro,' said Speedy. 'I like that series. Reminds me of the old days, cops and robbers.'

'But I think I do all right.'

'He's a fast learner,' the Comandante admitted. 'So, Molinari allegedly stole this design from *Ingegnere* Chiesa, who strikes me as a rather trusting individual . . .'

'A simple soul, an engineer down to his marrow. He couldn't see further than the pistons on a V-12. The *Cavaliere* ran rings around him.'

'He was an employee of Signor Molinari?'

'We're talking forty years ago, Comandante. Molinari had just broken from the big boys in Modena. It was still like a gang, or at least that's how the *Cavaliere*, a proper *furbacchione*, liked to make it appear – all for one,' he chuckled, 'and, it turned out, that one was Massimiliano Molinari. I dipped in now and again.'

'You, Speedy?'

'You thought you knew everything about me, Comandante,' he tapped beneath his eye, 'but I tell you. If you thought the criminal world was bad, you've never had anything to do with car makers. They make us look like clergy.'

'I'm not sure that's such a great comparison,' I said.

'It was after they released me, while my appeal was pending between the courts of first and second degree – maybe Molinari had been reading about my case – anyway, he got in touch through my lawyers and had me testing his cars. Who better? I would have kept it up, too, if you hadn't got me sent back on appeal.'

'You would have done better pleading guilty straight away – you would have done less time.'

'It's all relative, Comandante – this way I got to spend a year in the middle with my girl.' He shot her a fond look. She mumbled something bitter and turned to her computer screen. 'Anyway, by the time I'd got out, that was all in the past – "Scuderia Molinari" had become a real player on the F1 circuit, his high-performance *marque* was becoming firmly established, and the "old gang" had either been taken on full time, or given the elbow. And of course, they had legit, professional drivers. They didn't want to be associated with someone with my rep.'

'And Signor Chiesa was one of those who had been let go,' I said.

'From what I can understand, Molinari offered to take him on and include some kind of "retrospective bonus" for his "contribution". We're talking six figures by today's standards. But of course, Giorgio wouldn't have it because it was never about the money – well, not only. Like all artists, it was about having his name on his creation. That was the thing that really hurt, and in truth, he never got over it. He wouldn't even take the cash Molinari offered out of court – twice as much as that "bonus" – despite the *Cavaliere* knowing Giorgio hadn't a hope: his papers had gone missing, Molinari had all the witnesses on the company payroll, and the best law firm in Bologna behind him.

'Max just wanted to shut him up, I suppose, but if you ask me, it wasn't only about that – I might have made Molinari sound like a monster, but he's not entirely without a soul, in fact, he's a sentimental guy – sure, there's business, but he pays his debts, he always treated me fair and square, and he knew he owed Giorgio.'

'Apparently not enough to share the patent with him.'

'There's a line, isn't there, and that was Molinari's – if he had to choose between his business and Chiesa, you can bet he was going to choose Molinari Automobile SpA every time. That had *his* name on, right?'

The Comandante said: 'He took on Fabrizio Chiesa as one of his drivers.'

'You see? No hard feelings, I think, at least at the beginning, the fact he was Giorgio's son must have greased the wheels, so to speak – it was Molinari's way of repaying his old man. I mean, Fabri wasn't recruited immediately for the *scuderia*. He started doing my old job testing cars, but he had the background on the karts and Molinari was sufficiently impressed to back him on the lower formulas . . .' He drew deeply on his cigarette, sat back in a cloud of smoke.

'And then he had the accident,' I said.

'He was a great driver, Fabri. He had this . . . grace.'

'Do *you* think it was an accident?'

Speedy's bony shoulders jerked like pistons. 'Accidents happen.' He took a thoughtful puff. 'Even to experts.'

'Signor Chiesa apparently believed Massimiliano Molinari was behind it,' said the Comandante.

'He had a theory, certainly.'

'Which was?'

Speedy sighed. 'It's ridiculous – that Molinari got rid of Fabri because he was showing up his son, who was also in the team.'

'And you believed him?'

Those steeple eyebrows again. 'Molinari took the boy on in the first place. Fabri had risen, along with Max's son Niki, through the academy. The pair were firm friends! It's true, Molinari is ruthless, but to the extent that winning is everything to him – *everything* – and I certainly can't see him putting the fortunes of Niki ahead of the *scuderia*. If you want to know one thing about Massimiliano Molinari, know that.' He took a final drag. 'And frankly, why would he have Fabri killed if he could just have sacked him? I told Giorgio as much.'

'And what did he say?'

'He asked me to witness his will.'

'And I presume it was you,' said Giovanni, 'who recommended me to him.'

'Well, Comandante, the poor guy insisted, and who else would I suggest? I knew you were someone who wouldn't exploit the situation, and after all, if there *was* any truth to it, well, you were the only one to nab me, to ever get close!'

The Comandante looked around. 'Not always,' he said. Behind her computer, the daughter let out a joyless laugh.

Chapter 3

'I'll get it out.'

'How am I supposed to learn,' said Rose, hands on hips, 'if you do everything?'

'The best way to walk,' I slid between the sky blue Fiat Punto and my graphite grey Alfa SUV, 'is one step at a time.'

My daughter let out an exasperated *'che palle'* as I opened the Fiat's door and eased myself in, careful not to mark the Alfa's paintwork. Rose's regression to Italian was not a good omen – our common language was English – but as I had already noted, one hand gripped around the grab handle, the other hovering above the handbrake, once she was behind the wheel, she was *cento percento Italiana*.

I backed the car into the courtyard and turned it around to face the oak gates. Behind me, the doors to the garage, which housed three of the six family vehicles (if we included my brother-in-law Jacopo's Vespa) closed.

I had been the victor of the 'battle of the *bottegas*', which had resulted in the swelling number of cars crowding the courtyard of *La Residenza Faidate* being moved into the former workshops on the ground floor. Those stone-cool, whitewashed spaces, looked down upon by two storeys of 'Romeo and Juliet'-style balconies, had variously been used for printing, book-binding and, even further back, to display the exotic goods the Faidate had imported along the Silk Road. More recently they had been piled with junk or used as rehearsal rooms for Jacopo's friends' bands, something the Comandante had not long tolerated. Jacopo's cousin Alba had wanted to knock them through to create a sort of warehouse-style apartment, while I had proposed using the main workshops for cars and bikes while converting the one abutting her existing ground-floor 'house' (itself a former workshop situated just inside the Residence wall) to provide her with the space she and her new family required.

My plan had seemed like a perfect compromise, at least to me, but still took months of discussion, drama – Alba's operatic range turned out to be truly impressive – and intrigue (Jacopo had been, unsurprisingly, the weak link), a further six months waiting upon permission from the *sovrintendenza* (naturally, the fifteenth-century *Residenza* was listed) plus twelve weeks of work with all the upheaval that implied, before Rose and I were finally able to roar slowly along the gravel drive towards the opening gates.

'Ease up on the clutch.' I could smell rubber. Rose ignored me, her profile pinched with concentration.

She swung the car through the gateway, gliding as close to the parked cars as a shark to a surfboard before we rumbled along narrow Via Mirasole.

Clunk, clunk. She changed to first as she rounded Via Paglietta – without looking right, I noted, a task apparently left to me – and, clunk, clunk, into second gear.

We headed up the slope to the ring road.

'It would be easier . . .' she said in English.

'Please. Eyes on the road.'

'. . . if you let me drive the big car.'

'Because the Alfa's automatic, you mean? Your test will be for a manual.' Thank goodness – the thought of allowing her to drive my car brought me out in a cold sweat.

'They'll all be automatic soon,' she said. We stopped by the Q8 garage. 'Which way?'

'What do you mean?' I asked, alarmed. 'It's a one-way system, there's only one way to go.'

She nodded towards the junction. 'You might have wanted to head up Via San Mamolo.'

'I . . .' I leaned left. It was mid-afternoon and the Viale – Bologna's inner ring road – was quiet. 'All right.'

'What?'

'Do that – head for the hills.'

Bene.' She shot across the two empty lanes and, before I could say, 'check the other side' had swung left at the green traffic lights, scything over the opposite carriageway and up San Mamolo.

I clung to that handle, my teeth clenched as firmly as the Comandante's as we walked through Dozza, but I was resigned to the fact that driving in Italy – or with an Italian – is always partly an act of faith.

We whipped along San Mamolo, then Rose took the winding road uphill, the sign indicating the ancient hermitage of Ronzano, now part of a treatment centre for drug addicts. Also hidden here among the hedgerows were observatories, research centres, religious retreats and private villas; most of all the villas, modern houses sprawled behind iron gates with views across the city.

Soon even these were left behind.

The little Punto puttered across the rolling hills. It never failed to surprise me how swiftly you could move from the towers, porticoes and enveloping terracotta stucco of Bologna – a city still philosophically, if not actually, enclosed by walls – to what seemed like the heart of the countryside.

'Slow now, slow . . .' We glided around each bend, technically wide enough for two cars to pass, although thankfully this hadn't been tested yet.

It was about to be.

Rose's eyes widened as a white SUV came the other way. The seatbelt snapped across my chest and the hedgerow screeched along the passenger side as we lurched to a halt, and a panicking seventeen-year-old British girl materialised from behind that audacious Italian veneer.

'*Dad?*'

I looked up at the SUV being driven by a curly haired middle-aged bloke who probably owned a place around here and doubtless regarded this as his private road. I beckoned him forward. He rolled closer. To be fair, he was probably as reluctant to share the old Punto's paintwork with his car as I had been on mine.

'Now,' I said to Rose. 'Put it gently into first and steer it a little further over to the side.' Clunk. Roar. Rubber. We shifted a little further into the hedgerow and the car stalled.

'Don't worry about that,' I said as the SUV eased past.

Rose tried to restart the Punto. It, perhaps understandably, resisted. She tried again. It coughed and died.

'God!'

She was about to give it another go when I stopped her.

'Wait a moment – you both need to relax.'

'I'm never going to pass!' She covered her face with her hands.

'Take a couple of deep breaths and have another go.'

We waited. I checked the rear mirror but no one had yet materialised.

'Okay,' I said. 'Try again.'

This time it worked.

'See? You're fine. Although, it is true,' I said sombrely, 'we still haven't practised the most important element of the Italian driving test.'

'What's that?' she asked, startled.

I reached into my pocket and gave her my phone. 'Press this to your ear with one hand and try to steer with the other.'

She laughed: *'Dad!'*

There was a blast behind us – another SUV.

'Come on.' I took the phone. *'Avanti!'*

I had had my doubts about the country roads but after a while began to relax – they might not be as straight and smooth as the city, but there was a hell of a lot less traffic. Rose simply needed to put in some time behind the wheel – she was reasonably competent for a novice, and certainly not discernibly worse than many seasoned drivers.

We were properly in the Apennines now, lurching down dips, skimming hills. This part of the countryside had a brutal beauty. While the valleys and plains offered some of the best farmland on the planet, the hills had a wild, unhusbanded feel. If Tuscany was Lady Chatterley, then Emilia was Mellors, its peculiar characteristic the clay-grey *calanchi* – eroded rock faces that loomed like slagheaps and often ran into streams glistening like mercury. It was no coincidence the translation of *calanchi* was Badlands. It was a place where unshaven men went shooting for wild boar in ragged woods, and truffles lurked beneath secret trees; where you would come across a *trattoria* down a minor road and eat the best meal of your life, never to find the place again.

Ca' Nês – the name of the next village seemed familiar if the place didn't.

'Slow down,' I said.

'I am going slow.'

'What I mean is – slow right down, there's something I want to check.'

Rose stepped on the brake and we staggered nearly to a stop before rumbling through a tiny collection of houses. A wheelbarrow piled with the bruised buds of freshly harvested artichokes; a small, spired church with a boarded-up door.

We came out the other side.

'*Here*. This must be it. Pull over.'

'There's no parking.'

'To the side of the road.'

We got out. We were on the fringe of a bend. Looking back, I realised Ca' Nês would seem more impressive if you were approaching from the other direction – a grass and clay-grey cliffside raised the hamlet like a trophy around that church spire.

The curve was bordered by a chevroned crash barrier. I

followed it around to where the road sloped directly downwards for around a hundred metres before ending in another turn, although not as sharp as this one. You might be able to retain about half your speed as you rounded it before you put your foot down on the straight.

I took some photos, then walked back.

'They're pretty,' said Rose, admiring the flowers attached to the barrier. 'What are they?'

'You're asking the wrong person.' I took another photo, leaning closer to check if there was a card or any other kind of note. There wasn't, but the flowers were fresh.

'They're not the usual kind,' Rose said. I knew what she meant – although they were wrapped in tan florist's paper and tied at the bottom with a black ribbon, with their tiny blue petals and yellow, star-like buds, they were more like the kind you might pick from the wild or mix in a traditional bouquet of stemmed flowers rather than purchase on their own.

'There's no photo or anything,' said Rose. 'Do you think someone was knocked down?'

'Possibly,' I said. 'More likely, a car went over the edge.'

'But there are crash barriers.' She inspected them. 'Oh – I get it. They could have been erected after.'

'*Brava.*'

'Is this to do with that will thing you're working on with *Nonno*?'

I frowned. 'How do you know about that?'

'You were discussing it at dinner.'

'You were looking at your phone.'

'That doesn't mean I wasn't listening,' she said as if it was obvious.

'Well, I believe this was where the son died. I'm guessing he would have come speeding up the road then taken this corner too quickly and shot straight off.' We climbed over the crash barrier. I instinctively took her arm as we stepped towards an ash leaning precariously over the edge, roots gathered around it like old rope.

The cliff dropped into a ravine, the great clump of rock supporting Ca' Nês ending in a skirt of grey gravel that slid under a clump of trees.

'Ouch,' said Rose. 'He wouldn't have stood a chance.'

We backed away. 'Look at that.' Rose pointed to a deep ridge on the side of the tree. The bark had grown back but whatever had taken a chunk out of it had left its mark.

'Well-spotted. He could have clipped it as he went past.' I took a photo and we climbed back over the barrier. 'The Comandante is getting hold of the case files, we'll see if it's included. It would also be good to know where these flowers come from.'

'We can always ask.' Rose pointed to the house overlooking the curve.

'Hey,' I said. 'Who's in charge here?'

'Sorry boss.' She gave a mock salute.

'Come on, then, *capitano*.'

I buzzed the door, which set a pair of dogs barking. They sounded big. A scuffing sound. The voice of an elderly woman from behind the door.

'What do you want?'

Like the name of the village itself – Ca' Nês – she was speaking proper Bolognese dialect. I nodded at Rose.

'*Me?*' she mouthed.

'*You.*'

'We want to know who left the flowers at the site of the crash,' she shouted above the barking.

'Who are you?'

Rose looked at me again.

'*Friends,*' I mouthed.

'Friends.'

'*Of the family.*'

'Of the family.'

'I don't know,' said the old woman, both of us straining to understand her. Fortunately, she switched to – partial, at least – Italian. 'I don't go out. My grandson might know.'

'Is he here?'

'No.'

'Might anyone else know?'

'I don't know.' Rose looked at me. I shook my head.

'*Grazie, signora,*' she shouted. We walked back to the road.

'Why did you ask me to talk to her?' she asked.

'Old lady alone, speaking dialect.'

'I could barely understand her.'

'Me neither – which is why I thought rather than have a man with a foreign accent asking, it would be better coming from a woman with a Bolognese one.'

'I don't have an accent!'

'*Dai.* "I don't have an accent".' I exaggerated her slightly sibilant Bolognese. 'It's charming.'

'I don't speak like that!'

'I'm kidding. But I did think we might get further having a woman who's from these parts speaking to her.'

'My accent's not that bad, is it?'

'I was pulling your leg.'

'But I don't . . .'

'Hand on heart. You've got a lovely accent. Yes, there's a hint of Bologna, but everyone has one of those. Alba's is much stronger, for example. And let's face it, compared to me . . .'

'Your accent's actually not so strong these days' said Rose. 'You could *almost* be Italian if it wasn't for the funny way you say things sometimes . . .'

'Funny way . . .' A man was lifting the wheelbarrow and turning it back towards his house. 'Excuse me,' I waved. He put the wheelbarrow down.

He was wearing a red paisley bandana, his skin leathered from an outside life. A dormant roll-up was wedged in the corner of his mouth. He was a plump, grubby, country man. I wasn't going to bother with niceties.

'Can you tell us who leaves the flowers at the roadside? We came to pay our respects and saw them by the crash barrier.'

The man dug in his pocket and pulled out a lighter.

'What are you, family?'

'That's right.'

'Where are you from?'

'England.'

'So how are you family?'

'That's just it – we're over visiting. You know – the grand-parents emigrated. That's why we wanted to pay our respects.'

He relit the roll-up. 'No idea,' he said. 'But you're right, there's often flowers.' He looked as if he had just realised.

'It's been a long time, though,' I said. 'Since the accident.'

'Poor bastard. Went straight over. *Boof.* We called the

emergency services, made our way down, but couldn't get near, the thing was lit up like a torch. He probably died on impact. Hopefully.' He bowed his head. 'I'm sorry for your loss.'

'Thank you.' I looked back down the road. 'We were touched that someone still leaves flowers. You were saying you hadn't seen anyone?'

'We don't tend to go that way. All I would say is, well, there's not a lot of traffic up here, and now and again I do notice a car – and I say notice because it reminds me of the lad. And it's the kind of car you *would* notice . . .'

'A Molinari?'

'That's right – I mean that's the *marque* he was driving, who he worked for. And you don't see them that often.'

'Any idea what type of car it is?' He laughed:

'I'd be able to tell you if it was a tractor – maybe a Lamborghini! – but cars? It's silver and low slung, but not one of those flat ones. More like the type you see the footballers driving.'

'A sort of luxury one, then.'

'Like this?' Rose held up her phone, full of images of Molinaris. She scrolled slowly down. He pointed to one.

'Yeah, that sort of thing, only silver, like I was saying.' He gave us a curious look. He was no fool: his country wiles were telling him we were asking a lot of questions for relatives.

'I'm not sure if that rings any bells to me, does it to you, darling?'

Rose looked at me for a cue. 'No,' she said.

'Well, anyway. Thank you very much.' I steered us back down the hill. I could feel the man's eyes on us all the way.

Rose said softly: 'You're very slick at lying.'

'You have to think on your feet in this job, *capitano*. Generally speaking, people will take you for whatever you say you are.'

'You did that when you were a journalist?'

'Only when I was investigating something – you know that's how I met your mum, pretending to work in that coffee shop.'

She looked down at her phone. 'You lie to me, then?'

I laughed. 'No, although isn't that a trick question – what else would I say? But look at it this way: when I do lie, it's in the service of truth – as a reporter, it was to reveal what was really going on, like exploitative work practices or whatever. Back there, it was to find out what happened to our client's son.'

Rose continued scrolling. 'So you'd lie to get the truth out of me.'

We arrived at the car. 'To be honest, darling, I wouldn't dare – I don't think I'd get away with it.'

She gave me an appraising look. *'Slick.'* She raised the phone. The screen was full of those blue flowers.

'Forget-me-nots,' she said.

Chapter 4

'I'm very sorry,' I said to Signora Fernanda Chiesa, 'I'm sure she will be here soon.' The signora checked her watch.

'I hope so, I have a client call at five and will need to be back in the office.' We looked down the empty road. It wouldn't be the first time my colleague Dolores had arrived late or not at all recently – an abrupt change in her punctuality which was usually, dare I say it, almost British.

'You didn't leave the flowers at the scene, you were saying.'

'We have the cemetery,' said the signora. 'I've never visited the spot where it happened, I couldn't bear to.'

'And you've no idea who might have. You were saying your brother didn't have a girlfriend . . .'

'Naturally, he had girl *friends*. Fabri was a good-looking guy, a racing driver! There were plenty of plinky-plonkys . . .'

'I'm sorry?'

'Just what I used to call them – plinky-plonkys because of the way they tottered about on those high-heels, all those skinny young girls. They were proper *fighette* . . .' She meant the moneyed, designer-clad crowd on the fringes of which I was obliged to acknowledge my daughter had been known to hang. Was Rose a 'plinky-plonky'? Her pal Stefania definitely was, my girl increasingly less so – she had recently gravitated towards the more black-clad, tattooed and artsy crowd. Frankly, I wasn't sure which was worse. 'But they were kids,' continued Signora Chiesa. 'There was nothing serious. This is seven years ago. I can't imagine them remembering who they slept with the night before, let alone after all these years.'

'Someone said they spotted a silver Molinari Vernice coupé,' I said. 'It would be consistent with someone from a wealthy background.'

She shrugged. 'If there's one thing I learned from Dad and Fabri's involvement with fast cars, there's a lot of rich people in Bologna.'

'You mentioned Fabrizio visited you before the . . . incident.'

'He kept his bike, I mean, his motorcycle, in our garage because there was no space at Dad's, for tinkering, and so on. He popped in.' Her face hardened, as if trying to keep a lid on her emotions.

'And how was he?'

'Oh, normal. Just . . . normal.'

'Was he with you for long?'

'Not long, no. He was in the garage messing around with the bike, then away. I mean, he treated our place like his own.'

'And the bike?'

She looked surprised. 'What about it?'

'Do you still have it?'

She shook her head. 'Sold. It was really the only thing of value he possessed. Donated the proceeds to charity, in his name.'

'And he took that route . . .'

'There's a roundabout way home which is quicker, but he often cut across the hills. He said he liked the winding roads, practice.'

'And he didn't say anything that might help our enquiry? Anything out of the ordinary? Personal issues? Troubles?'

'Nothing,' she looked impatiently at her watch.

'Let's go in,' I said.

We were in Bologna's famous Via Fabbri of the folk song that evoked the angst of singer-songwriter Francesco Guccini in his 1970s hit *Via Fabbri 43*. But this afternoon we were down the road at 4B, home of the late Giorgio Chiesa, and his even later son, Fabrizio.

Compared to Bologna 'inside the walls', with its medieval and Renaissance porticoes, traditionally working-class Cirenaica, named after part of Libya conquered during the Italian state's early colonial adventures, might have been transplanted from industrial-era Turin or Milan. But it wasn't exactly ugly – the area had its own austere charm.

The grid of tree-lined streets consisted mainly of mansions divided into apartment blocks to accommodate workers' families, but there were also a few compact houses for the foreman class, like Fabbri 4B. It seemed a fitting address for Giorgio Chiesa. If the city 'inside' the now mostly demolished medieval walls was largely the preserve of students, professors, lawyers, doctors, private clubs and, well, private eyes, then this remained a quarter for people who got their hands dirty, who hammered and cranked and riveted, and who designed the objects of their toil – an *Ingegnere* like Chiesa.

Signor Chiesa had been dead a good few weeks and stepping into the narrow hallway was like entering a brick carcass. There's always a kind of hollow feeling about the homes of the recently deceased, especially if they lived alone. In colder seasons there might be that chill from the spent heating, in hotter ones a stuffy staleness due to closed windows. Now the weather was clement and the windows partially open behind the bars on the first floor, but there remained that unmistakable *still* to the place one might call soullessness.

We entered the living room where the only article that appeared to postdate the twentieth century was a newish flat screen TV. Upon the mantelpiece above an open, swept fireplace, cards of condolence jostled with silver and gold racing trophies. 'May I?' The sister shrugged, perching herself on the edge of a battered leather sofa and pulling out her phone.

I took a card. It felt brittle in my fingers and had a film of dust – what I thought were for the father, were for the son.

'He never took them down,' she said.

'You mentioned your father had left some kind of record about his investigations into Fabrizio's death?'

'Here.' She handed me a key. 'A lock-up,' she sighed. 'Boxes of the stuff.'

'And the bedrooms are upstairs?' She nodded. 'You don't mind . . .'

'Go ahead. We've already been through Dad's drawers to see if he left any further instructions. Money, jewellery, that kind of thing, to stop it getting stolen now the place is empty. We found some stuff from Mum, but not much else.'

'And your brother's room?'

'We didn't touch it. We'll have to clear it out soon, but I

wanted Niki to come first and see if there was anything he wanted. In fact, I wrote him we would be here, but he hasn't turned up either.' She shrugged.

'You mean Niki . . . *Molinari*?'

'He was Fabri's best friend, even though I suppose they were competitors. I thought he might like to see if there was anything he wanted since Dad had made such a shrine of it, and of course he would never have let Niki near it while he was alive, even if he had dared ask.'

'Because your father blamed him as well as Signor Molinari?'

Her cheeks puffed with indignation. 'It was *unthinkable* Niki could not be involved – Dad had lost his boy and Molinari had—' She closed her eyes, took a moment. 'Kept his. They weren't invited to the funeral, but still a lot of people from the *scuderia* turned up at the church. Niki and his dad must have slipped in at the back because we didn't see them until we were outside. They were keeping a low profile, to be fair, but Dad spotted them anyway and lost it. He had to be held back. It was a great mess.' Her eyes gleamed. 'But it was a long time ago, no? Time moves on, people move on.'

'Except your father.'

'Maybe it helped him make sense of what happened,' she said. 'Max Molinari was pulling the strings and it wasn't all just some . . .' Her business-like monologue faltered. 'Terrible accident.'

I could see the old man's front-facing bedroom behind me as I reached the top of the stairs. It was as stark as a butcher's slab – the stripped mattress, emptied wardrobe, cardboard boxes. Beside it, a similarly bare room, its faded pink walls pocked by Blu Tack where I guessed Signora Chiesa had once stuck photos and posters. A cramped bathroom came next, an old-fashioned shower head slung over the side of the bath like a dead hand, while in front of me the door was open onto what was clearly Fabrizio's 'shrine'.

It was dark – the shutters were closed – and murky like the domain of a teenage boy, although Fabrizio had been twenty-one when he died. But he might have been sixteen. It was not just the single bed with old racing magazines fanned upon a Le Mans coverlet, but the whole deal – the F1 and supercar posters, cheap trophies, runners-up medallions. Pirelli calendar, newspaper clippings, and Molinari caps. It had the obsessive focus of the fanboy. I somehow couldn't imagine Fabrizio taking a *fighetta* back here.

I thought about what his sister had said – I wasn't going to argue about her image of her youngest brother as a lady's man, but this room was his core – cars, cars and more cars, as well it might have been to attain the standards required in the sport. The single bed, the single purpose.

I opened the window and began to unhook the shutters.

'Fabri.' A man's voice behind me. 'Oh Fabri, Fabri, Fabri.'

I turned.

He stood silhouetted in the doorway like a figure in a *fumetto*, or graphic novel – a slender outline topped by a crest of thick, spiky hair. Only his marine blue eyes shone out of the gloom like a pair of artfully applied dashes.

Niki Molinari stepped further into the room. I would have recognised him even if I hadn't been researching the case. The *Carlino* was always boosting the local *scuderie* (and especially

Molinari's F1 rivalry with Ferrari, based further along 'Motor Valley' in old municipal foe Modena) and while it was not presently up there with the big three, it was holding its own in the top half of the grid. It only took a miscalculation by an inferior driver in a superior car, or a superior driver in an inferior car, for Niki Molinari to nip through and make podium, which he had achieved three times last season, twice as third, and once runner-up.

Niki frankly looked better in silhouette. With his bristled, pugilist's face dominated by a long, flat nose, he was definitely no pin-up, but I had to admit those blue eyes were really something. 'Go on,' he said. 'Crack the shutters.'

Sunlight streamed into the room. He picked up a magazine and flicked through it. 'Look,' he held it open towards me. '*Here we are.* I guess the old man couldn't cut me out for fear of messing up the article.' He chuckled. 'Fabri, you handsome bastard.' He set it back down. 'The place has barely changed since we hung out here – ah, the F190.' He approached the Ferrari poster. 'Four-cylinder V12. It sounded like . . . I don't know . . . *pure speed.*' He inspected the one beside it, a supercar in trademark Molinari green. 'The *Drago*, of course, of course. We said we'd have one each and race down the *autostrada* at three in the morning.' Niki Molinari grinned – an infectious, scoundrel's grin, but tears were falling freely. He wiped them away with the back of his hand. 'Fernanda said I could take what I wanted. But all this, you know, it's my youth – as much mine as Fabri's. My room was just like this. All right, I had a little more space . . . but it wasn't so different. It's like stepping back in time . . . Have you?' He meant a tissue. I shook my head. 'Damn it, I should have come prepared. Excuse me.' He left the room. I heard him loudly blow his nose in the bathroom. The toilet flushed. He returned with a handful of tissue paper. 'So, you're the guy the old man hired to pin Fabri's death on us.' His tone was jocular, but his eyes rested on me as they might a competitor.

'I wouldn't say that. Signor Chiesa asked us to look into it, that's all.'

'And do you think we did it?'

'I don't think anything. Like I said, we'll consider what happened and my boss will decide when our work is concluded.' The Comandante and I would do so between ourselves, but I often found it useful to evoke a higher power.

Niki blew that big nose again. 'Excuse me. You're very diplomatic, clearly not an Italian. British, right?' I nodded. He continued in faultless, lightly-accented English: 'Fernanda said something about that. Your Italian is good.'

'Your English is excellent.'

That cheeky grin: 'I've been groomed to be an international businessman.' True: I had read that in addition to being a top-flight F1 driver, he held an MBA. 'And in this business, it's more or less compulsory for all of us – for the media, I mean, publicity, all that shit. That was what Fabri struggled with most, back in F3. English. I would give him lessons.' His gaze drifted off. 'He taught me the rest.'

'Fernanda said you were best friends.'

'Charioteers.'

'I'm sorry?'

'That's how we thought of ourselves, from back when we were fifteen and racing carts. *Charioteers*. We loved that movie – *Ben Hur*. The original, obviously, not the remake. Christ, someone actually died in the race scene! We studied all the greats – Nuvolari, Ascari, Senna . . .'

'Lauda?'

He snorted. 'Yes, and Niki, too, although that was more Fabri than me, and Paps said the same – that he'd got the wrong one – though Fabri hated the comparison. I mean, what teenage boy wants to be compared to steady, disfigured Niki, when they can be his rival, dashing, womanising James Hunt? Who wants to be Alain Prost when they can be Ayrton Senna?'

'That must have stung – your father saying, in effect, you were the wrong one.'

'*Beh*. Dad's a mean bastard, but hey,' he grinned. 'I see what you're doing – looking for a motive, right? Well, you can have that for free. After all, Signor Chiesa was convinced! And as we got older, the stakes certainly got higher . . the instinct to win must overcome all!

'Would I have risked a shunt with Fabri? Hell yes, especially if we were on opposing teams. Might that have led to his death? There was always a chance, although since the halo,' I looked blank. 'Oh, a kind of bar around the cockpit, anyway, it makes it safer. But even so, there remains the risk, the reality. And really,' he considered it, 'that's partly the point.'

'What,' I scoffed, 'death?'

He gave me a surprised look. 'Yes death. What do you think people really come for? A race? *Dai*. It's the *risk* of the race, the *death-defying* speed. *Ben Hur*! The drivers we boys worshipped – Ascari, Villneauve, and yes, Senna, were all killed on the track.

'Now don't get me wrong, I'm not saying we *piloti* have

a death wish – I don't think for a minute Fabri did himself in – if you like, it's a *life* wish. *The sheer thrill of being alive.*' He rested a hand on my shoulder and fixed me with those dazzling eyes. 'Because isn't the moment you feel most alive when you're closest to death?'

I admit I was a little mesmerised, but his speech also felt rehearsed. 'I bet you say that to all the girls.'

'Ha!' He gave my shoulder a squeeze and said in Italian: 'You mean you don't want a kiss? Oh, come on!'

'I'll pass this time.'

'But to answer your question – did I kill him? You've got to be kidding. I loved him like a brother.' He pulled out a clump of tissue paper and wiped his eyes.

I thought: I never asked the question.

'We visited the spot where the accident happened,' I said. 'I imagine for someone like Fabrizio, the bend wouldn't have been a problem.' Niki shook his head. Of course not. I continued: 'So what do you think happened?'

'Ah, if you knew how often I'd asked myself that, mister detective. I still wake up in the early hours thinking about it . . .'

'And?'

'I've no idea.'

'None?'

He shook his head. 'That's what keeps me awake. I can't conceive how it occurred.'

'There were fresh flowers at the site, forget-me-nots.' He frowned. 'Not from you, then.'

'I'll never forget Fabri, but . . . I'm not a flower kind of guy.'

'A neighbour thought the person who left them drove a Molinari, a silver Vernice coupé. Ring any bells?'

Niki made a show of thinking about it before shaking his head, but he'd already given himself away – those wide nostrils flared bullishly at the make of the car. He might have been a decent F1 driver, but he would make a pretty terrible poker player.

'Think about it,' I pressed. 'You're sure?' He nodded insistently. 'All right. Well, if you don't mind . . .' I gestured around the room.

'Go ahead. Me too. Like a pair of vultures, right?'

'I've been called worse.'

The wardrobe was musty with old clothes. I dealt through them, surreptitiously checking the jacket pockets, but couldn't find anything. Shirts and jumpers were neatly folded, and although I reached over them to feel for anything hidden at the back, I didn't harbour much hope – everything had long-since been sorted through.

I closed the wardrobe and crouched to look under the bed. As I was pulling out a plastic tub, the doorbell went. The sound of Fernanda letting Dolores in. I heard my partner making an excuse about something coming up at work.

I opened the tub: resting flat on top, a burgundy Piquadro leather pouch or 'man bag'. I unzipped it, but it was empty except for a used napkin and some cake or biscuit crumbs. Beneath it: a tangle of medals, a small steering wheel – the kind used for carting – more F1 magazines. A shoebox. I removed the lid. A selection of Fabrizio's personal effects: passport, a couple of old mobile phones, a collection of rings, mainly cheap gothic tin things he might have bought from a market stall; a St Christopher medallion, a slim wallet of photos. I flicked through them – 'greatest hits' of Fabrizio in racing garb, looking as elated as only a teenage boy doing his favourite thing can. An F1 programme covered with autographs, an accumulation of crinkled foreign currency and coins, a slinky, stained white item I at first took to be a sock but turned out to be a driver's balaclava, a champagne cork, an empty polystyrene coffee cup (used) with an indecipherable ballpoint scribble, a Leatherman multitool, a blue handkerchief stained with motor oil, loose chewing gum sticks, an empty PEZ dispenser, a cigarette carton containing three presumably stale fags, and beneath all this, a notebook with sets of numbers written in a childish scrawl.

'*Ciao*,' I heard Niki saying curiously behind me.

Dolores replied with a more formal, and somewhat edgy, '*Salve*'.

'And who . . .'

'My colleague, Dolores Pugliese.' I took a photo of the writing in the notebook.

'*You're* a private eye?' I looked around, wondering what the hell she was wearing, but in fact Dolores was reasonably turned out in a formal, albeit almost certainly charity shop-purchased, black jacket, plain white top and faded jeans. A clump of her henna bob was tied back with a coiled elastic band. She might have jumped out of bed and exited her apartment in five minutes. Although she was young and pretty enough to usually pull it off, today she seemed a little less able – with those dark crescents beneath her eyes set against an uncharacteristic pallor, she looked as if she should have stayed under the duvet. She shot me a nervous glance.

'See the computer?' I pointed at the closed laptop on the desk. 'Can you ask the signora if it's working, and they have access, the passwords and so on.'

Dolores lifted the screen. 'We could just try turning it . . .'

'Go down and ask, please.' She nodded and left.

'You know,' said Niki, 'I always pictured private eyes as middle-aged guys.'

'Like me, you mean?'

He grinned: 'Like you.'

'You'd better watch your back then, we're everywhere.'

'I've nothing to hide.'

'Well, you must lead a very dull life. Not my idea of a racing driver.'

'Then you don't follow the sport. In truth, Fabri was ahead of the game – we all have to be straitlaced Laudas nowadays to have a chance to compete at this level. The times of Fangio downing a pint of champagne before jumping in the cockpit, even Hunt partying before a race, are long-gone. The girls, the bubbly, it's for the sponsors – brand, merchandising, *vero*? Take me – I'm an elite athlete!' He mockingly flexed his biceps, but I actually could see them strain inside his tight leather jacket. I didn't doubt he was super-fit.

'She said no.' Dolores was back in the doorway.

'No to what?'

'She took a look at it after he died but hadn't been able to access it as she couldn't find the passwords and her dad didn't know, but she said she didn't try very hard. Obviously everyone was very upset, and she didn't see the need.'

'Ask her if we can remove it for analysis.' I pointed to the pair of phones I'd laid upon the bed. 'Along with those.' Suppressing a yawn, Dolores headed back down.

'Up all night on a stake-out?' said Niki.

'Something like that,' I said.

'Do you want access to *my* stuff?' He produced his top-of-the-line iPhone.

'Not for now.'

'But seriously. If it means putting this to bed, you have my full support – full access! Jesus. I owe it to Fabri, and his dad, who I respected incidentally, at least until he turned on me . . . Which actually fucking hurt, but I somehow understood. He was a decent man.'

'He didn't have a problem with you hanging out with his son, then? Given the bad blood between him and your father?'

He shrugged. 'Never said a word, at least in my company. He was quite formal, but he was formal with all the kids. All adults for that matter. He probably asked his wife permission before he took his socks off.'

'And your father?'

'My dad? Likewise – I don't mean he was a stuffed shirt, only that he never said a word. If anything, he probably found the whole thing funny.'

'You don't think he took on Fabrizio to "get at" Signor Chiesa?'

'If you knew my father,' said Niki. 'You wouldn't say that. He won't spend a cent he doesn't think wouldn't further the *scuderia*. Emotions don't come into it – they're reserved for births, marriages and deaths, and frankly I don't know how many of *them* are written off as a business expense.'

'You don't paint a very sympathetic picture of him, Niki.'

'Oh, you know – father-son shit. I owe him everything. Not that I don't deserve it – there are only thirty F1 drivers in the world, and I'm up there with the best, so Dad's not wasting his money. But would I have got there without him?' He took in the room. 'I'm no Fabrizio Chiesa.'

Chapter 5

I watched Dolores unchain her bike from the lamppost outside Chiesa's house.

'I'm meeting the Comandante for supper at Da Vito,' I said. 'Join us.'

'Don't you want me to get the computer back to the office?'

'There's really no hurry. Isn't everybody already dead?'

We walked along Via Fabbri in the direction of the trattoria, a legendary eatery that had served Cirenaica for decades.

'You're okay?' I asked.

'What do you mean?'

'If you don't mind me saying, you're looking a little tired.'

'My time of the month. Heavy one. Honestly, I should take some iron.' I wasn't sure how to respond. I wondered what Alba – to whom I had delegated all my daughter's 'women's business', as I indelicately thought of it – would say.

'What do you think?' Dolores asked.

'What do I think about what?' I couldn't quite keep the panic from my voice.

'About the case,' she said. 'Do you think he was murdered?'

'The boy? Well, I think that's a bit of a leap.' I checked my watch. 'We're a little early.' There was a bar with some tables outside. 'How about an *apero*?'

'I really should be getting back to the office, Dan – Alba keeps hassling me about those CV searches.'

I pulled up a chair for her. 'Tell her – boss's orders.'

I asked for a beer, Dolores for sparkling mineral water. She sat scrolling her phone, spliced by the sun – one side bleached straw-gold, the other moon-grey. Neither the spring warmth or the shade's lingering winter chill appeared to bother her, but I thought: she would usually be happy to share a beer.

'Remember,' I said tentatively. 'We have a health plan, and while I realise you and Alba don't always see eye to eye . . .'

Dolores put on her eighties-style 'vintage' mirror sunglasses.

'She's actually mellowed a lot since she's had the kid,' she said. 'Look, I'm sorry I was late, I know I've been a bit shit lately. I had some stuff, then this period, it's really knocked me out.' With her eyes shielded by the glasses, I had no idea whether she was telling the truth, but she could certainly teach Niki Molinari a thing or two about poker. She began to roll a cigarette.

I watched my reflection ask: 'The "stuff" you mention. Is there anything I can help with?'

She shook her head, licking the fag closed. 'But thanks.' She lit up, releasing the smoke from the corner of her mouth.

Our drinks arrived. After the *cameriere* left, I said: 'So, how's it going with your cousin?'

Dolores looked amused. 'You mean – how's it going with *your* cousin?'

I'd never actually thought of Jacopo like that – he was my late wife's brother, so technically my brother-in-law, but in

the Italian context in which everybody seemed to be somebody's cousin, I had to admit it made sense.

Jacopo was dating the new receptionist – Dolores' *actual*
cousin Celeste. Celeste had come up from Naples to fill
Alba's maternity leave but Alba had decided she should stay
on when it came to an end. Alba had chosen to work mainly
at home, only coming into the office in Marconi two days a
week, where she took the reception desk, while Celeste went
to *La Residenza* to look after 'Little Lucia', as Alba's toddler
was known. And somewhere along the line, Celeste, 23, and
Jacopo, 32, had become an item. So far, so Italian. I was just
happy that thanks to the nation's creaking legal system, it was
unlikely I'd ever have to explain it to an employment tribunal.

Dolores' smile broadened. 'I think they make a great
couple,' she said.

'You didn't have it planned all along?'

'Not at all! I just knew Celeste was looking for a change, I
swear.' She let out a smoky laugh.

Despite snooping around Bologna together for years, I
had always avoided interrogating Dolores about her private
life, and she had made absolutely no effort to enlighten me.
God knows the atmosphere in Faidate Investigations, where
everyone else was not only related but lived in the same building, was febrile enough, so I think we both appreciated the
professional boundary. Which is not to say that when she had
first washed up on our shores with dreadlocks and stonking
military boots, I hadn't suspected she and Jac might become
an item, but as time wore on it became clear that not only was
Dolores not interested, even if she had been, Jacopo was far
too timid (if not actually intimidated) to ever make a move.

Celeste on the other hand had been quick to embrace the company culture and was soon fussing over the Comandante, coolly business-like with 'Signor Daniel', and apparently at ease with Jacopo leaning over her low-cut top as he mansplained the computer system. Within the month they were disappearing off for coffee and giggling in reception, until one morning I was bumping into Celeste breezily descending the stairs from Jacopo's apartment.

'If I hadn't known she was your cousin,' I said to Dolores. 'I never would have guessed.'

'She's a proper Neapolitan.'

'And you're not?'

'What I mean is – Celeste had a normal upbringing in the Spagnoli, and you don't get more "Naples" than that. I was brought up in the system.'

'*Raised by nuns?*' I echoed a remark once made by Jacopo. I knew Dolores had been orphaned at a young age, but not much else.

'Via Bosco di Campomonte,' she recited. 'The order of Santa Maria and Santa Immacolata. They made me memorise it – I was seven.'

'You couldn't have lived with your cousin's family? Other relatives?'

She examined the smouldering cigarette, but I could only see its reflection between her unadorned fingers. 'It was complicated. But don't get me wrong – I visited, they visited. I was invited to birthdays, weddings, picnics on the beach . . .'

'Then returned to the home?'

She shrugged. 'My auntie had tons of kids, it was almost like the orphanage at their place . . . and they weren't well off.'

'No one offered to foster, adopt you?'

She shook her head. 'I didn't want that. I didn't want other parents. In any case, I liked the nuns. They made me feel loved. I loved them.' She took another drag before stubbing out the cigarette. 'It was not like, I don't know, one of these institutions you read about – it was a place for girls, a women's world. Sure, there were some pretty tough girls, but on the whole it was fine. The nuns encouraged us to make the best of ourselves. It's thanks to them I ended up at university. I mean, maybe with Mum and Dad, but *my* relatives? Celeste got out . . .'

'Thanks to you.'

'The others – they're still in Spagnoli, the girls pushing prams, the boys . . .' She shrugged.

'And your parents – they died in a car crash.'

Dolores took a sip of water, nodded.

'All this,' I meant the investigation. 'You're okay with it, then. The job, I mean – it's not bringing back bad memories?'

Dolores took off her sunglasses. I don't know why, but I was surprised to see her hazel eyes calm and clear. 'Not at all,' she said, smiling at me almost pityingly, and I couldn't help thinking that one of those 'tough girls' in the orphanage had been Dolores Pugliese.

There was something about places like Da Vito that couldn't quite be captured by the new restaurants and bars proliferating in the city centre. The old ones like this exuded a disdain for the prevailing aesthetic that the painstakingly curated newcomers, for all their talismans of authenticity – from hung meats to artificially aged signage – couldn't replicate, and probably wouldn't want to. One could have too much authenticity after all, and they relied on tourists and out-of-towners for their trade. Even so, as we stepped into Da Vito's tatty entrance at seven o'clock on a sunny spring evening, I couldn't help feeling it would be best experienced through the fug of cigarette smoke around midnight, 1985.

A snap of Lucio Dalla, Bologna legend and Italy's Elton John, performing to diners back in the day, was stuck to the cracked entrance hall mirror, while a large faded photo of the late Vito and his wife took pride of place on the wall together with black and whites ranging from soccer teams to celebrities from the fifties and sixties.

We were waved through to the otherwise deserted dining room where the Comandante had a corner table. A half-litre carafe of red wine was set upon the red chequered table cloth, together with the old-fashioned, dinky glasses you otherwise only saw on the back of wine bottles to indicate the equivalent of a single unit of alcohol. Giovanni made to get up, but even before we could say no, an uncharacteristic wince had kept him in his place. Dolores and I exchanged an uneasy glance, but he appeared otherwise unperturbed.

'I don't think they've changed the menu since I used to come here,' he said.

'Which was?' asked Dolores.

'Oh, indubitably before you were born, my dear.'

'I always find it hard to imagine you as a young man, Giovanni,' I said.

He frowned. 'I was *never* young. I have simply matured.'

Dolores scrunched up her nose at the menu. 'Did they also have horse in your day?'

'In my day, dear, they still had unicorn.'

'I suppose they didn't have vegetarians then, either.'

'Vegetarianism was a key indicator of anarchism – an arrestable offence.'

'I would like to think he's kidding,' said Dolores.

'On the bright side,' I poured myself and the Comandante a glass of wine. I offered some to Dolores but she shook her head, 'isn't it wonderful that in today's world, a vegetarian,' I raised my glass, 'and a former comandante of the Carabinieri's Special Operations squad, can work together.'

'Just remember who's boss,' said the Comandante.

'Anyway,' I said. 'We've visited Signor Chiesa's house, got hold of Fabrizio's computer equipment, and been given this,' I held up the key, 'to a lock-up where our client stored his *boxes* of files concerning the incident – I'll ask Alba to lead on that. And – we bumped into Niki Molinari.'

'Oh?'

I recounted our meeting. 'The thing is,' I said. 'I believe he knew who the silver car belonged to, and therefore who was presumably leaving the flowers.'

I watched the Comandante digest this. 'Interesting,' he said. 'Although I feel obliged to point out that we have not been engaged to uncover an apparent love affair, rather the cause of Fabrizio Chiesa's death, suspicious or otherwise.'

'Unless this affair was the cause,' said Dolores.

The Comandante shifted uncomfortably. 'I had been hoping to have this wrapped up before I went in to hospital.' He sighed. 'Now with these additional *boxes* of files and this complication . . . Of course, if one digs, one is always likely to come across roots – the question is, to what are they attached?' He reached down and produced a thick grass-green folder from his briefcase.

'In the meantime, I've had a quick look – as far as the incident is concerned, everything appears to be included. Crash report, autopsy . . .' I raised my eyebrows. 'No silver bullet, I'm afraid. Because it occurred in a remote location, it took some time for emergency services to arrive, then considerably more for them to access the site itself – Fabrizio had gone off a cliff, after all. The body was thoroughly incinerated. This meant, strictly speaking, it was difficult to say whether COD was pre- or post-incineration, although according to the report, he was not wearing his seat belt and was, in fact, um, difficult to detach from the impacted control console, engine, and so on. I should warn you,' he tapped the file. 'The photographs are . . . disagreeable.'

'Toxicology?' The Comandante shook his head.

'From what they could tell, there were no traces of alcohol, drugs, and so on, although again, the body was so charred the tests were extremely limited in their scope. The organs had the consistency of "cooked meat".'

'Vegetarianism doesn't seem so bad now, does it,' said Dolores. Still, I noticed she poured herself a glass of wine.

'I presume they were able to confirm it was actually him,' I said.

The Comandante nodded. 'Dental and DNA.'

'The crash report,' said Dolores. 'Skid marks?'

'Before the bend. A sharp turn to the right, but it was too late. Their hypothesis was that the car subsequently spiralled downwards before impacting with the cliff.'

I pictured the scarred tree Rose had noticed, the car clipping it before helicoptering over the edge. 'So it doesn't appear as if he did it on purpose,' I said.

'It doesn't appear so, no,' said the Comandante.

'And his father would have known all this?' asked Dolores.

'I expect as part of his inquiries he would have secured copies of the reports. You will probably find them somewhere among his files.'

'So everything points to an accident,' Dolores said.

'But Signor Chiesa wouldn't have *believed* it was an accident,' I said. 'Which is what we are doing here.'

Dolores took out her tobacco pouch and began to fill a cigarette. 'Seems like a waste of time, though.'

The Comandante looked amused. 'What about this love affair you mentioned? I think it is time we undertook a client consultation. Do you have that photo you shared with us, Daniel? The one of Signor Chiesa in the restaurant . . .'

I took out my phone and brought it up. 'Oh, I understand.' I laid the phone upon the table. 'This is the same spot where the photo was taken.'

We looked down at the three faded men.

'*Salve*, Signor Chiesa,' the Comandante said solemnly. 'We will examine your files, which may take us a little time, I'm afraid.

'And now we have uncovered this apparent *love story*. Presuming this is not something we turn up among your records, how would you like us to proceed?' The Comandante nodded, as if responding to our phantom client. 'I see.'

Dolores shot me a questioning look. I could only shrug. 'What actually sparks my interest,' the Comandante continued. 'Is not so much the affair *per se* as, if Daniel's intuition is correct, Molinari junior's desire to conceal its existence from us, which may be worthy of further consideration. What do you say, signor?'

My phone buzzed. I admit I jumped, and I was not the only one.

I tapped the screen. 'Well, there we have it,' I said. 'A message from Niki Molinari inviting me to the circuit.'

Chapter 6

Autodromo Enzo e Dino Ferrari materialised as I turned the corner of a quiet, tree-lined street in the suburbs of Imola.

A smooth asphalt-grey racetrack was visible on the other side of a fence, the lip of a grandstand grazing the distance. I followed the road until I came to a sign signalling the entrance above a modest-looking, closed ticket booth. I took another road inside the fence until I arrived at a vast, empty car park bordering the track. On the far side stood a cluster of buildings that wouldn't have looked out of place on an out-of-town industrial estate. Only the modest white tower bearing the yellow Ferrari logo signalled their true provenance.

I drove diagonally across the car park towards the buildings, pulling up just before the slip road where various cars and lorries were parked at the rear of a line of mostly shuttered single-storey cement sheds, which I took to be the paddocks. Black cables spilled from the rear of a SKY TV truck, stretching across the road into the only one that appeared open.

As I got out the car the brightness startled me into reaching for my sunglasses. Spending almost all my time 'inside the walls' of Bologna or snooping around its built-up sprawl,

I was unaccustomed to being exposed beneath such a broad sky. Beyond the race track's enormous car park and clump of buildings, there was only a bare line of trees and, on the other side of the circuit a little distant from the new stand, an abandoned one greened by weeds, resembling a terraced hill.

I was contemplating this monument to Grands Prix gone by when suddenly – the chainsaw of a car tearing along the track.

Whoosh, it was gone.

Another. It might have been an approaching jet as it thundered past then vanished again, leaving only a rumble that may have been inside my ears.

No amount of Grands Prix on the TV, I thought, could prepare you for that.

I began to better understand Niki's florid, almost mystical talk, which had perhaps been his purpose in inviting me. If, indeed, he had had one.

I set off for the paddock.

'Where do you think you're going?' I looked down at the palm raised in front of me, its skeletal fingers ending in talon-like, crimson nails; at the woman in a dark green Molinari jumpsuit, the zip ending well below the cleft of her cleavage, dyed blond hair combed back and huge black, jewel-encrusted Armani sunglasses.

'I've an appointment with Niki Molinari.'

'He didn't mention anything.'

'I'm sorry about that, but as I said, I've an appointment.' I noticed a big fellow with an earpiece, dressed in similar Molinari get up, drifting towards her.

'And as I said – he didn't say anything to me.'

'Well, I can't help that.' I began to step around her, but the muscle was now in my way.

'Niki's not available.' She smiled humourlessly. 'I'm so sorry. Why don't you try fixing a time with the office.'

'I have a feeling I'm speaking to the "office".'

'What can I say? It's a shame you've come all the way out here, but he just doesn't have the time.'

'Isn't that for him to decide?'

'No. You see, mister.' She chewed her gum like a teenager, even though she had to be at least fifty years old. 'Here on the circuit, his time is my time. We're only permitted two days of production a season, and this is one of them, so every minute is costing more money than you could conceivably be charging.' Even through her sunglasses she was apparently able to suss my cheap OVS suit, quite a trick. 'And look, honestly, I couldn't give a shit what he gets up to in his own time – who he's fucking, what he's promised, how much he owes, whatever, really, I don't give a damn, but I answer to the boss, just as he does, and the *capo* will have my balls on a plate if we waste any time, so I'm sorry,' she said with impressive insincerity, 'but Niki doesn't have time for you.'

'Succinctly put. But this has nothing to do with Niki's . . . hobbies, it's strictly business, and my time, cheap though it may be, is also money. Niki requested my presence, so please inform him that I'm here.'

The woman took an almost Kung Fu-style step back that would have only really worked on her letterbox-red heels had we been in a Tarantino movie. 'Then what the hell do you want?'

'That's confidential.'

She lowered the sunglasses to reveal unexpectedly tender eyes. 'Oh come on, you can tell me – I keep all his secrets.'

'That may be so.' I smiled, impressed, as so often with Italians, how she was able to turn her demeanour on a dime. 'But this is a matter between the two of us. He's certainly welcome to share it with you if he likes. I'm very sorry, but it shouldn't take long.'

'You're not from the courts, here to serve him a summons?'

I laughed. 'Certainly not.'

The woman pursed her lips. 'What's your name?'

'Daniel Leicester.'

'Davide,' she said to the muscle. 'Tell Niki there's a British. Daniel Leicester, claims he has an appointment.' As he headed off, she said in English. 'What's a British doing here anyway, speaking Italian?'

'You say that almost as if it's an offence.'

She looked amused. 'Well, it's certainly not normal.' She looked brazenly at my bare ring finger. 'Love, was it?'

'Not many people come here for work.'

'Some of our drivers,' she said. 'Our engineers. And our Principal is a British, but he doesn't speak the language like you, in fact he doesn't speak any Italian. So, what's your line of work?'

'I can see what you're doing.'

'Oh come on!' She flashed a whitened smile.

Behind her, Davide emerged with another man in a Molinari jumpsuit (which would be a theme – apart from the Sky TV team, I would be the only one who did not look like a would-be racing driver). The man's 'winter sun' tan and healthy head of combed white hair did little to soften features that would have made you think twice about crossing him back when Giorgio Chiesa had begun his legal campaign, and despite now being technically an old man, Massimiliano Molinari appeared to have lost none of his vigour.

'You'll be the English detective.' He brushed past the woman as he reached out to shake my hand. Molinari senior's grip was rough and strong, as if he had spent a lifetime delving into machinery and tightening bolts. 'Niki told me you were coming. Are you a fan of F1?'

'I take an interest.'

'But I bet you've never been this close, eh?'

'That would be correct.'

'Come.' He placed an arm around me. The woman smiled frigidly as he led me inside.

'Of course, this is all a set-up for the cameras.' Max Molinari famously spoke with a heavy Bolognese accent – I recognised it more from sketches by comedians than interviews with the man himself (which probably said something about my preferences) – and I had to concentrate to fully understand him as we moved through the paddock.

'It would all be full on race day, which is coming up.' He winked. 'So we thought we would use one of our production days to familiarise the team.' In fact, the pit *was* full – of people. But instead of their equipment, the various squads of engineers and goodness knows what else, were collected in teams across the concrete floor using strips of tape to mark out their areas. Another group was carrying out a timed drill, fully decked out in gloves and helmets, of what even I could recognise as a practice pit stop, albeit without the tyres and other tools they required. It would have been comic watching them rush from one end of the pit to the other, playing out their actions, shouting 'selecting tyre, removing tyre', if they hadn't clearly been taking it so seriously.

To the side sat a dark green Formula One car. Again, the telly didn't do it justice. What struck me most was its size. It was huge – more than a metre longer than my family SUV parked outside – but barely hip height, the cockpit slotted in behind an engine that took up almost half its body. Enormous black wheels melded into the machine like the limbs of a monstrous crocodilian emerging from lake mud.

'That's it,' the producer shouted, 'just do it how you normally would.'

The cockpit was occupied by a helmeted driver, his visor up, although as I was standing at the rear, I couldn't tell if it was Niki. It was surrounded by half-a-dozen team members, all wearing crash helmets. One held a Molinari-branded screen up in front of the driver, another a drink, which he was taking from a straw. Two others were pretending to discuss what was on a laptop, while more were knelt by the front wheels on either side.

A cameraman began to move gradually along the car. He reached the end and straightened up.

'Okay,' called the producer. 'Sorry guys, I'm going to have to ask you to do it again, this time from another angle.'

One of the cars I had seen hurtling by outside rumbled into the pit lane. Max Molinari nodded.

'Last year's model,' he said. A bunch of engineers gathered

around it, while the woman who had assailed me stood waiting for the driver to lift himself out.

Niki Molinari handed her his helmet and pulled off his white balaclava, his hair matted with sweat. The woman was saying something and indicating the camera crew, but he spotted me and came over, leaving her holding his helmet up distastefully by the rim.

'I see you've met Dad,' he said.

'How was it?' asked Massimiliano.

'Same old Imola,' he said. 'Which is the trouble – the kerbs. There could definitely be some crunch if it gets tight.'

'*When* it gets tight,' growled Massimiliano. He swore. 'We lower the floors according to the new regulations, but they haven't taken account of old circuits. So – do we soften the suspension, and thereby make the car less competitive, or limit the amount of track we use and cut down kerb riding?' He looked at me as if I might have the answer.

'The real question is,' said Niki, 'do we limit the car or the driver?'

'Or put another way,' I said, seeing as they had chosen to include me. 'Do you trust the superiority of the car or the skill of the driver?'

Massimiliano grunted, Niki grinned. 'So,' said Molinari senior. 'Niki told me you were carrying out Giorgio's final instructions.' The engine of the new car suddenly roared into life.

Snapping his headset over his ears, Massimiliano gestured towards the pit mouth.

The three of us emerged onto the track as last season's car was wheeled back inside. We began to walk up the empty lane. Molinari senior pulled his headset down around his neck. 'I suppose it was inevitable there would be a . . . How to put it? "Epilogue" to the Giorgio saga. That fucking injection system. If I'd known . . .'

'You would have still put your name on it,' said Niki. His father harrumphed.

'Yes. But I would have made damn sure that malicious prick didn't have any grounds whatsoever to make a claim.'

'He clearly believed he had been wronged,' I said. 'Whatever the facts may be.'

'Just as he believed his son was murdered,' said Massimiliano. 'Whatever the facts may be. If you ask me,' he tapped his temple, 'there was always something not quite right about the man. The father was not worthy of the son.'

I supressed an impulse to defend my deceased client. Instead I said: 'You were very fond of Fabrizio.'

'Fond?' He looked at me as if I was mad. 'He was a great driver. The best I'd ever seen.' I was conscious of Niki walking like a shadow beside us. 'He was undoubtedly set to be our number one,' Massimiliano continued obliviously. 'At least for as long as we were able to keep him. Would he have gone to Ferrari?' He chuckled. 'If he was prepared to come to Molinari in defiance of his father – certainly! But that was the point – he was purely there to win. The boy would have inspired us to make the finest cars on the track. You might think it's all about engineering, aero-dynamics, but it's as much about art, and what is art? It's inspiration!' From the existential musings of the son to the 'art' of the father, I had never imagined there was so much to motorsport.

'Yet Signor Chiesa believed you were behind Fabrizio's death,' I said.

'*Son of a bitch.*'

'Apart from Signor Chiesa's long-standing dispute with you, can you think of any other reason why he might have reached this conclusion?'

'What more do you want? He never came up with anything, did he?'

'We are currently going through his files.'

'Good luck with that. As far as I could tell, he seemed to think I'd got rid of Fabri so Niki could have a place on the first team. Or was it you who got rid of him, son?'

Niki shrugged. 'Variations of both.'

'Fabrizio was driving a Molinari when he had his accident,' I said. 'I don't suppose the car could have been tampered with?'

'Oh,' said Massimiliano. 'It could certainly have been tampered with. Any car could be. Have you read the police reports? Did they indicate it had been?'

'No, although given the state of the wreck, it may have been difficult to tell. The car would have been serviced at specialist garages, I imagine.'

'It would have been serviced at ours – it's the only one in Bologna, and after all, the car was actually *company* property – Fabri was given it gratis, to fly the flag, so to speak. We even paid for the petrol! You're welcome to speak to the staff there, be my guest.'

'And another Molinari,' I said casually, 'a silver Vernice, has been spotted near the site of the incident. We believe the driver is leaving flowers at the scene. That wasn't you, was it?' I'd couched the question with flippancy but he ignored it anyway. 'Then, I'm guessing the Vernice would have probably been purchased in the local area, which means through your Bologna dealership. I was wondering if I could speak to them and see if I can get an idea of who the owner might be.'

'Personally, I wouldn't have a problem.' Molinari senior turned those ice-blue eyes on me. 'But there are data protection issues even here in Italy – you know, *La Privacy* – and I don't think our customers would approve of us sharing their details with . . . third parties.'

I looked back at him just as coolly – everyone knew that in this land of laws every one was open to interpretation, and not only by the courts.

'Max!' A middle-aged man came marching up the lane. He called in English: 'Bianca said you were dawdling out here.'

'Ah,' said Molinari. 'It is your compatriot.' A wink. 'He's not half as polite as you.'

'Those fucking kerbs! Typical of the wankers in FIA – you know they want to bugger things up so the European tracks aren't viable. It'll be bloody Mumbai, Oman, and Kuala fucking Lumpa if they have their way. We'll spend the rest of our lives in the damn desert or jungle, for fuck's sake.'

'Jeremy,' Molinari said. 'I should introduce you to a fellow Brit, Daniel Leicester.' Jeremy's red-brown beard clung flat to his face like a climber to a mountainside. The clean-cut ruggedness suited him well, like a trust-funded adventurer. He gave me a brazen once over and proffered his hand. 'The pair of you should have a beer some time,' said Molinari. 'Perhaps you can make fish and chips together.'

'If you knew anything about fish and chips,' I said. 'You

would know they're not the kind of thing you can make at home. Or find in Bologna, for that matter.'

'There's a decent fried fish place by Mercato delle Erbe,' Niki pitched in. 'They have chips, too.'

'I've tried it,' I said. 'It is many things, but it's not fish and chips.'

Jeremy checked his expensive sports watch. 'We've only got three hours, Max. We should get out there and measure up those kerbs.' He gave me a dismissive nod and headed back to the paddock.

Molinari senior let out an avuncular laugh and slapped me on the back. 'I'd better get going,' he said. 'You should come to lunch – I'd be interested to know if you actually manage to dig anything up, and of course if we can help speed the process along . . . Those kids have lost enough already; it seems a shame for them to waste their legacy too on account of Giorgio's obsessions.' He set off back down the track. 'And I'll have a think about this silver car of yours,' he called. 'See if there isn't something we can do.'

I was left alone with Niki, who was gazing down the lane to the first curve. 'To be honest,' I said. 'I've never actually been to a Formula One circuit before.'

Niki continued to focus on the track, his expression absent its usual whimsy. He might have been strapped into a car's cockpit, tearing down the lane trying to wrest a millisecond's advantage over Leclerc or Verstappen.

'It reminds me of cricket,' I said. This shook him from his reverie.

'What?'

'The difference between the perception and reality. On

TV, the camera shoots over the bowler's shoulder, so when you're watching a match, the length of the pitch appears short and the ball slow, whereas when you're actually playing a match, the pitch is bloody long and the ball, which has the consistency of concrete, is hurtling at you at what seems like a hundred miles an hour. I tell you – you're bloody grateful to be wearing a box.'

'Box?'

'To protect *your* balls. Yeah,' I nodded thoughtfully. 'This is a bit like that.'

Niki shook his head in wonder. 'Only a British,' he said, 'could compare motor racing to cricket.'

We walked back down the lane and out through the Molinari paddock. As we passed the new car, Massimiliano Molinari and Jeremy were crouched beside it, taking measurements.

Chapter 7

The Alfa was the more sensible choice, but Rose was keen to get some driving practice and when she proposed the Punto, I knew her grandfather would bend to her will, regardless of his difficulties getting in and out of the tiny car. I was glad my daughter had expressed no interest in joining the family firm because within a week Giovanni would have undoubtedly promoted her to the boss of me.

I insisted however that the Comandante sit in the front and I drove up to the hospital – Rose could take over on the way down.

Ospedale Rizzoli was actually only a short walk from our home – across the Viale, a little way along Via San Mamolo, then up the road that ran alongside the park of San Michele in Bosco, where Rose or I often walked the dog. I doubt the irony of a world-famous orthopaedic hospital being sited at the top of one of the tallest hills overlooking Bologna was lost on anyone, but I suppose if you could make it up there unaided, you had no real use of its services.

A large part of the hospital was housed in the former monastery of San Michele, which must have been a spiritual powerhouse back in the day, the vaulted corridor stretching to a point of light as we followed the nurse to the Comandante's room. The other bed was empty for the time being, and Rose sat upon it while I took the chair.

Giovanni began to unpack. I thought he might say there was no point in us hanging around and to leave him to it, but he seemed in little hurry for us to go. When he had finished hanging up his clothes, he asked Rose if she wouldn't mind seeing if it was possible to buy a can of Coca-Cola. He dug into his pocket. 'And one for yourself, if you would like.' My daughter jumped off the bed, happy to have something to do despite the long walk back down the corridor. Giovanni finished setting out his neatly folded pyjamas upon the bed. He placed the collected works of Balzac next to them. I picked it up.

'In French.' I was impressed.

'I have already read them in Italian.'

'Of course you have. Any good, is he?'

'Well, he is certainly more "fun" than Proust.'

'I can imagine.'

'And as for *La Comédie humaine*, which is actually the extent of my reading . . .' He permitted himself a little smile.

'What?'

'I admit, that is eighty-five novels.'

'Blimey.'

'It contains the gamut of human experience – envy, avarice, spite, and a sprinkling of virtue. Most of all, the majesty of money as the arbiter of all things.'

'Is that how you see the world, then?'

'That was how the author saw it. The roots of nineteenth-century Paris were far more visible than our own – money, or the lack of it, spelled the difference between a cursed or blessed life. Without sufficient income there was neither the education nor, limited though it was, medicine to shield the individual from the grimmest of outcomes, regardless of their other attributes. Despite the fine words and costumes in the works of Honoré de Balzac, his world is far more brutal than any of these modern dramas you watch on television with their violence and foul language.'

'He was the James Patterson of the nineteenth century is what you're saying.'

'Who is James Patterson?'

'A highly successful thriller writer.'

'That would be more like Victor Hugo,' said the Comandante. 'But Balzac's novels were certainly popular, and he wrote at a tremendous rate – he published the entire cycle in ten years. He dropped dead at fifty-one.'

'I'm not surprised.' I laid the book back beside his silk pyjamas.

'You know where all my documents are, I take it.'

'By "documents", I presume you mean your will, and so on? I wondered why you had asked Rose to go on a soft drink expedition. Really, Giovanni – you don't need to worry, these kinds of operations are among the most routine. I've known of people being discharged on the same day.'

'I am not worried,' the Comandante replied peevishly. 'But as you know, I like to have everything in order.'

'In the top drawer of the shelf,' I recited, 'in your safe, the combination of which I have memorised.' It was a random six-digit number, so far as I could tell; the safe was nothing

too flashy – albeit hidden behind his wardrobe – but I suspected if you didn't know the combination, it would be a
bugger to break into. 'And among your papers, I presume,
is also an exhaustive reminder of my other duties.' The
Comandante nodded, apparently satisfied. But levity aside,
I did understand – nothing had been the same for either of
us since Lucia had been snatched away a decade past, and
nothing ever would.

Her daughter Rose returned with two cans of Coke Zero
and a Franciscan.

'Daniel!' Don Filippo gave me a hug. In his 'cappuccino'
cowl, complete with a hefty wooden cross upon his barrel
chest, he was a big man with a bowl of brown hair verging
on the medieval. He was given to bemusing his flock at the
nearby church of Santa Annunziata with sermons encompass-
ing Nietzsche, *Dancing with the Stars* (the Italian version of
Celebrity Strictly Come Dancing, a big hit among the nuns,
apparently) and the films of Pedro Almodóvar. It had always
surprised me that the Comandante, an observant Catholic
whose religion definitely leant more high than low (and
who I knew had politely declined membership of Opus Dei)
should attend a church run by Franciscans, but I suspected
it wasn't so much choice as custom – Santa Annunziata had
always been the Faidate church and always would be, regardless of the order in charge. Personally, despite marrying in
the church and agreeing for Rose to be raised in the faith,
I was neither Catholic nor particularly religious, but on the
occasions I had attended – the usual births, weddings, con-
firmations, and so on – I had to admit Don Filippo gave
good mass.

'He was looking for *Nonno*,' said Rose, turning pale 'You're going to be all right, aren't you, *Nonno*?' She looked at me. 'You said this is just routine, right?'

'It *is* routine,' I said. 'Don Filippo's just popped in to say hello as it's near the church.'

'It's near the church,' agreed Don Filippo, who I noted avoided adding it was routine. 'I was saying to Rose, we could really do with her help with our youth group – she could give English lessons.'

'Now there's an idea. You often talk about volunteering, don't you, darling?' I was stretching it a bit, although she had recently been making noises about going to Africa to help build schools, which cost thousands and seemed like a glorified vacation to me. Don Filippo's proposal sounded far more affordable, albeit with less bragging rights.

'I'd love to,' Rose said hollowly, 'but what with my studies, and Dad's teaching me to drive, I'm pretty tied up.' The priest nodded sagely.

The Comandante cleared his throat. 'Thank you for coming, Don Filippo. I realise you must be very busy. Please, take a chair.'

'Is *Nonno* really worried about his operation?' Rose asked as we walked back down the corridor.

'You know he doesn't like hospitals.'

'But what's the priest for? To give him last rites?'

I laughed. 'Don't be silly. Although admittedly he may be a little nervous – the older one gets, the more anxious one tends to become.'

'I would have thought it would be the opposite – you've

lived a long life, so you should be pretty relaxed.' I looked into her bright, blissfully uncomprehending eyes.

'I'm afraid life doesn't seem so long when you're looking at it from the other end. In fact, the older you get, the quicker time seems to pass. But the operation is genuinely routine. I'm sure he'll be back at the disco this time next week.'

Rose laughed. 'I don't think *Nonno*'s *ever* been to a disco!'

'Go on, then.' I handed her the keys.

'But Dad,' she said. 'There are *others*.'

We were standing in the car park of Rizzoli between two lanes of parked cars while others circled, waiting for a space.

'Weren't you complaining the other day I did everything myself?'

'But that was when it was the garage at *home*.'

I crossed my arms. 'You're learning to drive girl, so drive.'

'And you're not afraid I'll hit the others?'

'Not really,' I said. 'I'm only bothered about mine.' I whispered: 'If you hit another, just put your foot down and we'll scarper.'

She scowled. 'That's *so* Italian.'

'Look who's talking.'

The Punto was parked front-first between a white Range Rover Evoque and a black BMW 3 Series. Both were reasonably new and dent-free. I had been joking, of course, about taking off if she scraped one, but I did have to suppress a sudden urge to call a halt to this experiment as she daintily opened the driver's door and slid inside.

'Wind down the window,' I called.

Scrape. Clunk. The car jerked backwards. Fortunately, it

had been parked reasonably straight, otherwise it might have taken the wing off the BMW.

'Carry on,' I called. 'Take your time.' A car had halted beside me – an old man behind the wheel and his wife, presumably waiting for the space. I smiled at them apologetically; they looked blankly back at me.

The car bucked back again. This time, for reasons known best to Rose, veering towards the Range Rover. 'Wheel to the left,' I shouted, stepping back while waving my hands like an airport controller. 'Left!' The Punto broke free of the space, swinging blessedly away from the Range Rover, albeit that its nose almost shaved the Beemer.

Unfortunately, Rose was now sat facing the couple in the lane between the parked cars which, needless to say, was one way. The pensioners looked stolidly at her, the old man making a remark to his wife, who replied equally stoically. Life might seem short for some, I reflected, but for others it might appear very long indeed.

I looked over my shoulder. Enough was enough. I came around to the driver's side. 'Okay, darling,' I said. 'You did very well, but I'll take it from here.'

Rose considered the couple, who had acquired a further two cars behind them, then around at the choice confronting her – a tight three-point turn or long reverse.

She put the car into neutral and went around the other side.

I steered the Punto backwards until we reached the end of the lane, then swung it around before we switched places. 'I didn't think about that,' Rose admitted. 'Being around the right way.'

'One thing at a time,' I said. 'You did well reversing.'

'I only backed it out, Dad.'

'Under pressure. Now – down the hill.' We left the car park, following the narrow, winding road bordered by mansions and hedges until it arrived at the rear of the parkland that constituted the Giardini Margherita. We continued down until we reached the Viale.

'Where to?'

'Straight ahead.' I indicated Via Castiglione. We crossed the ring road and navigated the former gatehouse, all that remained of this section of the walls that had once encircled Bologna. We entered the old city and rumbled along a cobbled street between salmon- and yolk-porticoed facades, our path further constricted by cars parked on either side.

Castiglione became one way when you reached the gatehouse which marked the inner ring of the city's fortifications, so Rose followed the system around.

'Now where?'

'Wherever you like,' I said. 'Just drive around a bit.'

Moving onto smooth tarmac, my daughter swung down a sloping, narrow street and continued towards the centre.

As soon as you passed into the old city, you effectively stepped back half a millennia and certainly this far in, Bologna's backstreets maintained their medieval dimensions. The city's extensive one-way system helped, but in Italy's cities there are no truly one-way streets. Helmetless cyclists, skateboarders and, increasingly, grown-ups on electric scooters barrel obliviously towards you before swerving aside at the last moment, so it was no less nail-biting accompanying Rose 'inside the walls' than upon the Viale or country lanes.

We were caught in traffic along Via Carbonesi when Rose said: 'Ooh look, there's Dolores.' She waved, but Dolores didn't notice her. 'I wonder where she's going.' The traffic snailed forward and we caught up with her walking along the curb beside us. Rose was about to tap the horn, but I stopped her. 'I was only going to attract her attention,' she protested.

'Hang on a moment.' I knew *that* walk, *that* look – Dolores was following someone.

'What is it?'

'I think she's working.'

'You mean she's got a mark?' I looked at Rose in surprise. 'Mark', another term she had apparently picked up when I hadn't thought she was listening. 'Who?' Rose stretched over the steering wheel.

'Just concentrate on the job at hand,' I said. 'We've still got time to hit someone.'

'But who do you think it is? Can you see anyone?'

I made an effort to look around the SUV ahead of us, but it was no good. I considered our current workload. Since being promoted to 'Investigator', Dolores had been responsible for her own portfolio of jobs and clients, albeit I had palmed off the more boring stuff to her like background checks for corporate clients and insurance claims. We discussed our workload at weekly catch-ups, and of course divvied up commissions that required more than one investigator, but I couldn't recall Dolores saying anything about fieldwork at the last meeting – a lot of evidence could be dug up online these days, which was cheaper for clients. But that didn't mean she wasn't on the trail of someone who was claiming disability or for a workplace accident that she considered routine.

The rear of a car loomed into view.

'Watch it!' Rose broke sharply. *'Pay attention.'*

'You're doing the same as me,' she said. 'Trying to see what she's doing.'

'But I'm the passenger – you're driving. There's a big difference.'

The traffic ahead cleared. 'Go on then. And, please, keep your eyes on the road.'

We moved forward, past the lofty Renaissance facade of the church of Sant Paolo Maggiore, then over the zebra crossing and onto Via Barbiera.

We swept past Dolores, who still hadn't appeared to notice us. But she was definitely moving along Barbiera's high portico at the peculiar pace of the hunter, maintaining a rigid distance that caused her to slow when her prey did, and pause, or at least bend to tie her laces or look in a store window when they did the same.

As we left her behind, I scanned the few others walking ahead of her – an old lady with a fluffy, powder-pink jacketed *Bolognese* dog, a young woman pushing a buggy; finally a man in late middle-age, maybe his early sixties.

He looked vaguely familiar, but that could have simply been because he appeared the most likely candidate. He was strolling unconcernedly beneath the portico, between the burnt-orange shadows; past the graffiti, designer furniture stores and trendy bars. With his perma-tan, spume of straw-blond curls, the gold in his ears and dangling around his neck, he could have been a ladies' hairdresser, the proprietor of a wellness salon, or perhaps come to Bologna on business from his beach club on the Rimini or Riccione strips. (I flipped through these settings in my mind but was still unable to place him).

Rose pulled up. I looked away as the mark passed us by. Out of the corner of my eye, I noted Dolores hanging behind.

'Do me a favour, darling,' I said. 'When we get to the junction, cross over onto Sant'Isiaia, then take the first right towards Piazza San Francesco.'

Rose crossed at the lights and took the turning, following it along until we reached the corner of the piazza where the imposing basilica dominated the far side of the square. The road was tight with parked cars, but there was a gap by a gateway.

'Great, just pull up here.'

'But it says no parking.'

'Don't worry, I'm just going to pop out for a moment – you stay in the car. Move if anyone comes along.'

'But I'm not allowed . . .' I looked at her.

'*Dai,*' I said, and in a rare break from our habitual English, continued in Italian: 'Take it easy. I'll just be gone for a moment. Everything will be fine.'

I left her gawping as I got out of the car. I dashed across the square, then along the road running beside the huge bulk of the church in time to spot the mark emerge from Barbiera and turn north down Marconi in the direction of our office.

But he didn't get that far – he joined the queue boarding a bus heading the other way (I noted the final stop – Stadio, the football stadium).

I stepped back as Dolores turned the corner. She sidled up behind the queue, pretending to check a restaurant window, while actually monitoring the bus in the reflection. She

waited for another two passengers to board behind the mark
before jumping on herself.

The bus pulled out.

I walked thoughtfully back to the car – or at least where
the car should have been. Instead, I found it, engine running,
in the middle of the street facing the other way.

Rose was sat holding the steering wheel, her cheeks flushed.
'You turned it around,' I said as I got in. 'Brava!'

'I thought I'd better get some practice.'

'You didn't hit anything then?'

She glanced in the mirror. 'Well, Papa,' she said. 'Maybe it
would be better if we didn't hang around.'

Chapter 8

We parked the Punto without further incident in the car park beneath our office. Rose went to her *liceo* (Minghetti, just around the corner – the family tradition was Galvani, where the families of *Bologna Bene* tended to send their kids and which had latterly become English immersive, but as language was not an issue for Rose, we/she had plumped for Bologna's other 'top' school, which had a reputation for being more arts-orientated and, frankly, a little more laid back) while I went up to the office.

Faidate Investigations was housed on the fourth floor of a relatively modern office block that had been constructed during the post-war boom. Although Bologna's old city had mostly avoided Allied bombing, Via Marconi, with its proximity to the railway station, which had been the Germans' – and remained Italy's – transport hub, had not been so fortunate. In fact, the only old-style edifice that appeared to have survived unscathed was now the local branch of Deutsche Bank.

The reception had that mid-morning feel, the metal blinds splicing the elongated room with noirish shadows. The sofa where clients would be asked to wait, perhaps leafing through the latest issue of *Carabinieri* magazine, was empty.

'How's the Comandante?' Celeste stood up behind the marble-topped, baroque-style desk, but because she was very small, even upright she remained mostly concealed by the large Apple computer screen.

'He seems to be all right,' I said, coming around to the side of her desk so I could see her properly. 'But he was clearly a little nervous.'

It still felt odd finding her here instead of Alba. The pair couldn't have been physically more different – Alba's ancestral origins in robust Emilian farming stock were self-evident, while Celeste's, springing from the 'Spanish' district of Naples, suggested as much Greek and Castilian as Italian; in any case, a definite tendency towards the compact. Yet, while Alba had a personality as big as she was, Celeste, like many a Neapolitan woman, projected an aura far greater than her physical size. She might have been compact, but compact like a suitcase nuke.

Sadness swept her face. 'The poor man. Who's with him at the moment?'

'Well, when we left, his priest had popped in.' I checked my watch. 'But he'll have probably left by now.'

'And Alba?'

'She'll be with Little Lucia.' That much was obvious – otherwise, Celeste would have been.

'And Claudio?' She meant Alba's boyfriend. 'Couldn't he look after her?'

'He's working, I guess.'

'So,' I could feel a definite charge, as if the atmosphere was about to snap with static, 'you're saying no one is with him at the moment?'

'He's fine,' I turned my palms up, as if to deflect whatever was coming. 'He's got a good book. Several, in fact.'

'*Magg rutt o'cazz.*' Her Neapolitan sounded as if she was trying to rid a bitter taste from her mouth. She gave me an exasperated look. '*And Dolores?*'

'Ah, your cousin – I wanted to have a word with you abou—'

'I mean – is she going?'

'I don't think so, and to be honest—'

Celeste ejaculated another string of Neapolitan curses. I took a wary step back. She switched off her computer and flung her things into her fake (albeit a very good fake) Hermès handbag.

'I was going to buy *Sfogliatella* from La Borbonica on my way to see him this afternoon,' she said. 'When, and if, you see my cousin, tell her to bring some.' She gave me a look every bit as dismissive as the one I had received from Jeremy at the Imola circuit. 'In fact, don't worry, I'll message her myself.' She plucked her jacket off the hanger and began to head for the door. I felt the sudden urge to assert my authority over the twenty-three-year-old interloper.

'And who's going to staff the reception?'

Celeste swivelled around with a Medusa-like glare.

'Jaco,' she yelled. Jacopo came rushing out.

'You're to mind reception.' He gave her the thumbs-up. She pushed through the double doors and, plainly not having time to wait for the lift, clattered down the stairwell.

I was seized by a vision of her as my future sister-in-law

and the mother of an additional clutch of grandchildren for *Nonno* Faidate. I wasn't sure how I felt about that. I didn't think I would have much choice.

'You don't get it, then,' I said to Jacopo as he was setting up.

'Get what?' he said from beneath the desk.

'The evil eye.'

'Oh, she's from Naples. It doesn't mean anything.'

'So's Dolores.'

Jacopo's head emerged from below the desk. 'She's the exception.'

'Dolores said something similar. I spotted her before I came in – she was trailing someone, followed them onto a bus heading to the stadium. You wouldn't happen to know what she's up to, would you?'

Jacopo slid out. In the old days, it would have been better to leave reception empty rather than have the tattooed would-be *punkabestia* greeting clients, but now I had to admit he looked almost respectable. 'She never tells me anything these days. Shouldn't *you* know what she's up to?'

'I suppose I should.'

I left Jacopo fiddling with cables and went through to the back offices. Photos of the Comandante during his time in uniform lined the corridor, along with our various framed qualifications and licences from Prefettura. It didn't look unlike the hallway of the notary in Osteria Grande, give or take a grandfather clock.

With Celeste on her mercy mission, it would be just Jacopo and me in Marconi. I passed the Comandante's office, which resembled the study of a gentleman's club, and Jacopo's gloomy plastic jungle of glowing computer screens and cables.

Dolores' office blinds were up and the room was bleached bright with sunlight. Her desk was typically clear, except for leads where she had unplugged her laptop, the hardback books she balanced it on when she was Zooming – a graphic novel on seventeenth-century female artist Artemisia Gentileschi and a giveaway hardback on the interior décor of a banking foundation – the usual framed photo she had of the cow she had cared for in her urban farming days, and a batch of documents in her in-tray. I picked them up – mainly CVs to run checks on, along with her work phone bill, some travel receipts, and a half-completed expenses sheet.

A cloud darkened the room, then quickly passed. Something winked at me from the bin next to her desk, red like a warning, or traffic light. I hesitated. I wasn't averse to going through people's litter, but this was one of my colleagues.

I plucked out the wrapping. The backing had caught my attention – the silhouette of an attacker fleeing fire-red flames signalling pepper spray to the strength of two million SHA, or heat units, more than twice the minimum required to give an attacker a very bad day.

I opened the blinds in my own office and gazed down on Via Marconi. The pepper spray could be something Dolores always carried, although I had never noticed it before. But it was legal in Italy and could be found in the purses of many women, along with their keys and phones, especially if they were going on a night out. And in our line of work, particularly if you were a woman, I would imagine it would be handy to have to hand. I'd sometimes thought about it myself. In fact, Dolores could have probably got a licence to carry a gun if she had wished, a privilege currently denied to me as a non-citizen, although my application (for citizenship) was in an – extremely long – queue.

But I still found it unsettling. I came back to this 'stuff' she had apparently been dealing with. Was she feeling threatened? Was someone connected with an old case harassing her? Someone in her private life?

I switched on my desktop computer – I was not nearly as mobile as the young folk – and clicked on the Excel sheet that supposedly tracked the team's work, which I had instituted now Dolores and Alba were playing more independent roles (the Comandante had steadfastly refused to participate in 'this Anglo-Saxon managerialism' as he put, and when Alba faithfully quizzed him every week in the hope he might cough something up, he frostily replied: 'the business of detection').

I clicked on the folder containing Dolores' current portfolio and ran the cursor along it. Her work was laid out, I was pleased to note, as neatly as her desk.

She was technically my junior, and mostly occupied with the firm's bread and butter work like background checks on job applicants, which mainly involved phoning around former employers and searching the internet and sites like Linked In. She had two active insurance jobs that might involve fieldwork – a disability claim from a woman who had a medical certificate claiming a back injury after being required to lift heavy goods at a supermarket (the company were disputing the severity of the injury) and another from a clothes store claiming on stock damaged by a flood in the basement. The fact that the store itself appeared to be going out of business had led the insurance company to ask us to look into the claim. It was just possible that the store owner might have been the guy Dolores had been following, but I doubted it.

Dolores had also begun taking on some 'relationship' work, but opening the folder I saw there was only one active investigation – a gay couple who were living together, but one of whom suspected the other of still seeing his wife and trying to have a child with her. This *had* involved some 'fieldwork' by Dolores and she had followed the couple to a fertility clinic. But the man in question – a handsome thirty-something lawyer – was definitely not the individual Dolores had been trailing.

She had closed a further two – both straight professional couples; classic cases of grown-up kids and straying husbands, quickly resolved with a report and photographs passed to the wife. We – or rather, I – had a further five 'relationships' open, but these were for clients we called 'the ladies that lunch', wealthy women of a certain age whose husbands kept mistresses, visited high-class prostitutes, or were closeted homosexuals with entirely alternative lives, and wished to be kept abreast of their activities. I suspected that some of the 'ladies' rather enjoyed the prestige of having an English detective on a sort-of retainer, and our meetings usually involved my taking them to lunch at Pappagallo or Diana for what amounted to a gossip. I graciously paid for the meal, which I then charged to expenses.

I stayed in the office through the day until finally that afternoon I heard Dolores talking to Jacopo in the reception. She popped her head around the door.

'All right, boss?'

I looked up and pushed back my chair.

'Hey,' I said. 'I saw you this morning getting on a bus to Stadio.' She stepped fully into the room, crossing her arms.

'What time was that?'

'I guess around eleven. Surely you haven't got that many buses today?'

'There was the bus heading up to the Residence, and the one coming back – I was a bit pushed for time. My bike's at the repair shop.'

It was true – that route did pass close to home. 'What were you doing back there?'

'Checking how Alba was progressing with the files, I felt a bit bad about leaving her to it. You know, we had the boxes delivered today.'

'Yes, of course we did.' I played for time. 'How did it go, then?'

'*Mamma mia*. The lock-up was piled high on either side. We had to use Claudio's van in the end – I counted them, there were forty-two.'

'With the workshops gone, where did you put them all?'

'The basement.'

'And how was Alba doing?'

'I think we may all have to pitch in. I'll have to help, and maybe Celeste and you too, otherwise it'll take forever . . .'

'I'll speak to Alba this evening,' I said. Dolores was turning to go when I added: 'You know, when you were saying before that you had "stuff" you needed to sort out, are you sure there's nothing I, or we here, can help with?'

Dolores nodded emphatically. 'That's all sorted now.'

'No safety issues, or anything that might somehow be

connected with your work here? Or in your private life?'

She looked amused. 'Why?'

All right, I'd pick up that gauntlet. 'So what were you doing trailing that guy in Via Barberia?'

'When?'

'This morning. Rose and I passed you in the car.'

'Nah-ah. I was walking down Barberia, yeah, but on my way to the bus stop. Like I said, my bike's—'

'In the repair shop.'

She let out a nervous laugh: 'You think I was trailing someone?'

'That's what it looked like.'

'Nah.' The corners of her eyes crinkled with amusement. 'I guess you checked my log?' I shrugged, yes. 'Well then.'

'That's what I was asking.'

'Then I don't know what to say, honestly.'

Dolores Pugliese was twenty-six years old, but for the first time, despite still being got up rather like a student intern – and the typical Italian university career might last well into one's mid-twenties – she seemed to fill out the doorway like the professional woman, the Investigator on a *contratto a tempo indeterminato*, she actually was. I decided to take a different tack.

'You realise you're not permitted to work off-the-books, right?'

She jabbed a finger at me. 'I'm accused of moonlighting now?'

'Oh come on, Dolores.' I sat back.

'Dan,' she said. 'You've got the wrong end of the stick.'

'And the pepper spray?'

She didn't so much as flinch. 'You've been going through my trash?' Her amused expression returned. 'Aren't there laws against that?' She laughed. 'Don't we break them all the time?'

'I'm worried about you,' I admitted. 'That's all. I would like to think . . . Well, not that we don't have any secrets, but if something was going on . . .'

'Nothing's going on, I swear! I always carry bloody pepper spray. Of course I do!'

'Of course you do,' I mumbled.

'Is everything okay?' Jacopo called down the corridor.

'Fine!' Dolores shouted back. She smiled at me. 'You really don't need to worry, Dan. One daughter's enough, eh?'

Dolores left. I contemplated the empty doorway. There had to be a good reason why she hadn't told me about the guy she was trailing, and not just because it had been on company time. Was it connected to the purchase of the pepper spray? It seemed likely, whatever she might say.

What was she up to? And why wouldn't she tell me?

Chapter 9

Bologna had once been a city state which granted citizenship to newcomers only grudgingly and came to tolerate the overlordship of the Papacy as the least worst way of avoiding dominance by more rapacious powers. So while a Bishop sat in impotent splendour in the sumptuously frescoed Sala Urbana in Palazzo d'Accurzio, the real power lay across Piazza Maggiore in the hands of the consuls who sat judge over mercantile affairs in the Guild Hall. These were drawn from families whose names pop up again and again upon Bologna's grand *palazzi* – Bentivoglio, Pepoli, Isolani. And while one branch might become too big for its boots and be hounded from the city by its rivals, you could be sure that within a few decades, or centuries, another would rise to prominence. And for at least four hundred years, my adopted family, the Faidate, had served them. The fortunes of the grand houses might rise and fall, but the Faidate continued to prosper regardless of the political weather.

But while the city, with its protective walls, remained the sole realm for the ever-cautious and calculating Faidate, for most of its rulers, Bologna was a kind of dormitory – a place to do business and politics; to display wealth, first through the towers that loured over, and frequently toppled down upon, the city, then their more stable and striking *palazzi*, only appropriate for the royalty of a republic. Yet 'inside the walls', Bologna was a crowded, fetid place of disorder and disease. You might require a presence in the city to keep your finger on the pulse, but almost all the ruling clans had their 'seats' among their principal source of wealth – the rich Emilian farmland.

The oldest families owned *rocche*, castles like the one set upon the hill in little Dozza. But the 'new' old money exported the fashion for *palazzi* from the city to their flat farmland and, unencumbered by neighbours, constructed huge edifices across the Piadana Plain. The ones on the periphery of Bologna sometimes came to be swallowed by the city – a former hunting lodge turned into a museum bordering a transport depot; a family *palazzo* taken over by an obscure branch of local government, its grounds sacrificed to a housing estate. But other *palazzi* continue to stand among vast acres of farmland that may or may not be still in the family.

Yet few of these grand buildings are actually occupied by their original owners, and many stand empty. Not necessarily abandoned – huge expense may have been expended, often by ancient banking foundations, to preserve their frescoed hallways and chambers – but they are rarely used as intended. Heating and air-conditioning costs are prohibitive. Improvements that might affect the historical integrity of the buildings, never mind harm the art, are forbidden by the authorities. In short, while the old money may have divested itself of such liabilities, new money doesn't feel inclined to put up with stone-cold/stifling-hot piles in the middle of mosquito-crazy nowhere. They've got Cortina and the Seychelles for that.

But there are always exceptions.

I was half an hour outside Bologna, on the Imola road, a little way beyond Osteria Grande. The car's sat-nav sent me straight through Lungo Campo, the 'town' that was the single address I had for Palazzo Pepoli-Molinari and which seemed to consist of a few houses and a bar, before I found myself out the other side among cabbage-green fields of what was actually broccoli.

Looking in the rear-view mirror, I spotted what I had missed – a series of buildings set back from the town with a huge *palazzo* at their epicentre, its rows of rectangular, cell-like windows looking over the surrounding countryside.

I followed my nose to a narrow gravel road with a canal on one side and a hedge on the other until I arrived at a pair of open wrought-iron gates integrated into a sturdy wire fence that was concealed behind a hedge. Driving through, I noted the famous Molinari 'double M' worked into the fretwork. At least I was in the right place.

I drove down a dirt road bordered on either side by fields of greens. At the end a procession of overgrown cypress screened a lemon-yellow *palazzo*.

The size of the trees, which dwarfed the cars parked in front of them, only served to emphasise the scale of the build-ing behind. While Palazzo Pepoli-Molinari probably dated back to the Renaissance, it was more beast than beauty. Show off all you like in the city, it seemed to say, but here in the countryside with its unlovely cash crops and rudimentary roads, it's all business.

The cars had been too far away for me to tell at a distance, but as I pulled up I could see they were all Molinaris. Here was Niki's sleek Domino supercar. Beside it, a pair of gleaming 'Molinari green' SUVs that made my Alfa, of which I was, I confess, pathetically proud, seem like a tugboat next to superyachts.

And at the far end, a silver Molinari Vernice coupé.

I pulled in beside it.

Although I was screened by the trees, I was quite aware I might be being watched – I imagined a place like this would be bristling with surveillance equipment – but what the hell.

I peered in through the tinted glass of the Vernice at the maroon leather and walnut interior, which was otherwise empty save for a half-litre bottle of mineral water. I walked around the back and took a photo of the numberplate.

I followed the tree-line to where the drive fanned out to the entrance – a comparatively modest set of steps leading up to a pair of oak doors. I pressed the bell. There was no name, intercom, or camera I could see.

I stepped back and waited. I had no doubt I had been heard and was not going to give them the satisfaction of trying again. Instead, I placed my hands behind my back and turned to look down the road, breathing in the scent of spring, in this case the herbaceous, bath-salt aroma of the cypress, uncommon in Emilia, but which clearly served a purpose – to mask the pervasive whiff of manure.

The door opened behind me. An angular young woman in a modest black dress, her collarbones underlining her frame beneath the cotton. But she didn't seem starved or anorexic, simply built that way, as if for efficiency. Her black hair was combed back as neatly as the rest of her. She didn't ask me who I was or my business, simply ushered me inside.

I followed her along a vaulted hallway frescoed with dallying deities. Modern abstract and figurative paintings lined the grey stone walls. We passed a vast hall that had clearly been restored to its former, frescoed glory, rows of seats set out upon timeworn parquet to face a podium and screen. On our right, a broad stone staircase, modern statuettes occupying alcoves where once, presumably, had sat busts of stern-looking Pepoli, or their favoured humanist heroes.

The woman opened a pair of tall glass-paned doors that looked onto a garden and led me down some steps.

Further functional Renaissance-era edifices were dotted around the garden, including an intricately tiled tower I took to be some kind of former pigeon loft, although an array of antennae and satellite dishes now nested upon its roof.

In contrast to the main *palazzo*, these buildings were to a more human scale, but they were big enough – the woman led me along a path to a three-storey villa set above a ground floor that had once clearly been used as some kind of store, its half-dozen arched entrances now closed by steel shutters painted terracotta to match the villa's facade.

A further set of stone steps up, and the woman opened the front door.

Massimiliano Molinari emerged from a *soggiorno* where a huge tan modern sofa sat opposite a large flat screen TV tuned, naturally, to a programme about motor racing.

He grasped my hand with both of his. 'Did you find the place okay?'

'Well, I found the place eventually.' He laughed.

'It's a bit out of the way, but it helps keep us out of trouble.' In contrast to the main building, the villa had a homely feel, at least if you lived the kind of life featured in the Sunday supplements. Plenty of tasteful art, designer furniture and family photos. But, with the exception of a framed silver photograph featuring Niki spraying champagne from the podium, and a very old one of Massimiliano knelt proudly beside an early Molinari prototype, there was no other car memorabilia.

Niki Molinari appeared from the far door. Father and son locked onto me with those brilliant blue eyes, like a pair of Midwich Cuckoos. 'It's an impressive set-up you have here,' I said, 'although you could have just told me about the Vernice.'

'But Mum's never met a private eye,' he grinned. 'She was curious.' I looked between them.

'The car belongs to your *mother*?'

A beautiful young woman popped her head around the door.

'It's ready,' she said.

Niki smirked. 'My sister.'

The dining room was at the rear of the house, overlooking a series of gardens and out-buildings. There were five of us – myself, Molinari senior and his wife Aurora, who bore the unmistakable mark of Bologna's plastic surgery boom of the 1980s which had left many a wealthy old lady with the bloated features of the recently drowned; Niki, and his sister Agnese, who as yet had no cause to go under the knife. I suspected, as is traditional in Italian households, Aurora was boss at home and had been responsible for the interior décor. I doubted her husband had actually been forbidden to express his taste, I simply suspected he had no interest in anything outside automobiles. Aurora seemed to read my mind.

'The only place Max really spends any time is that one.' She waved the serving ladle towards a building opposite with heavy oak doors. 'His workshop.'

'I like to tinker,' he said.

'Dad's got one of the largest vintage collections in Italy,' said Niki. 'He pulls them apart, then puts them back together again.'

'I pay a thousand people to design future Molinaris,' said Max. 'Mostly young people, but they're forever re-inventing the wheel. The key to our future is rooted in the past.' I could imagine him delivering that from the podium. Molinari senior appeared to share his son's knack for dropping rehearsed lines.

'You'll know Speedy, then,' I said.

'I'm sorry, who?'

'Vladimir Bonnacini. He specialises in servicing vintage cars, has a garage in Imola.' Max still looked blank. 'He mentioned he tested cars for you in the early days.'

'Well, a lot of guys tested for us,' said Molinari. 'But this Speedy character sounds interesting, I'll have to look him up.'

We commenced our *primo* – tortellini dusted with parmesan and a garnish of spinach leaves, as if we were at a restaurant.

'You don't really think young Fabrizio was murdered, do you?' asked Aurora. 'It was a tragedy, yes, but . . .' She glanced at Max. 'It was such a shame what happened with Giorgio.

We were friends in the old days, me and Giusepinna – his wife – we often went shopping together. If you ask me, that was when he actually began to, you know, go funny – after she died. He never got over it – then came this . . . mechanical system that gave Maxi so many sleepless nights, and then, of course, his son.

'It was almost as if Giorgio was looking for someone to blame for all his misfortune. Some kind of, I don't know, *plan* to make sense of it all . . . But you've found nothing, I presume?'

'Not very much, signora.' I turned to Agnese. 'Are you connected with the family business?'

Having ignored me apart from a brief acknowledgment, Agnese Molinari paused her fork half way to her mouth, then set it down. Massimiliano gazed curiously at his daughter. Niki assumed a supercilious smile. Aurora simply looked sad.

'My work, detective,' she said solemnly, swallowing me with her huge brown eyes, 'is the most important of all – to produce new Molinari.'

Agnese was spectacularly beautiful in the way daughters of brutish yet highly successful men and their trophy wives have a tendency to be, as if evolution was rubbing it in the faces of the rest of us. But she also clearly had a brittle edge, as if God was adding: 'Be careful what you wish for.' My usual style would have been to make light of her remark, but I sensed she was too self-absorbed to have much of a sense of humour, especially about herself.

'Do you have children, then, signora?' I asked gently.

'Three.' She turned to her father. 'Jeremy wants to send Michele to his old school in England.' Aurora let out a little gasp.

'But Agnese . . .' she began. Her daughter held up her hand.

'Did he mention it to you?' she asked. Massimiliano Molinari frowned. He wasn't looking quite so relaxed now. Even Niki had lost that smirk.

'You know we only talk shop,' he muttered.

'I would have thought the future of your oldest grandchild – your heir, but one,' she glanced at Niki, who was staring at her intensely, 'would have been "shop"'.

'You know what I mean.'

'But he's only seven,' said Aurora.

'Asshole.' Niki was looking at his father, although he presumably meant the company's Principal.

'He says it will "make a man of him",' Agnese began to warm to her theme, 'that he needs to get a "decent British education". He seems to be quite keen on the idea.'

'He's only seven!' Aurora exclaimed, her rubbery mask wobbling. 'How could he even *think* of it?' Glances were exchanged between the other family members. 'You can't let him,' she said to Massimiliano.

'I'll have a word,' he said gruffly. 'Obviously, I wouldn't want him to send the boy away. But it is a family matter.'

'*Our* family.' She banged the table and the crockery jumped. Max Molinari gave her a sheepish look. I knew more about Molinari senior now, who I had of course Googled. I had read the articles associating him with a string of younger women who all shared the same long dark hair as both wife and daughter. I can't say it surprised me – I presumed it came with the territory in this hyper-macho world which was all about machines, a mechanical place where everything had its function and all that counted was the latest, most powerful model; an objectified world then, within a universe of things. Yet everything was comparative – while in England a motor mogul might simply trade in his old wife for a new one, even the divorce bill in its way signifying how high he was up the ladder, in Italy there was something to be said for retaining one's spouse while being associated with younger women, a failure to square this particular circle revealing an essential weakness in one's character – a loss, and therefore unacceptable – which inevitably gave the marriage a different dynamic.

'I'll speak to him.' Molinari senior said firmly.

Now Agnese looked at me. 'Jeremy says British private schools are the best in the world. Is that true?'

'I couldn't honestly say,' I said. 'It's not something I've given much thought to.'

'Because you know, in Italy it's the opposite – you only send your child to a private school if they can't keep up at a state one.'

'The local school is fine,' insisted Aurora. 'And he's so young!'

'Are the state schools in Britain so bad?' asked Niki.

'Not at all,' I replied. 'Of course, there are always some that are better than others.'

'So why does everyone send them private?'

I looked around the curious faces with a sinking feeling. Never had the chasm between myself and Italians felt so great. How could I begin to explain the peculiar dynamics of Britain's class system, which at the end of the day was less about facts than feelings?

'Well,' I said, 'only a tiny minority of children actually do attend private school.' I could tell by their expressions they found this unlikely. I realised that all the British people that entered their orbit probably had. 'Anyway, there is the perception that the educational standard is superior, not least because there are fewer to a class.'

'Less competition,' Niki said triumphantly.

'The facilities also tend to be of a higher standard.'

'That's a good point,' said Massimiliano. 'Our schools are falling apart.'

'And I suppose, from the parents' point-of-view, there's also the sense that their children are mixing with those from a similar background . . .'

'You mean contacts?' Niki asked quickly. 'People who will get them work?'

'I'm not sure it's quite as crude as that, at least any more. But,' I admitted, 'I don't suppose it can hurt.'

'These British are always making fun of us Italians,' observed Massimiliano, 'but it's really not so different.'

'And,' I added, thinking on it, 'a private education does appear to instil a certain confidence.'

'But why is that?' said Niki, who seemed genuinely confused. 'If they haven't been pitted against the best, what have they got to feel so confident about?'

I looked helplessly around those puzzled faces. 'I suppose they learn the right way to hold a knife and fork?' Now they looked even more confused. 'I'm being facetious, but when you put all these things together, it must help pupils feel more sure of themselves – after all, that's what their parents are paying for.'

'It might work in England,' said Agnese, 'but here they would think he was a snob.' I could see what she was saying, although part of me was also thinking – doesn't *every* Italian boy grow up thinking they're special?

'Anyway,' Aurora pitched in. 'His future is *here*, not England – he will go to Galvani and the friends he meets there will serve him for life.'

Niki asked mischievously: 'And Jeremy, what do you think of him?'

I shrugged. 'I've barely met the man.'

'But did he strike you as a nice guy? A humble guy?' He added in English: 'Or a bit "snob"?'

'It's really not for me to say,' I replied in Italian. 'Although in my experience, good and bad, like intelligence and good looks, are distributed pretty equally regardless of what school you went to.'

Niki clapped his hands. 'Now that's the truth! I'm an ugly bastard even though I went to Galvani, while Fabrizio who went to the technical school, well wasn't he a stunner!' He looked pointedly at his sister.

'And what school did you go to, Signor Leicester?' asked Aurora. 'A private or state?'

All eyes were again on me.

'A grammar,' I said.

'And what's a grammar?'

'Let me put it this way,' I said. 'They taught us Latin but my mum made my tea.'

We had finished lunch and an elderly, black-clad woman every bit as slim and elegant as the one who had shown me in and who may have been her grandmother, began to tidy up the plates together with Aurora, whom I suspected was putting on a show for the guest. I had decided this was as good a time as any to ask Agnese some pointed questions, but Niki said: 'Come, let me show you the murals.'

Even Massimiliano seemed to share my sense the game was over. 'Niki,' he said. 'I'm sure Daniel will want to be getting away.'

'We'll only be a minute,' he said like a kid with a new friend. He came around the table and almost hoisted me to my feet.

I had already noted the staircase in the hallway that curved upwards into the light also curved downward into gloom, and it was this way we went, a light clicking on automatically as we descended.

'This was always my favourite part of the house,' Niki said, pushing open a plain wooden door into darkness. I followed him through and strip lights blinked into life.

We were on the ground floor of the building, which was actually more like a huge basement with whitewashed, vaulted ceilings. Parked around us must have been a dozen classic sports cars.

'This building,' said Niki leading me between them, 'is actually older than the one at the front which they threw up when they got rich but never had the money to complete, so, like today, it was used mainly for show and guests. It was here the family lived, and they built it like this so their tenant farmers could drive their produce right in, and it could be stored. The family lived on top of their produce in the same way their *contadini* lived with their livestock, the pigs and that, on the ground floor.'

'Only to a grander scale.'

He laughed. 'Yeah. Now of course Dad uses it for his collection.'

'And very impressive it is.' Niki didn't respond. It was as if the many millions of euros' worth of fast cars meant nothing to him.

'Look,' he said. 'There's one.' He was pointing to a column with the crude cartoon of a tank drawn in charcoal. 'And here, see, another.' Upon the next column a slightly superior hand with a rudimentary grasp of perspective had sketched a line of riflemen crouched behind sandbags pointing their carbines towards an unseen enemy. 'But these are the really great ones.'

Niki beckoned me over to where on the walls around a flame-orange Lamborghini Aventador an even more talented hand had created black and red frescoes depicting an injured soldier being carried between his comrades, then lying in a hospital bed, a fondly caricatured doctor seizing the top and bottom of a comically broken leg, then, in the next scene, snapping it back together while the soldier yells in pain. On the adjacent wall the soldier was sat convalescing in a bath chair, his plastered leg, busy with scribbles and slogans, sticking out in front of him, while a grotesque nurse with huge knockers stood behind him. In the background was a charcoal sketch of what was clearly Palazzo Pepoli-Molinari, which, perhaps due to the Germanic hand, reminded me of Colditz.

On the final wall, the soldier was depicted marching off in full kit, his rifle over his shoulder, the doctor waving as the buxom nurse wiped her eyes. A pair of SS flashes were clearly visible on the soldier's collar.

'First it was a German military base during the war,' said Niki. 'Instead of Dad's cars, they put their vehicles here. Then at some point it was taken over by the SS and they used it as a hospital. They put a big red cross on the roof, but that didn't stop the Allies as they bombed it anyway, which actually turned out to be good for us because unlike the main house that meant there wasn't much historical stuff left to preserve – the only intact frescoes were these, which of course the *sovrintendenza* insisted we keep!

'I used to love it down here,' his hand traced the lines of the cartoon, 'before I knew what it all stood for, I mean – before I realised the same guys who drew this probably slaughtered innocent families in the hills, never mind the rest. I begged Mum and Dad to turn this space into my bedroom. Can you imagine? Alone down here in the cold and the dark? Crazy! But Dad hadn't entirely filled the place up then, and in my mind I would have had the best of both worlds for a little boy – the company of soldiers and fast cars.'

'You're still a little boy, though, isn't that the truth, Niki?' Agnese was slouching against the wall, the fighting fit SS soldier apparently marching towards her. Her arms were crossed; a sly, sibling smile played on her lips.

'You take life seriously enough for the pair of us, sis.'

'Oh, life's a comedy all right. Like a cartoon by the SS.' They stared at each other, locked in a hundred historical battles.

It was up to me to break the spell: 'You're the one who's been leaving the flowers.'

'I'm sorry?'

'The flowers at the site of Fabrizio's death.'

'What about it?' She looked back at her brother, who couldn't restrain his rubbery grin. 'Hold on – you mean you came all this way for me? Did Dad know about this?' She answered her own question. 'Naturally. That was why he insisted I didn't bring the kids. And Jeremy is at the plant in Forli.'

'Daniel kept asking about your car,' said Niki. 'It was bound to come out.'

'And why couldn't you have just told me?' I asked. Niki's cool eyes – his father's eyes – drilled into me.

'I thought I'd better check with Dad.'

'So why didn't either of you mention it at the circuit? Oh.' I realised. 'Jeremy.'

'Yeah, *Jere*—'

'*Basta*, Niki,' said his sister. 'If he's so interested, I can tell my own story. In fact, now you've lured us down to your playroom you can fuck off.'

Niki chuckled, holding up his hands before sidling out between the cars. As he disappeared back around the corner, he gave me a playful wave.

'I apologise,' I said. 'This was nothing to do with me.'

'You're just doing your job,' she said. 'But you're a man in a boys' world. You realise that, don't you.'

'Boys with their toys,' I said, looking around.

'We're all their toys.'

'And Fabrizio?'

She rolled her eyes. 'You want me to say he was different? Oh, I doubt it. I doubt it very much. He would have probably gone the same way in the end with the clothes, the watches, the cars, of course the cars. Women, too, no doubt, even if . . . Well.' Her eyes gleamed. She teared-up as casually as her brother, I thought, even if she didn't possess his hard, watchful eyes. 'But he wasn't like that yet – he was too young, innocent, which is what drew me to him. Along with his fantastic good looks! You think I'm deep? I'm not so deep.

'I was the "older woman", all of four years, but at that age it may as well have been thirty. He was my brother's best friend, although I didn't realise that until after I had noticed him. I mean – I spent most of my time trying to avoid Niki.'

'This was before you were involved with Jeremy?'

'Oh, please. We'd been married two years. The shine had already worn off. When I was growing up, I'd sworn I would never get involved with a car man, but I was getting over a professor at the university – I studied finance, he was my prof, but not old, simply a PhD student. Anyway, needless to say, he broke my heart. Then Jeremy appeared on the scene, ten years my senior. He was Molinari's new Principal, hired to breathe some life into the *scuderia*, and he seemed so different to the others surrounding Papa. But I realise now it was simply that he was British. All our case studies on the business course were from the UK or US. I loved the Anglo Saxon way of doing business, and he arrived with his British directness after all these fucking *mammone*, mamma's boys, and for me as much as the *scuderia* it really was a breath of fresh air.' She sighed. 'But of course, it didn't last. I eventually realised he was just as fucked up as the others, only in different, unknowable, *unfathomable* English ways. And now he wants to send Michele away, turn him into another fucked-up Englishman I won't understand.' Her eyes narrowed, her face contorting with what appeared to be real hate as she ran her hands down her sides. 'Son of a bitch.'

'Perhaps he just thinks it's best for Michele,' I said softly. I didn't feel particularly inclined to defend Jeremy, but I may have succumbed to a little national pride.

'Sure,' she nodded mockingly. 'That's what he says.'

Well, I was not here to provide marriage counselling: 'So you had this . . . *storia* with Fabrizio after you were married to Jeremy, and you've been leaving flowers ever since. Forget-me-nots.'

'A sort of memorial, no? I'm sentimental that way.' Her eyes fixed challengingly onto mine.

'You loved him.'

'Of course I loved him.'

'Would you have left Jeremy for him?'

'I . . .' She blinked, and the tears finally tumbled. I would have offered her a tissue had I had one. Instead, she wiped them with the back of her hand, just like her brother. 'That was never a question I asked myself.'

'Yet, seven years ago . . .' I stopped myself. My stomach knotted. A triumphant smile had appeared on Agnese's lips.

'Your father knew,' I said. 'Your brother knew. Did Jeremy know?'

'I have two younger daughters.' Agnese examined her fingers. 'Jeremy says I can send them to any school I like.'

'You're saying – because he presumes they are his?' She shrugged.

'He certainly seems less interested in depriving his daughters of their mother.'

'But how did he learn about you and Fabrizio?'

She tutted, shaking her head. 'I thought we had it under wraps. Jeremy was away a lot, busy with work and so on.

He barely had time to fuck me. In fact, it was only after I realised I was pregnant, I made . . .' She stuck out her coffee-sulphured tongue. 'God, I even disgust myself. And then Fabrizio was dead.'

'Did your family know about your affair before or after?'

'It must have been before, although I certainly didn't realise at the time, but following the accident, well, it became clear. I think Fabri must have told my brother, or Niki guessed, I don't know. In any case, Fabri was no angel, he was just some kid.'

'Yet Niki didn't say anything?'

'You think Niki is the kind to stick up for the honour of his sister? He would have probably asked for all the details! To Niki, everything that's not about Niki is a joke.' She made a mean smile. 'At most, he would have probably stored the information for later use, maximum advantage. You have to understand that about Niki – behind the clown he's a competing machine, just like Dad. He probably told my father at some point, I don't know when – when he felt it would most serve him, probably. Neither of them ever said anything to me. They didn't need to.

'In fact, believe it or not, Niki's the subtle one – he doesn't actually require the applause so long as he has the win, whereas with Dad it's all about the crowd, he can't help himself. The remarks he's made about Michele, his good looks – "I don't know where he gets them from!" – how he would "become a racing driver like his father". He said that one Christmas when Jeremy was with us, in Italian, but even though Jeremy can't speak Italian, or pretends not to, I'm sure he picked it up. And Dad knew he would.'

'But why would he say such a thing in front of your husband?'

Agnese looked at me as if I was stupid. 'Because he hates him, of course. No, not because he's a "protective daddy". You have to understand – Massimiliano Molinari hates everyone, because the true competitor *must* on a very deep level. To dominate, totally, means to destroy, if necessary. Even when it might be against their wider interests, such as the future of their grandchild. My father felt *compelled* to put Jeremy in his place, he couldn't resist.'

'And how did Jeremy react to this?'

'He didn't! He was as relaxed as ever. Even when we were on our own, I was on tenterhooks waiting for him to say something and he never did, and in fact that was when I began to wonder if he had known all along.'

'You mean about the affair?' She nodded.

I felt myself on a precipice. I had begun to think that, having cleared up the car and Agnese's sentimental role, presuming that our client's files contained nothing new, we would be able to close the case. But I felt obliged to ask: 'Then do you think Jeremy could have had something to do with Fabrizio's death?'

'I'm not sure what they did to him at that school where he's so keen to send Michele,' she said. 'But for Jeremy, winning's everything, too.'

Chapter 10

Niki Molinari accompanied me back to my car, linking his arm with mine.

'Sis spilled the beans, then.'

'She did, but if you had told me earlier . . .'

'Then you might have missed Mamma's cooking! Well,' he chuckled. 'She oversaw it. The true genius is Maria-Rosa.'

'The old lady?'

'That's her – the *other* old lady, the one without the Botox. She actually did most of the looking after us when we were kids, but Aurora takes the credit for that, too. In truth, she and Dad were always away at the track.'

I took in the sumptuous grounds. 'Not a bad place to grow up.'

'You think? Just me and sis, a couple of kilometres away even from the town, if you could call it that, let alone the city. A chauffeur to and from school. Everyone hated us – the kids, teachers, who were all communists, obviously, in this part of the world, even the house staff, whose lives we made hell because we were so damn bored. To be honest, I don't think even Maria-Rosa cared for us much, although she did her job.

I didn't have any real friends, or family, until carting, until Fabrizio. To be honest, I sometimes think the main reason Dad took any interest in me even then was because he wanted to get Fabri.'

Walking around the main house and emerging at the front, I began to see this world through that child's eyes – a great open prison.

'So I suppose for you, being sent away to a boarding school wouldn't have seemed so bad.'

Niki scoffed. 'Yes, if only that was Jeremy's motive! But to be fair to Agnese, and I try not to be,' he winked, 'she's done her best to avoid that kind of life for the kids. Although they live out San Lazarro way, it's a nice suburb with plenty of other families, and she's a stay-at-home mum who always cooks their "tea", as you put it. Yes – she may seem bitter, and don't get me wrong, she's certainly got some issues, but she loves those kids, which is another reason Jeremy has targeted little Michele. The fucker could be Sicilian – revenge served cold, all that.'

'Because of her affair with Fabrizio.' I paused. 'Which your father apparently knew about, which was why he was also cagey about her car in Jeremy's presence. Was it you that told him?'

Niki laughed. 'Is that what Agnese thinks? I told Dad to somehow win a point in my favour? Well, you can tell her she's got it around the wrong way – it was *him* who told *me*. He loves a gossip, the old man, but this was one morsel he didn't dare tell a soul, which was probably the only reason he told me, the single person such a suspicious bastard felt he could trust, although only because I owed him everything, obviously.'

'Obviously.'

'He was already plotting how he could get Jeremy out of the picture, had even asked his lawyer to see how Sis, and he, could extract themselves with the minimum financial damage.'

'You're kidding. With Agnese's agreement?'

'Oh, she knew none of it, he just assumed she would go along.'

'But what if she didn't?'

Niki thought it through. 'Then he might have exposed it himself.'

'But why? I thought he brought in Jeremy to turn things around at the *scuderia*. Isn't winning absolutely everything to him?'

'Precisely,' said Niki.

'I'm sorry, then why . . .'

'Because it would have meant even more little Fabris, right?' He rapped his knuckles against his skull. 'Principals come and go, grandchildren are forever. Agnese spoke of his "dynasty". I'm sure it's not been lost on Dad that not only was Fabrizio able to serve him up a boy – a future driver – but Jeremy's second-rate sperm has only managed to squeeze out girls.'

'Nicely put.' But I had to admit that among these folk it did have a ring of truth. 'And do you think Jeremy realised? I mean – that he might not only lose his wife, but his job, too?'

'Jeremy is many things,' said Niki, 'but he's no fool.'

'So what you're suggesting is you and your sister believe Jeremy might have had something to do with Fabrizio's death.'

'He certainly had everything to lose.'

We were arriving back at the car. 'Have you and Agnese discussed this?' He gave me a solemn shake of the head. 'Because, if you don't mind me saying, it seems a little neat – Agnese wants to stop Jeremy from sending Michele away to school . . .'

'Dad will never permit that. He wants to keep his little Fabri close. It could be Jeremy's just flexing his muscles, wants to remind Dad he has a hold over him, that it's not just one way.'

'And I don't know what your relationship is with Jeremy . . .'

Niki let out a cough like someone had poked him in the gut.

'I honestly can't say he's done a bad job,' he admitted. 'He's got the *scuderia* onto pole. Well, I have . . .'

'But you're number two, right?' I said brutally. 'To Moyen. And there are always younger drivers looking for your slot. How do I know this isn't a way for you to cast suspicion on Jeremy, have him replaced by someone more . . . pliable?'

Niki nodded. 'You don't, detective. But hey, you're the one who came sniffing around.'

'And as a top driver you must know an opportunity when you see one – a competitor drops behind, a space opens up . . .'

'That's a good metaphor, signor Leicester. You should be a writer.'

We had arrived at my car. 'Okay, Niki,' I said. 'What are you going to do to help me?' If he had thought this much through, I figured Niki must have a plan. He didn't hesitate.

'I'm not just a driver,' he said. 'These days, an F1 *pilota* has to be a computer tech, too. I spend most of my time in the office.'

'You have access to the company's systems, is what you're saying.'

'Full access,' said Niki. 'That's what the MBA was for – Dad's supposed to be grooming me to take over one day, although of course he expects to live forever.'

'Would you have access to Jeremy's calendar from seven years ago? His emails? What if he's wiped them?'

'It's all archived.'

'He uses a company phone? Is the bill itemised?'

'It is.'

'And you realise that you would probably be breaking a fistful of laws by sharing the information with us without official authorisation?'

Niki rolled his eyes. 'If no one knows about it, what does it matter? If we find something out, then it won't matter.'

'All right.' We shook hands.

'Before I forget.' He produced a folded envelope from his back pocket. 'VIP passes for Imola, as you're such a fan. Paddock-access. They're like gold dust, so don't waste them – I got two. I thought maybe that colleague of yours could join you, she looked like she could do with a break. And I might even have a little something for you by then.'

I had switched my phone to silent, so it was only when I got into my car and was checking it that I noticed the missed calls – scrolling through them, most recently from Rose, earlier Jacopo, then Alba and finally, but first, six from Celeste.

I called my daughter. Before I could say anything, she wailed:

'*Nonno*'s dying!'

'What?'

'He had a heart attack during the operation!'

'You say "dying",' I said carefully. 'He's still alive?'

'He's in intensive care. We're all at the hospital. Where are you?'

'But he's still breathing? His heart's beating?'

'I . . . yes, I guess. I mean – he's *alive*. But I don't know how much of that is down to the machines.'

'He's stable?'

'I don't know – where are you? Why aren't you here?'

'I've been working, my phone was on silent. I'm coming now. If anything changes, call me immediately.' I was about to add not to worry, that everything would be okay, but stopped myself. My daughter knew only too well that wasn't always true.

I drove swiftly to the hospital, cursing the Comandante much of the way. I wished I had been tougher with him over his smoking. In Italy everyone seemed to smoke and get away with it, yet there was no reason why the gods of heart disease should single Italians out for special treatment.

I was angry with Giovanni for putting his family through this when they had already had it with Lucia – Rose's mother, Jacopo's sister, Alba's cousin, my wife. And I was angry, I realised, with him for leaving me like this. I would miss the old bastard dearly, I thought.

Ludicrously, I found Jacopo and Dolores smoking on

the hospital steps. A little further along from them, a pair
of nurses and a doctor were also puffing away. I might have
snatched the cigarettes from their mouths and crushed them
on the ground but seeing Jacopo's expression – it was his
father in there, after all – I gave him a hug.

'Well?'

Dolores spoke for him: 'It's touch and go.' She gave Jacopo's
elbow a squeeze 'They had done the op and were stitching
him up when he had a massive seizure. They got his heart
going again, but he's hooked up to all sorts.' She looked me in
the eye. 'They're not being very reassuring, Dan.'

I said to Jacopo: 'That means nothing.' Italian doctors
were notoriously poor communicators, either concealing a
patient's prognosis to not upset them, or going straight for
the (proverbial) jugular to cover themselves.

I headed up the steps, found the three women waiting in
the corridor outside intensive care – Rose, Alba and Celeste.
In a sense, you couldn't have found greater contrasts: Celeste
the small-boned Campanian with big hair, Alba, the robust
Emilian, and Rose, who had supped deeply from not only my
English, but some long-buried Celtic roots with her rainwater
pale skin and natural auburn hair. Yet sat along the wall they
could only belong to one family, even if Celeste wasn't, yet,
officially a part of it. They looked at me as one.

A doctor pushed through the double doors dressed head-
to-toe in hospital blues. She drew down her mask. 'Signore,'
she said as they stood up. She noticed me – 'Sir.' – but she
addressed Rose, who not only stood taller than the other
women but, at seventeen, was clearly considered a 'responsible adult' by the doctor. I was struck by an unsettling vision

of her in some Bolognese hospital corridor one day, playing sentinel for me.

'Your grandfather is being medically sedated while we try to work out what the problem is. He was lucky it happened here – anywhere else, he would have certainly died.' Celeste crossed herself. Rose said:

'But it occurred because he was being operated on, right? Otherwise, it might not have happened in the first place. Wasn't his heart checked beforehand?'

The doctor shrugged defensively, her chin disappearing beneath her mask. 'He was checked, along with his medical history. There was nothing to indicate he would have a problem.'

'Except that he did.'

'Look,' said the doctor.

'I'm sorry, doctor,' I said mildly. 'My daughter is upset, as are we all. Let's talk about what we'll be doing next.'

'As I was about to say,' she looked at me, relieved, 'at the moment, we're administering drugs to restore his blood flow. The next step will be to give him an angiography . . .'

'What's that?' asked Rose.

'It's a kind of scan which will enable us to see what is going on inside his heart, and depending on the results of that, he may have to be transferred to Maggiore for some kind of invasive procedure.' She dared to look at the other women. 'I'm sorry, I can't tell you much more than that.'

'But,' I said, 'you've got his heart working again, so he's "stable", right?'

The corners of the doctor's eyes creased. She chose her words carefully: 'As I said, it is lucky it happened here because we had the facilities on hand. Until we have undertaken further tests, we can't say much more.'

'So what you're saying is – he's all right for now, but you don't know if it will happen again.'

'I'm sorry, I can't say much more. Now, if you'll excuse me ...' She pulled her mask up, backing away to push through the doors.

'Oh Dad.' Rose wilted into my arms.

Now I did say it: 'I'm sure he will be all right. The doctor has to be cautious, that's her job. But the Comandante is in the best place, and in a sense, the doctor probably is correct to say we were lucky it happened here – if anything occurs again, they'll be right on it.'

She looked up through those auburn strands. 'He will be okay, won't he?'

'I think he will,' I said solidly. 'Your grandfather is not going anywhere.' Rose looked searchingly into my eyes. 'We need to stay calm and strong, as he would expect.'

I let Rose go. 'Why don't you all take a break?' I said. 'Get some fresh air. I'll wait here.'

The women looked at each other and moved silently away. I took a seat, placed my hands on my knees, my mind wiped clean by shock. Only gradually did I permit new thoughts to enter, and when they did, to float freely – a memory of the Comandante's solemn pre-operation instructions, my flippant response. What did the old man really think of his son-in-law? I looked into those watery eyes and saw acceptance, although I wasn't sure that was altogether such a fine thing – it was as if he was watching a leaky boat depart from port, but it was the only one available and the future of his family depended on it.

Then Rose addressing the doctor, neither deferential nor afraid to reveal her ignorance, rather un-Italian characteristics she had probably picked up from me one way or another. And while I had had to step in to avoid her alienating the medic, one thing was clear – my girl could stand on her own two feet, and as a parent, what more could one hope for?

The ICU doors moved a fraction. I glanced up to see I was being observed through the porthole. The doctor disappeared, emerging a moment later accompanied by a nurse.

They were about to walk past me, but I rose. 'Doctor, from what you were saying, it doesn't sound good.'

The doctor looked longingly down the corridor. She said to the nurse: 'You go ahead.' She felt in a pocket for a pack of cigarettes and handed it to her.

She scanned my face. 'It was a massive heart attack. It was a miracle we were able to save him, frankly. In fact, we lost him a couple of times. It was almost as if he wanted to go.' She glanced over her shoulder at the ICU. Her voice dropped. 'I might have let him, but the others – they were determined to drag him back. Was there any reason he might have wanted to die?'

She was young, for a doctor at least, in her early-thirties, but she clearly meant what she was saying.

'He's lost his wife and his daughter,' I found myself saying. 'Maybe it was something to do with that?'

The doctor nodded thoughtfully. 'Maybe they were reaching out to him.'

I didn't say anything. I couldn't quite believe I was having this conversation.

'How is he?' A voice behind me. I turned to find Don Filippo.

'I was just explaining to the signor,' said the doctor. 'It's touch and go. We can provide some PPE if you'd like to perform the last sacrament.'

'Not necessary,' said Don Filippo. 'I've already given it to him.'

Naturally, I told the family none of this when I met them on the hospital steps.

'We'll make sure there's always someone here.' I nodded to Celeste. 'The rest of us should be ready to attend at a moment's notice.'

Alba elected to stay along with Rose, while Celeste and Jacopo would head back home, where they would be only a short ride away. Dolores volunteered to go back to the office, although as I watched her set off on foot, I wondered if that was where she was really heading.

I was left alone on the hospital steps, my mind drifting back to the doctor's suggestion that the Comandante's wife and daughter were beckoning him on. Certainly, according to Don Filippo, he had been prepared for this eventuality, but the priest had also been at pains to emphasise the sacrament was not exclusively for the dying, 'only that your father-in-law wanted a little insurance'. This certainly sounded like the Comandante. In any case, I preferred this version to the doctor's, which sounded almost as if Giovanni had been planning his exit.

I decided to head home myself. I had parked the car on the road leading up the hill to avoid having to wait for a free space in the car park, so I would take a shortcut through the hospital. I walked back up the steps and set off down one of those long corridors.

I passed through a room with a display of glass cases devoted to the hospital's role developing orthopaedics, and into a rectangular cloister. I followed it around to an arched oak door, which opened into the church of San Michele, by the side of the altar.

The church's semi-domed apse was the usual blitz of baroque. As far as I knew, San Michele was rarely used, yet there were half-a-dozen polished pews set on this upper level, while the main body of the church down the steps was empty.

I was about to descend when I noticed the figure knelt in the first row, her hands clasped in prayer, a silver crucifix suspended on a dainty bead rosary in front of her. I could tell by her bunched-up curly hair, the narrow olive neck sprouting from the puce puffa jacket, it was Celeste. I was both unsurprised and surprised by this show of faith: Dolores excluded, Neapolitans might be accused of displaying their religion like they did their jewellery, conspicuously. The Englishman in me instinctively found this suspect and wondered if Celeste had known I would pass this way. Highly unlikely: I hadn't even said I was leaving. And presuming she had gone to such extraordinary lengths, what had she to gain? Nothing, frankly, from me.

Meanwhile, the burgeoning Italian in me had learned circumspection. Ostentatious displays in a culture where appearances were often considered a mirror to one's soul were best taken at face value. Italians, after all, were no less sober in their own way than the British – something, to my shame, it had taken me a while to fully appreciate.

I would leave Celeste to her prayers.

'Wait.' I was half-way down the steps. Now, hypothetically,

the shoe was on the other foot – she might think I was following her. But Celeste said nothing, approaching me with
her puffa-jacketed arms wrapped around herself, the rosary
nowhere to be seen. Her pretty face was grey, eyes bleary with
tiredness or tears. She accompanied me down the steps and
along the aisle of the church, making a little curtsy and cross
as we left. We took the path down through the woods.

Despite the baroque interior of San Michele and that
Mediterranean, aquamarine sky, Celeste seemed somehow
out of place as we walked through the budding green and
brown, as if her natural habitat was balconied city backstreets
draped with washing, posters of Maradona and Napoli FC
flags.

'I apologise,' I said. 'You were right about the Comandante.
Having someone there, I mean.'

She shrugged her bony shoulders. 'Rose came, for the
operation.'

It hadn't occurred to me that my daughter would go to the
hospital of her own accord. 'And,' she conceded, 'you weren't
to know it would end up like this.'

We continued in silence through the greening oak and
beech trees, clumps of bluebells and spikes of asparagus; the
air was fresh with the flowery scent of spring.

'You've moved out of your cousin's now?' It seemed like a
politer way of asking Celeste if she had moved in with Jacopo.

She frowned. 'Jac didn't mention?' I shook my head. A
Neapolitan expletive. 'I hope it's all right. I brought over my
stuff a few days ago.'

'Welcome, then. You'll have to come to dinner – it's not
far.' She laughed.

'I didn't realise, otherwise I would have said something. You northerners! You'll have to come to ours, too. I'll make *parmigiana*!'

I felt sentimental for the days when Alba and Jaco were single, and the entire family had sat in our kitchen to be served Emilian staples by Alba, who was now fully occupied with Little Lucia and her partner Claudio, both of whom had large appetites. Would the three of us (I inevitably included Giovanni in my calculations) welcome another domestic goddess to our table, this time dishing out Neapolitan dishes? I certainly fancied the prospect, but knew in reality those days were over – we might be treated to the occasional *parmigiana*, *sfogliatelle* or *struffoli*, but Celeste was no Alba. She had not escaped domestic servitude in Naples to swap it for Bologna.

'Will your cousin miss you?' I was genuinely curious. Although Dolores had found her the job and they lived together, they barely interacted at work.

'She'll be happy to get her bed back!'

'You mean you slept in her bed? She took the couch?'

Celeste looked puzzled. 'No, the same bed. Otherwise, we wouldn't be able to use the couch.' I wasn't sure why this surprised me. I was still probably more the stolid Englishman than I imagined.

'You must be close, then, you and her.'

She considered this. 'Not really. I mean, she's part of the family, so . . . You know she grew up in an orphanage?' I nodded. 'She was always the *testarda*, Dee, the stubborn one, that's what Dad said. Just like his brother, her father.'

'But what's being stubborn got to do with the orphanage?'

She looked at me as if I was crazy. 'She didn't have to stay!

She could have lived with us. Mum and Dad pleaded, but she wasn't having it.'

That wasn't what 'Dee' had told me, I thought.

'So why did she turn them down?'

'Oh. Hell, I can't say for sure, I was just little. But there must have been a lot of emotion, obviously, after what happened.' She loosened her hair band and released her curly locks around her shoulders. 'Maybe something about if she couldn't have them – her parents, I mean – she wouldn't have anyone. At the time, least ways. Afterwards, she just said she got used to it, the orphanage.'

That much, at least, seemed to chime with what Dolores had told me. 'And her father, what did he do?'

Celeste looked surprised. 'I thought that was why you gave her the job.'

'What do you mean?'

'Her dad was a Carabiniere, right? I figured it must have been some old connection through the Comandante.'

I stopped dead. 'I didn't know that.'

'Then how did she get the job?' Celeste asked with genuine curiosity.

We gazed at each other in mutual puzzlement, tiny Celeste stood above me on the path, so we were eye-to-eye.

'I came across her during an investigation,' I said. 'And she helped me out . . . So, you're saying *Dolores's dad was a Carabiniere?*' I shook my head in wonder. 'And her mother?'

'Oh yeah, her, too. That was how they met. I know, it's crazy isn't it, considering how left-wing Dee is now, and how straight her mum and dad must have been, although I never really knew them, I was too small. But let me put it this way – in the family photos Dee's dad is the only one wearing a tie.' She sighed. 'A beautiful couple. It was terrible what happened.'

'The car crash,' I said. Celeste frowned.

'No,' she said. *'The bomb.'*

Chapter 11

There was very little about it online: after all, it had happened almost twenty years earlier, and bombings had been as routine a means of assassination for the *Camorra* – the Neapolitan mafia – then, as they were today. What distinguished the event was that the victims were a pair of military police officers, and there was more about the actual fallout from their deaths, in which the authorities came down hard on the clans, than the actual event itself.

Celeste had heard the story that had been handed down through her parents, aunties and uncles, and numerous siblings – that Dolores' mother and father had been setting off for work from their apartment just outside the Spagnoli, near Piazza del Plebiscito. The car was kept in a steel-shuttered garage beneath the building, which was used solely by them, secured with the best locks and alarmed, so it was a mystery how the bombers managed to get in. It was also a miracle seven-year-old Dolores hadn't been with them – she was being kept at home that day because she had a fever, and in fact her older cousin, Celeste's sister Camilla, who at the time was out of work, had come over the night before to look after her.

Dolores's father had started the car and manoeuvred it out of the tiny garage so her mother could get in. She slammed the door and they set off, but before they got to the end of the street there was a huge blast.

The apartment windows were blown out, and after picking herself up from the kitchen floor, Camilla's first instinct was to rush to Dolores' bedroom. She found the girl on the balcony, stood barefoot in her nightdress upon a carpet of broken glass. In that instant Camilla realised what must have happened. She shouted for Dolores to come inside, but it was too late – she had seen the burning car with her parents in it.

She began to scream.

'She had to be sedated,' said Celeste. 'And actually, despite Mum and Dad saying she could stay with us, the doctors were worried about her mind, they actually put her in hospital with shock for a while. I suppose seeing your mum and dad die like that . . . anyway, so from there she went to the nuns. The family talked about a sister visiting her in hospital, and that was why she had gone – actually, everyone was rather bitter about it, they said the nuns had brainwashed her, stolen her from us, and I remember when she came over as a teenager, she was *very* religious, but despite everything – I mean, I was there when they asked her once – she always said she didn't want to leave. I can actually remember being quite jealous – it seemed like a great way to escape my brothers, who were always beating me up, and my sisters who were, you know, *sisters*.'

'Did they ever get the people who did it?'

Celeste made a dismissive tut. 'They got *people*.'

'But why? It's not normal for the mafia to hit police officers, is it? It must have been something serious . . .'

'I don't know, nothing official was ever said, although Dolores's father was senior, you know, a *maresciallo* in the drugs squad, so it must have been something to do with that.'

'And her mother?'

'Would you believe it? She was an accountant! She had been transferred over from the Guardia di Finanza, the tax police, which was how they met. She spent all day in the office keeping an eye on their expenses, I never actually saw her in a uniform. She would have been better off doing ordinary book-keeping, Dad said.'

I closed my laptop and left our apartment, descending to the ground floor and crossing the courtyard to Alba's house. I opened the front door (there were few locked doors in the Faidate Residence, at least during the day).

Where once I would have stepped into a 'snug' *soggiorno* fronting a kitchen with a bedroom and bathroom upstairs, now Alba's ground floor ran the length of the east side of the courtyard with the expanded living room looking out through warehouse-style windows onto the grass. A mezzanine provided additional space for a spare bedroom-cum-office for Claudio, while the kitchen, which had also been knocked through, now stretched along the far wall, reminding me a little of the counter at my old school canteen, quite honestly. But the apartment was airy and not unpleasant – certainly trendier than our place on the second floor, which hadn't changed its layout in at least a hundred years, although I wasn't sure I would swap our view over the rooftops.

It had seemed like the sensible thing to encourage everyone to get back to normal, notwithstanding our hospital duties.

'It was what the Comandante would have wanted,' I had said.

'What he would *want*,' Rose had corrected. 'Don't talk about him in the past tense, Dad.'

'My bad Italian,' I replied. She had shot me a sceptical look.

Jacopo and Celeste were sat on the floor, having picked up where Alba had left off. So far, the team had got through twenty boxes, which were piled at the end of the room. There was plenty of space; for all the trendy magazine and news-paper supplements Alba had waved in our faces during the planning phase, she seemed to have run out of energy (or money) once it came to furnishing the living room, which consisted solely of a flat screen TV, a pair of burnt-orange IKEA shaggy rugs, and a three-seater black fake leather sofa bought on discount from Poltronesofà. It included a console in the armrest from which you could operate an automatic footstall, and where Claudio was now duly reclining, tapping away at a laptop balanced on his big belly while Little Lucia sat upright in her playpen surrounded by plastic bricks she was enthusiastically banging together.

I crouched beside the pen, reaching over to build a tower while she looked on with fascination. As soon as I had fin-ished my art-deco-inspired edifice she swept her plump arm across and demolished it.

'*Brava,*' I said. Claudio peered over his phone.

'Oh, hey, Dan.'

'How's the babysitting going?'

'No problem.' He scratched his three-day beard. 'I don't know what they complain about.'

I walked around the pen to where Celeste and Jacopo were sat on the island of a rug surrounded by boxes.

'It's mainly court records, apparently,' I said.

Celeste looked up. 'Tons – the depositions of the defence as well as the plaintiff, lots and lots of patent submissions, designs, manuals, that sort of thing.' Her eyes widened. 'You didn't want us to go through them, did you?'

I laughed. 'Don't worry, it's stuff concerning his son's death we're interested in, and then any files or notebooks containing information we don't already have.'

'There are a couple of boxes,' said Jacopo, 'Alba had set aside from the patent stuff – there's a copy of the crash report, coroner's report, even autopsy stuff he seems to have got hold of, along with safety information on the car, that kind of thing. He also hired an agency to look into Niki and Massimiliano Molinari,'

'Really? Which one?'

'Sherlock.'

'Of course.' I suppose I should have been grateful Britain's fictional detectives had made such an impact upon Italian culture that they were shorthand for 'sleuth' – it had certainly not done my career any harm. However, there were few who could resist addressing me by the forename of Mr Holmes sooner or later, and certainly no shortage of private investigation agencies in Italy named after Sir Arthur Conan Doyle's most famous creation – with an accompanying picture in the window of Basil Rathbone in a deerstalker, in the case of Boris Malprese, who ran his one-man show out of a unit in a Casalecchio shopping mall. I bore Boris no ill will, he did for the *casalinghe*, or housewives, of the suburbs what we did for the jewellery draped 'ladies that lunched', and I didn't doubt his professionalism – a former *Ispettore* for the Polizia di Stato he had jumped before he was pushed for fiddling his expenses (maintaining two households, a long and entirely predictable story) but he was basically a good cop who got referrals from his old contacts in the *Polizia* as well as walk-ins who couldn't miss Rathbone puffing away from a discreet corner as they worried about their husband's extracurricular activities while doing their shopping. But Boris also offered the full range of services, which was presumably why our client had chosen him before deciding to entrust us with his legacy (and thinking on it, while I might hire Boris to spy on the Molinaris, I'm not sure I would give him a blank cheque – he had half-a-dozen mouths to feed, after all).

His report was in the single box set aside for material that might merit further investigation. I had to smile – the document looked impressive, professionally bound, probably at one of the printshops that proliferated throughout the city, with a matt-black cover and titled in silver serif script CONFIDENTIAL, *Assignment undertaken on behalf of Sig. Giorgio Chiesa* above Basil Rathbone's profile, which had been worked into a logo. It was as large and thick as a novel. I opened it randomly – a transcript of an interview (paid – €300 cash) Boris had undertaken with a mechanic at the Molinari garage detailing the ways Fabri's car could be sabotaged (various) but denying any knowledge of anyone actually meddling with it. Useful. I flicked back to the front, where Boris respectfully presented the findings of the investigation . . . blah blah, I turned over. An introduction setting out the terms of reference, then Boris's activities, their appendices making up the bulk of the document, followed by a summary of his findings divided into three questions:

1. *Could Massimiliano Molinari have been involved in the death of Fabrizio Chiesa?*
2. *Could Niki Molinari have been involved in the death of Fabrizio Chiesa?*
3. *Could a third party have been involved in the death of Fabrizio Chiesa?*

I read the third part first, not least because it was conspicuous by its brevity:

3. *Could a third party have been involved in the death of Fabrizio Chiesa?*

    Although the investigation was limited to the possible involvement of Massimiliano or Niki Molinari, we cannot rule out the possibility that another person(s) may have facilitated the death of Sig. Fabrizio Chiesa. Sherlock Private Investigations SpA recommends further action in this direction in pursuit of the truth.

I liked that last flourish – 'in pursuit of the truth' – a very Boris touch, but he presumably didn't have much joy. He would have understood that clients engage private eyes as much for their obsessions as 'the truth', and Giorgio Chiesa's obsession was with Molinari father and son. He was looking for *proof*, not truth.

But it was always possible Boris's recommendation was founded upon genuine suspicion rather than opportunism and I would have a word with him. If he had anything useful I would bung a couple of hundred his way, so he would get his mitts on some more Chiesa cash, after all.

1. ***Could Massimiliano Molinari have been involved in the death of Fabrizio Chiesa?***
   There is no direct evidence associating MM with the death of FC. According to MM's phone positioning (access price, appendix 5) he was in Bologna within 30 metres of his members club (Domino) in Via Castiglione at the time of the incident. I have examined the computer of FC and not found anything in this or his emails to suggest anything suspicious.

'How are you doing with Fabrizio Chiesa's laptop?' I asked Jacopo.

'It's on the to-do list.'

'Well keep it there for now – it seems Sherlock had already hacked it.'

In fact, there appears to have been no direct communication between them, the only references are in respect to team meetings, etc. As discussed, I did attempt access into MM's means of communication

He tried to hack his phone and emails, I thought. That must have been expensive.

but was unable to do so using standard means, and we agreed that I would not proceed further, due to cost. I made discreet enquiries with former and existing employees and associates of MM, as well as with FC's friends and acquaintances (payments in appendix 7) and could find no evidence of motivation.

> **2. Could Niki Molinari have been involved in the death**
>   **of Fabrizio Chiesa?**
>   *There is no direct evidence associating NM with the*
>   *death of FC.*

Boris had gone through the same process with Niki and come to the same conclusion. He did note:

that a motive – as a competitor for a place in the first team – is a possibility, but I could not find any evidence of this, or indeed anything pointing to animosity between the pair. That does not mean NM was not involved – premeditated murderers by their very nature can be good at concealing their intentions – but I saw no reason to believe he was.

I nodded appreciatively at Boris's assessment – he might be happy to keep charging Signor Chiesa for his services, but he was too professional to deliberately lead him on. I would put Sherlock, AKA Boris Malprese, on *my* to-do list.

I laid the report aside, picked another batch of papers out of the box. Invoices from Sherlock, black-and-white paper print-outs of photos of both Molinaris, beneath them, a memory stick.

'You checked the stick?'

'It's all photos,' said Jacopo. 'Only, the colour versions of those.' I flicked through the papers – there were dozens of them. Giorgio Chiesa had clearly decided to save money and do the surveillance himself, although to what end is moot. Boris would have almost certainly advised against it – surveillance was labour intensive, risky and, I flicked back to the beginning of the report, the investigation had taken place more than a year after the death of Fabrizio, presumably after Signor Chiesa had exhausted his options with the police. It wasn't as if he was trying to catch Max with one of his mistresses, and it was hard to tell what the photos would actually achieve except provide Giorgio with a sense that he was doing something. Meanwhile if the Molinaris spotted him, they would at best think he was making a fool of himself, at worst stalking them, and he would leave himself open to criminal proceedings.

Here was Niki exiting a *palazzo* in central Bologna, another of him with the same woman at the park; with a different young woman at the circuit, both 'plinky-plonkys' as Fernanda Chiesa might put it, with the same shoulder-length hair and figure-hugging designer gear. Now he was chatting to the mechanics in the pit (presumably shot from the grandstand at Imola); sat with *another* woman at a bus stop, leaving the HQ of Molinari Automobile SpA, and yes, looking straight at the camera and waving. He had clearly known Signor Chiesa was photographing him and didn't appear overly concerned. He certainly didn't look like a guilty man, but then he didn't look particularly discomfited by the odd behaviour of his best friend's father, either – he seemed to have that same smile for every occasion. Was that truly him, or was it the Niki I saw coolly considering the curve at Imola? To achieve all he had, albeit with help from his father, life had to be far from a joke. Like Sherlock, I wouldn't put planning past Niki Molinari; whether he had actually done anything, however . . .

I flicked through photos of Molinari senior, one after another with a string of similarly self-satisfied older men, sat outside bars . . . at a car show . . . entering restaurants – I recognised one – Da Vito. I turned the page over. Scribbled in pencil: a set of letters and numbers in columns.

I pulled out my phone. It was the same sort of thing I had seen in Fabrizio's notebook.

I held the paper up. 'Have you any idea what these are?'

'Alba reckons they're timings of cars,' said Celeste.

It was as if the numbers came into focus. They filled the blank page. The top line read – *Mc1/7/84.1/6*

86.1/6/86.0

248.3/6

85.4/7

86.8/7

85.6/ X

McLaren, I guessed. Lead driver? (1).

Seventh place on the pole? (7).

Then 84.1 seconds for the first lap, where they took sixth place (6), followed by the times and positions for the subsequent laps with an X marking where the car had for some reason retired from the race, judging by how the other cars – Fr (Ferrari?), Rb (Red Bull?), Ml (Molinari?) – covered line after line, and page after page of photos to complete the approximately sixty laps in a typical Formula One race.

I looked back inside the box. Beneath a further batch of printed photos, many of which had similar lists of numbers on the back, sat a nest of betting receipts.

I grabbed a handful. The slips were not just about winners and losers, although there were podium positions among them. There were bets on the timings of cars, bets for other cars to retire or come last . . . every permutation possible was being wagered, although the amounts were modest, averaging around five euros. Giorgio Chiesa wasn't going to break the bank with his habit, but he wasn't going to get rich either.

'He liked a flutter,' I said. 'Although he apparently kept it under control. I saw a similar thing among his son's stuff.' I thought back to Fabrizio's room, the unlikelihood that he would have ever brought Agnese Molinari there. If his father had even had an inkling about their affair, he would have been sure to have set Sherlock upon her.

'But where does she live, precisely?' I said out loud.

'Who?' asked Celeste.

'Agnese Molinari. Niki said out San Lazzaro way, with her husband, Jeremy Frost. Because it was never properly established, was it.'

'What?'

'What Fabrizio Chiesa was actually doing driving up there – his sister said he liked to head home through the hills even though it was the long way around, so he could practise taking the curves. But San Lazzaro's also on the other side of that range. Fabrizio could just as easily have had an assignation with Agnese and, who knows, someone could have been waiting to drive him off the road.'

'Who?' asked Celeste.

'Her husband.'

Chapter 12

Rose was still at the hospital and our dog, Rufus, a dirty-brown Lagotto Romagnolo, was beginning to roam menacingly around our freshly laid lawn, so I thought I'd better take him for a walk. I needed to pass by the office anyway.

We were turning the corner onto Via Marconi when I spotted Dolores coming out of our building. It was a bright, hazy evening and the portico was busy with people still enjoying the novelty of spring, lingering by the bars for an after-work *aperitivo*, or dawdling before shop fronts. With Rufus padding placidly off the lead beside me, I began to follow her, at first with the intention of catching her up and confronting her about what I had learned from Celeste, but then, as my doubts about how to approach the topic crept in, just following.

An experienced snoop doesn't expect to be snooped upon any more than a hunter expects to be hunted, although in this case I was at the disadvantage of being known to my mark, plus having a dog in tow (albeit that Rufus's anosmia was a definite plus – he wasn't about to waylay me with arresting odours) so I had to fall further behind than usual and made sure to keep to the sides of the street where we could blend more easily with the shadows.

Dolores headed south up Marconi.

It soon became clear where she was going, so now I placed Rufus on the lead, and we crossed the street to stay out of her eye-line. Sure enough, she stopped at the bus stop opposite the church of San Francesco while we lurked beneath the portico. I vaguely wondered if I had time to dash back and get my car before her bus arrived. I looked down at Rufus, who gazed up at me with his disconcertingly human eyes as if to say – you've got to be kidding.

In any case, it was too late – here it came, the 22 for Stadio.

'Popping into *La Residenza*, is she?' I asked Rufus. Of course, I had checked with Alba, and Dolores had indeed stuck her head in that last time, which didn't surprise me – she was nothing if not thorough – but it didn't mean anything. I looked around for a cab, but I was not in London or New York. Here, taxis had to be called, which wasn't much help to private eyes who needed to instruct a cabbie to ride tail. Then I spotted the one thing that almost never arrived when you needed it – another bus.

As the first number 22 pulled out with Dolores aboard, I scooped up Rufus, as hefty as a furry three-year-old, and dodged the busy traffic to make it to the other side. Still clutching the dog beneath one arm, I signalled for the bus to stop. For a moment I thought the driver would ignore me, but it drew up at the last minute and I got on at the rear door. It closed behind me and accelerated away. I took a seat at the back, setting Rufus on the floor. He gave me a questioning look but when he didn't receive an answer, laid flat at my feet.

Our bus was just far enough away for the first vehicle to be visible beyond the intervening traffic. The 22 rumbled up tight Via Nosadella, seemingly defying the laws of physics and avoiding the parked cars, then turned north on Via Saragozza before winding its way around to Via d'Azeglio, which would be the stop to the Residence, if that was where Dolores was really heading. But there was no sign of her alighting. I might have missed her – everyone was out that evening as if emerging from hibernation – but I didn't really believe Dolores would travel anywhere inside the walls by bus, broken bike or not. She was an eco-zealot and, given the choice, would walk.

The bus swung west onto the Viale. Up until that point, it had been almost empty, but now a group of men got aboard and stood in the middle, blocking my view ahead. As we pulled out of the stop, I peered through the grimy window to see if I could spot Dolores.

Nothing.

We were reaching the end of the route, so her destination had to be somewhere along Via Saragozza, which we had returned to after our roundabout diversion. The street continued south 'outside the walls', stretching for five kilometres, first on the flat, then uphill to the church of San Luca, which overlooked the city like a salmon-coloured wedding cake. But we wouldn't be going that far. Before we arrived, the bus would turn off and terminate at Stadio, the stop for the red brick stadium, home to Bologna FC.

Via Saragozza was even thicker with traffic than usual. The portico was crowded with soccer fans bearing the traditional *rossoblu* colours of Bologna, and I realised the guys in the middle were probably *tifosi*. It was midweek, there shouldn't have been a match today, at least in my mind, but then I guessed it had to be some kind of cup. In any case, my bus was going nowhere in the jam of cars, vans, and, of course, buses.

I stood up, and looking over the heads of the fans, could see the passengers in the bus ahead begin to alight.

I picked up the dog and made my way through the good-humoured clump of guys.

'We're stuck,' I said to the driver. 'Would you mind letting us out?' He glanced at me through the Perspex screen, then returned his eyes to the road.

'That one ahead is,' I pointed out.

He shrugged. I doubted it was about Rufus, who was gazing at him placidly from beneath my arm. Dogs were a common sight on buses. I suspected it was me – I didn't often experience prejudice, but now my British accent had softened into generic 'foreign', my status appeared to have deteriorated in the eyes of those who didn't know better. To the bus driver, who probably came into contact with a lot more Italian-speaking Albanians or Romanians than Britons, I was likely just another *extracomunitario*, the technical and pejorative term for someone who came from outside the European Union, which in common parlance still applied to Romanians, who were now members, but not to Britons, who were now not.

'All right.' Rufus and I headed back to the middle of the bus and I pulled the emergency release. The guys let out a cheer and we poured onto the street. There was a shout from behind, followed by an agitated blast from the bus's horn.

Bloody *extracomunitario*!

We joined the throng heading towards the stadium, the claret-red and blue of the good-humoured Bologna supporters peppered with the green and black of Sassuolo, a side which perennially bounced along the bottom of Serie A. The *rossoblu* may have been especially cheerful anticipating success against their Emilia-Romagnan rival. Bologna supporters, like West Ham fans, took their victories where they could get them.

I did my best to weave through the throng while Rufus tolerated the frequent hands descending to ruffle his woolly fur. I searched the packed portico ahead for the beacon of Dolores's henna bob, but without much luck – she was swallowed by the mass of men. The best I could do was keep moving forward.

We flowed with the tide along the portico, past pastry shops and bars, florists and pharmacies, until we reached the part where the road forked up to San Luca. Doubting Dolores had gone on a pilgrimage, I trooped with the supporters towards the red-brick bulk of the stadium.

Rufus barked – he couldn't smell, but there was nothing wrong with his eyes – and began to strain against the leash. Dolores was sat outside a kiosk off the main drag. I tried to pull Rufus back into the crowd, but it was too late – perhaps the bark had drawn her attention, or she had been on the look-out. In any case, she had made us, and waved me over.

Rufus led me excitedly forward. 'No wonder they gave you away,' I muttered.

'Hey!' Dolores delightedly opened her arms to the dog. Peering around his fluffy head, she said: 'What are you doing here? You can't take him into the stadium, can you? I didn't even know you were into football.'

'I was just coming this way.'

'Long walk,' she observed.

'Fancied one, didn't we, Rufus?' Hearing his name the dog swung around, but seeing there were no treats involved, dropped to the ground and made his way to a water bowl by the kiosk. 'We just got caught in the crowd.' I added with fake levity: 'Never mind me, what about you? I didn't know you were a fan of *I Rossoblu*.' She shook her head, closing her mouth around the pair of straws protruding from a bottle of fruit juice.

'Then what are you doing here?' I pulled up a chair.

'Oh,' she said. 'You mean when I'm supposed to be at the office?'

I smiled. 'I've never tried to impose hours on anyone, so long as they get the job done.'

Dolores drew on the juice, eyeing me coquettishly, and entirely mockingly. I picked up the gauntlet. 'All right. *Basta*. Enough playing around, Dolores. What's going on? You're not thinking about leaving the agency, are you?'

This caught her by surprise. She let the straws go and straightened up. 'Why would you think that?'

'We're partners,' I said. 'There's clearly something going on you're not telling me about. In fact,' I said, 'there are a lot of things you haven't told me – like what really happened to your parents, for example. And that they were Carabinieri! Were you never planning to share that little detail with us?'

'Why should I?' She dug into her pocket and pulled out her tobacco pouch. 'Heh,' she said. 'That was Celeste, I suppose. Well, it was never a secret. I guess it had to come out one day.'

'What do you mean "it was never a secret"? You told us they died in a car crash.'

Dolores daintily filled her cigarette paper, her fingers trembling a little, I noticed. 'True,' she said. 'But that was years ago, to Jac, when I began working at Faidate.' She licked the paper closed. 'I didn't like talking about it.' She looked at me pointedly. 'I still don't.'

'You told me it was a car crash.'

'*You* told *me*, I didn't say anything.'

'*Come on.* You didn't say no. It's a pretty big deal. "Dolores Pugliese – the daughter of a pair of Carabinieri assassinated by a bomb."'

She lit the cigarette. 'Maybe I don't want to be *that* Dolores Pugliese. How about maybe I just want to be myself?'

'All right, I get that – it's your business. But you can understand it's shaken my confidence, given you've also been,' I chose my word carefully, '*concealing* what you've been up to. Following this guy – I saw you, Dolores, even Rose saw you, we passed in the car – then buying pepper spray.'

'Really,' she insisted. 'That's just for protection.'

'I've never seen it before.'

'Do you usually go through my pockets? *Or my litter bin?*'

'The last time you got the bus here. What for?'

Dolores let out an exasperated sigh. She twirled the cigarette between her fingertips. Again, I had the sense I was dealing with a fully grown woman, no longer the student *punkabestia* in big boots I had come across leading a dairy cow through Bologna's backstreets. Naturally – Dolores had grown up over the intervening years, while I had simply grown old. But she remained in her twenties, she remained my subordinate. And, I thought, an orphan.

'Tell me.'

Dolores scanned the other tables set outside the kiosk. 'It's my uncle. This is where he does business sometimes.' She looked around. 'But apparently not today.'

'Uncle?'

'My Uncle Gigi. Short for Luigi. I called him "uncle", anyway. He was my mother's second cousin, I think. Look.' She flicked through her phone, tapped on a photograph. 'That's him.' It was the one from Speedy's office I had shared with the team.

Giorgio Chiesa awkwardly raising a toast with two others, one Vladimir Bonnacini, or Speedy, the other apparently 'Uncle Gigi'. I squinted. I could just about see the resemblance between the ageing 'hairdresser' with the spume of straw-blond hair, and this leaner, younger fellow with chestnut brown curls trimmed short, a tight T-shirt showing off his muscles.

'Uncle Gigi, then,' I said. 'What about him?'

'I hadn't seen him since my parents died. No one had – he disappeared.'

'So you're saying he was somehow involved in their death?'

'I barely noticed at the time. Why would I? Uncle Gigi was the last person I was interested in. But it came out after. He lived in the same condominium. . .

'We knew everyone, the families had lived there forever. Not *all* related, but all – I don't know – trusted. Uncle Gigi would have been in his thirties, still living with his parents, couldn't hold down a job, a bit of a joke – they were always saying he needed to find a nice woman, which was how it was, you know . . . Just one of the things my parents and their neighbours chatted about – it was open house, in the condominium doors weren't locked. People came and went for coffee, a chat, we kids were in and out of each other's homes. Everyone was an uncle or auntie even if they weren't.

'My parents were Carabinieri, so respected. But there was no sense of threat. They weren't judges. There was caution, yes. People always made sure the condominium front doors – there was a proper one and a gate – were locked, but that was normal, it was Naples! But no one tried anything against individual police, not if they could help it. Not if they didn't want the world crashing down on them.

'Anyway, Gigi hung around. I don't remember him specifically inside our apartment . . . or maybe, for Christmas, birthdays, when everyone else popped in, otherwise nothing particular that I could put my finger on. But the key to the garage hung with the others on a coat peg by the door, so would it have been hard to slip inside the apartment, make a copy? No.

'And then he had gone. I didn't hear it directly. I mean, it must have been a year or more after, on one of my visits to Celeste's house, an "occasion". The women gossiping in the kitchen. Something about Gigi's parents not being there, shutting up as I came in and pressing me tightly to their bosoms, lots of love and lamentation.

'But I knew something was up. I didn't ask them, I asked my cousins. They said they were sworn to secrecy – but have you ever heard of a kid able to keep a secret? – I bribed one of the young ones with sweets.

'Gigi had disappeared soon after the bomb, the police were looking for him, he was nowhere to be found. And that was that.' The cigarette had gone out. Dolores relit it and took a puff. 'Trail went cold. Case went cold. Life moved on.' Rufus had returned and she scratched him under his chin, which was most appreciated. 'I moved to Bologna,' she said. 'And so, it seems, did Uncle Gigi.'

'Then you're going to inform the police.'

Dolores leaned back. 'Well, I want to make sure it really is him, first.'

'You know it's him, Dolores, you've said so yourself.'

'It was a long time ago.'

'So? You know the police don't take kindly to their own being killed.'

'I know that.'

'Well then.'

'Oh, you know how it is, Dan. Anything could happen.'

'Or nothing – that's what you think.' She shrugged.

'But we have contacts,' I said. 'The Comandante, our contacts in the Carabinieri. I know they could ensure the information reached the right people, that it didn't get lost, something was done.'

'True.'

'You've discovered where he lives? Works?'

'More or less, yes.'

'Then you've done their work for them. All they have to do is pick him up.'

Rufus lay on his belly. Dolores surveyed her cigarette, which had gone out again. She considered it for a long time.

'But *I* want to talk to the Comandante,' she said finally. 'Explain, I mean, in my own words . . . I mean about not saying anything . . .'

'Of course, although you realise he's not likely to be very talkative for a while.'

'*Beh.*' She sighed. 'I suppose after all this time, it can wait a few more weeks.' She cupped the cigarette and took another light to it.

'I'm sorry if I gave you a hard time, but you had me worried.'

Dolores looked surprised. 'Like I said, Dan . . .'

'I know – you can look after yourself. But we all need someone to worry about us.'

She cocked her head, a smile playing at the corners of her mouth.

'Sure,' she said.

Chapter 13

As we walked back down Saragozza, I explained what I had learned about Jeremy.

'He's got the motive,' said Dolores.

'And the means? I guess it's possible – he knows all about cars, and Massimiliano said they could be tampered with. Jeremy could have been watching his wife . . . Honestly, anything's possible – he might have confronted Fabrizio, drugged him, beat him up and sent his car off the cliff. Unfortunately, we won't be able to trace the position of his mobile phone or anyone else's going back that far. Fundamentally, we need Jeremy to incriminate himself.'

'And how are we going to achieve that?'

'Niki told me he's going to hack the system, see what computer records he can dredge up. Maybe Jeremy will have let something slip.'

'And what about Agnese?'

'What about her?'

'Might she have been behind it?'

'How so?'

'She knew she was pregnant with Fabrizio's child. Did Fabrizio know? Maybe he was threatening to tell.'

'It's true – she mentioned making the child appear like Jeremy's. But really, she's still leaving flowers for Fabri after all this time.'

'Guilt?'

'There was me putting it down to love.'

'You men are such soft touches. And there's still Niki Molinari himself, Fabrizio's number one competitor.'

'And best friend.'

'So he tells *you*.'

'Fabrizio's sister Fernanda seemed to think so, too.'

'Maybe they were in it together!'

'*Dolores.*'

'I'm just thinking "out of the box" like you always tell us. Have you noticed, by the way that every sibling in the Chiesa household is an "F"? *Fabrizio*, the older brother, *Francesco*, and the sister – *Fernanda*.'

'Or that Fabrizio shortened is *Fabri*,' I said. 'Which is the same as Via Fabbri?'

'Of course! "Fabri in Via Fabbri"!'

'Be that as it may, let's try to remember that our client is looking down upon us, and may not be very happy about us billing him for flights of fancy. We need to stick to firm leads and, frankly, close this case as soon as possible.'

'That's what Signor Chiesa's thinking, is it? From up there? You don't really believe that, do you?'

Given that my late wife remained a lingering presence in my life, I suppose I did feel a certain responsibility to *Ingegnere* Chiesa.

'At the end of the day,' I said, sounding disconcertingly like King Charles, 'I suppose one might as well behave as if one does.'

'There's no God,' Dolores stated simply.

'Celeste told me that when you were young, you were very religious.'

'I might not believe in God,' said Dolores. 'But I sure as fuck believe in the Devil.'

When Niki Molinari had talked about his sister choosing the suburban life, I wondered how often he had visited her at home. While it was true that Villa Brilla was on the fringe of San Lazzaro, and only a few minutes by car or bicycle from its modest, yet discreetly affluent centre, their home was hardly a three-bed semi.

Massimiliano Molinari had apparently purchased the villa as their wedding present. It was set back from the road behind a screen of bushy alder and a set of solid battleship-grey iron gates. You could have drawn a straight line between Fernanda Chiesa's home on one side of the hills, and Agnese Molinari's on the other.

I had come prepared like a 'proper' private eye. I parked my car by San Lazzaro's placid main square and removed a fold-up bike from the boot. The bike didn't look too ridiculous – it wasn't the type commuters carried around the London Underground, it was just compact enough to fit in the car – and I might have been heading off for a ride in the countryside, a popular local pastime.

But despite my helmet and other cycling garb, I was only going a few kilometres outside town. I turned down a dirt track bordering a vineyard, got off and wheeled it between the vines towards the line of poplars that masked Villa Brilla from even the vintner's prying eyes. I rested it against a tree and pulled the binoculars out of my backpack. There was a green link fence in front of me, but more to keep the livestock in than prowlers out. Half a dozen alpaca were munching at the grass in front of a Palladian-style villa, intermittently raising their long necks to look around with their typically satisfied expressions. The 'villa' itself was a handsome, peach-coloured pile that might have been constructed in the nineteenth century as a summer house, but was more than adequate for the all-year requirements of the modern well-to-do.

Agnese's Vernice was pulled up outside, behind the sinister bulk of a Molinari-green SUV that was closer to the size of an Armed Personnel Carrier than family car. I had the image of Fabrizio glancing up and seeing it in his rear-view mirror as he was about to take a sharp bend.

The front door opened – a man and boy, the latter wrestling with a large black holdall he was grasping with both hands. The trunk door of the SUV floated upwards and the man stood by it as the boy struggled towards him with the bag. It was Jeremy, sure enough, his legs set apart as if ready to take a punch, or deliver one. The boy arrived at the car and together they lifted the holdall inside. The little chap seemed happy enough helping out his dad, or vice versa depending on the bag's contents. Through the binoculars I noted that he had Agnese's black hair, and that aquiline Chiesa nose. The kid couldn't have looked more Italian.

I stepped back from the fence as the car rumbled up the drive, Jeremy visible behind the steering wheel almost at head height. The car truly was a monster, and you saw few of them on the local roads. But that was not Molinari's strategy, at least according to what I had read online. Its main market was the

Gulf, where it had developed a string of dealerships thanks to its connections with royalty, whose princelings splashed out hundreds of thousands for garish customisations. In contrast, Jeremy's paintwork was markedly restrained.

Apart from the video camera for the intercom at the gate, I couldn't spot any CCTV. I supposed there was little cause – the *palazzo* would probably be alarmed, but the family was not the sort to invite intruders simply by virtue of who they were. Jeremy might have had a profile by stint of his role as Principal alongside the 'bigs' from teams like Mercedes, Ferrari and Red Bull, but despite their best efforts, Molinari had yet to consistently make podium, let alone seriously compete for a world championship, so he seemed more likely to invite respectful curiosity rather than outright fanaticism. But the key thing was – if Fabrizio had been visiting Agnese here, he would not have been picked up on camera.

I walked with the bike along the side of the vineyard in the direction of the road. But Jeremy could have found out any time. Maybe he turned up unexpectedly one day and discovered Fabrizio's car in the driveway. . . Who knew how long he had suspected until he decided to make his move. Would he have had murder in mind? Not necessarily – following him toward an assignation with his wife, he might have decided to pull him over and – who knows? – reason with him, or perhaps engage in a little fisticuffs. But then something akin to road rage had overwhelmed him, or Fabrizio had panicked, and – goodnight Vienna.

I was chewing this over as I arrived back at my car, opening the boot and folding up my bike, when a Molinari SUV pulled in. Jeremy Frost stepped out and, without appearing to notice me, strode towards the shops.

I watched him disappear into the *edicola*, or newsagents, through my car's upraised trunk window, then slammed it down and nipped around to the front. I jumped in and pressed *start*. The Alfa coughed. I pressed it again. It spluttered. I looked around the cabin. Had I forgotten to do something? I put the car in drive, tried again. Another mute cough. If this had been Rose, I would now be sat on the passenger side saying . . . What? I had no idea. I was doing everything correctly. I pressed the button again. The car hiccupped. I glanced up at Jeremy coming back towards me, a *Financial Times* under his arm. I momentarily considered ducking, but it was too late, he was looking straight at me.

Jeremy gestured to wind down the window.

'Sounds like a loose connection,' he said in English.

'I beg your pardon?'

'To the battery. Open her up.' I reached under the dashboard and the bonnet clunked upwards. Jeremy's thin lips curled with amusement. 'You'd better get out,' he said. I did as I was told, but instead of going to the front of the Stelvio, he headed to the rear and had me raise the trunk.

He looked down at the muddy bike. 'You've been cycling,' he observed.

'Keeping fit.'

'Good job.' We lifted the bike out. 'If this doesn't work, you might have to use it to get home.' He removed the trunk carpet. Beneath it sat what I presumed was the grey bulk of the battery, and beside it an array of pristine tools I had never set eyes upon before, let alone used. He selected a spanner and tightened a bolt on one side of the battery, then another on the other side. He looked at me.

'Go on, then.'

I went back around the front of the car and closed the bonnet before climbing into the driver's seat.

I was almost disappointed when the car started first time.

Leaving the engine running, I got back out. 'Cheers,' I said. Jeremy handed me the spanner with a wry smile.

'Bianca, our track manager, told me you're a private eye. Niki in trouble again?'

'Ah,' I said. 'Confidentiality and all that.'

'I couldn't give a damn so long as it doesn't affect his performance on Sunday.' He frowned. 'That's not likely, is it?' I shook my head. I suppose I owed him.

Jeremy seemed satisfied. 'I would get the poles cleaned,' he said. 'But don't let them tell you the battery needs replacing, that's their usual trick – they'll sell yours on as new.'

'Will do. Thanks.'

Jeremy Frost nodded and got back into his car. He pulled out without a further glance in my direction. If he was a guilty man, I thought, he was remarkably incurious. He hadn't exhibited an iota of surprise to find me near his home – either a sign of genuine innocence, or overcompensating for guilt. Wasn't it a bit of a coincidence to come across me here? Yes – but an innocent man would put it down to just that, coincidence.

In any case, ambivalence was not enough to condemn a man, unfortunately. It may have been this that led me to call in on Sherlock's on the way home – once again, I felt as if I had nothing.

*

'The competition.'

Would-be clients who tremulously opened the frosted-glass door to Sherlock Private Investigations SpA might have been a little disappointed if, instead of finding a Basil Rathbone or, for the younger generation, Benedict Cumberbatch-type Holmes leant back in an upholstered armchair pensively sucking his pipe, they were confronted by Boris Malprese cleaning his ears with a Q-Tip. His eyebrows arched like a pair of bushy black caterpillars beneath that broad, creased brow bordered by a fulsome wall of grey-flecked hair that reached his temples and no further. Boris was an earthy but not an ugly man – he looked like someone's uncle, the local butcher or, as in his case, the kind of ex-cop that would steer you towards a confession as if you were sharing a drink at the bar, and slap you fraternally on the back before you were led to the cells.

'I don't think of us as competitors,' I said. 'More like colleagues.'

'Ooh, you with your silky English manners. Come, take a pew.' He checked his computer. 'I'm free . . . for the next couple of days.'

'Business slow?'

'It's this new divorce law that's streamlined the system. *Come on* – it must have affected you lot, too. It's made it all too damn simple.'

'Well, you know, a lot of our work these days is corporate, and our clients . . .'

'Are as rich as Croesus. Whereas my lot want everything on the cheap, and now that breaking up has become a lot less expensive, they don't need to do the research, or catch hubby with his pants around his ankles. I could do with getting into corporate. I could scrub up – you're looking a bit casual, if you don't mind me saying. Run here, did you?'

'I was out . . . Well, the look's cycling. I was actually on a job.'

'Fieldwork. Nice.' He rubbed his large, hairy-knuckled hands together.

'Which is why I popped in.'

'And there was me thinking it was social.'

'It's a funny one.' I explained how we had, literally, inherited his case. Boris didn't so much as blink. No time for hurt feelings – he was all business. 'Given this, we've also got hold of your report.'

'Then you will have seen I pretty much cleared Chiesa's "chief suspects".'

'He was quite obsessed . . .'

'He was. Look, Daniel, if you want to grill me about it . . .'

'I was thinking – a consultancy fee?'

'That would be appreciated. And since you mention it, and we would be collaborating, I was wondering if you could give me a sniff of that corporate stuff. As a sub-contractor, maybe?'

Boris was certainly competent, but could I trust him not to undercut us? Of course not. If there was one Italian saying I might have tattooed on my forehead after all these years as a reminder every time I looked in the mirror: *Fidarsi è bene, non fidarsi è meglio.*

To trust is good, to distrust is better.

'I'll think about it.' He gave me a lingering look, and understood – if he wanted to win my trust, he would have to earn it.

'So,' he said. 'His suspicions were mostly bullshit.'

'Mostly?'

'Do I think that Fabrizio Chiesa was murdered? On the basis of my brief, no.'

'On the basis of your brief?'

'You'll have seen Chiesa wanted me to dig up dirt on Massimiliano and his son. I dug around a bit. I couldn't find anything solid that would link them to his death. Honestly, Daniel, regardless, it just looked like an accident to me.'

'So why did you say "mostly"?'

He pursed his big lips. He would have made a great trumpet player. 'Their world. F1, supercars, all that.' He chuckled. 'It's more your clients than mine, so you'll know, money's a bit like the sea – it washes in, washes out on a bed of sand, *shifting* sand . . .'

'That's almost poetic.'

'First time anyone's said that, although now you mention it, it's not really sand I'm thinking of. More like grit. More like slurry. Sea tar and broken shells and plastic bottles, cigarette stubs, in short – dirt.'

My eyes widened. '*Dirty money*, you mean? Money laundering?'

He held up his hands. 'Now let's not get ahead of ourselves, *gioventù*. I'm just observing – wherever there's money swimming about in Italy, well, you've got to wonder where it comes from, haven't you?' Those eyebrows wiggled.

'Was this why you asked to expand the investigation? You smelled something,' I winced at another aquatic metaphor, 'fishy?'

Boris laughed. 'Well, as they say, a fish rots from the head down. Something felt a bit off. You know there was all this business about Molinari pinching Chiesa's fuel injection system. To be frank, the shenanigans around that might have influenced my thinking – rookie error on my part, probably.'

'Shenanigans?'

'Chiesa went on as much about it as his poor boy.'

'The court case.'

'That, and the robbery. He had, or at least claimed to have had, a whole bunch of stuff stolen – blueprints and whatnot – which would have proved the system was his, but before he could bring it to court it went missing.'

'Yeah, I seem to recall his pal Bonnacini mentioning something about that.'

'Speedy?' Boris nodded knowingly. 'So he had it all put in a lock-up after that, right? Because he didn't want to keep it at home. Look, all I'm saying is it set alarm bells ringing, and it may have coloured my general approach to the case. Certainly, Molinari seemed to have gone from humble start-up to supercar-F1 team exceptionally quickly, and I'm guessing that would have required a massive *injection* of cash. I would have liked to have had a closer look into his investors, all that, on the off-chance Fabrizio might have stumbled across something that led to his demise.'

'Even if Molinari had some . . . questionable investors,' I said, 'why would they want to bump off one of his most promising drivers?'

Boris held up his hands again. '*Right*. I just had some unanswered questions. You know how it is.'

I pulled out my phone. 'Do these men ring any bells?' I began to flick through the photos I had taken of Chiesa's fieldwork.

'Where did you get them from?'

'Your client decided he would cut some corners.'

'Cheapskate. Hold on.' He prodded a thick finger. 'Marco Barbieri from Maserati. Oh, and that guy there's Andrea Rizzoli, a Ferrari bigwig.' He continued to swipe through. 'No. No. . . nuh.' He came to Niki. 'Oh boy, he gets around doesn't he? Some guys have all the luck. No. No . . .' His finger hovered above a picture of the manager, Bianca, and another guy stood up in the VIP area of some race, flutes of fizz balanced precariously upon uprights. 'Her that shall be obeyed, right?' I nodded. 'Yeah, I recognise her, the other guy, no.' He continued flicking through.

'How about this?' It was the one with Speedy, Chiesa and Dolores's Uncle Gigi.

'Well, the client, obviously, and our retired wheelman. The other one, no.'

The next photo was the series of numbers. 'Do these mean anything to you?'

He considered them. 'Where did you get these?'

'Here and there – among both Chiesa junior and senior's stuff.'

Boris expanded them on the screen and licked his lips. 'I do like a puzzle. Now let me see . . . Well, it's got to be connected to racing, right? They'll be the teams. That will be positions . . . times?'

'I found pages of them among the father's files.'

'Racing fanatics, the pair of them.'

'That's all it is, you think? I can see that, of course, but for some reason I had the sense that there might be something else there. I found a stack of gambling slips, although they were for modest amounts.'

'Could be something, could be nothing. Anything can be evidence – but of what?'

'Funnily enough another former policeman said much the same thing.' I cleared my throat.

'The Comandante, you mean. How is the old hound?'

'Getting older. He's just had a hip op. and taken a turn for the worse. In fact, the family's holding a vigil for him at the hospital.'

'It's that bad?'

'He almost died, but,' I checked my phone, 'he appears to be stable at present.'

'Christ, then send him my regards. If you like, I can take a further look at these numbers while your crew are otherwise occupied.'

I wouldn't have usually farmed something out like this, but we were stretched. And, I thought, in a way we did owe him. It would also make up for the fact I wasn't likely to introduce him to any of our corporate clients.

To trust is good, to mistrust is better.

I forwarded Boris the pics.

Chapter 14

'It should be banned,' grumbled Dolores.

'You're your usual sunny self.' I eased the car a few inches further forward.

'For the congestion alone! All this traffic belching fumes into the sky!'

'This is a hybrid, you know.'

'*Beh.* They're just as bad.'

We moved a little further forward. Finally, after around half an hour stuck in the suburbs of Imola, the entrance to the circuit came into view.

'You're aware the process of making electric cars damages the environment,' I said. 'And what about those poor Africans having to mine the stuff for the batteries and so on?'

'Did I say I liked electric cars?' said Dolores. 'People should ride bikes.'

'To Imola? All right, I guess that's possible. But Rome?'

'Train.'

'I like trains,' I admitted. I spotted the VIP entrance and began to manoeuvre the Alfa towards it.

'And horses,' she said.

'What about horses?'

'They could bring them back, for the slightly longer journeys. Or for old people.'

'You mean who can't ride bikes?'

'Precisely.'

'But they can ride horses?'

'Carriages.'

'Oh, of course.' I managed to steer the car around the main queue and reach the VIP entrance. I showed our tickets and the man took them to check in the cabin. 'But what about their farts?' I asked.

'What *about* their farts?'

'Isn't that the problem with cows? Releasing methane into the air? Isn't that a major contributor to greenhouse gasses?'

Dolores scowled. 'When did you become so interested in the environment?'

'Since Rose had to study it for geography. It's all green stuff now.'

'Anyway,' said Dolores, 'if they banned meat, then there wouldn't be a cow problem.'

'True,' I said. 'There wouldn't be cows.'

'There would be dairy.'

'Terribly exploitative,' I said. 'Isn't that why you became vegan?'

'Oh,' she snapped. 'Stop talking like you give a shit!'

The guy returned with our VIP lanyards and waved us through. We drove along the empty lane, passing the long queue of spectators' cars in silence.

The lane took us to a car park at the rear of the paddocks. I found a slot and pulled in. 'Look, Dolores,' I said. 'I really didn't mean to . . .'

She scowled: 'Not everything's a laughing matter, Dan.' She popped her seatbelt and got out, slamming the door behind her.

'Although people taking themselves too seriously, might be,' I muttered.

If I had felt exposed when I had first visited the circuit, now grey clouds domed the elliptical stands and, despite the sea of parked cars, regiment of juggernauts, many thousands of spectators watching or milling about the merchandising stalls, the gloomy sky only seemed to amplify the sound of the monsters prowling the track.

An attractive young woman, predictably sporting a dark green Molinari jumpsuit, met us at the entrance.

'They're finishing their warm-up lap,' she explained. 'Please, follow me.'

I had naively expected a paddock pass to be precisely that – to allow us to squeeze in among the hundred or so worker bees we could see gathered around computer screens, tweaking obscure lumps of machinery, rehearsing the kind of drills I had witnessed before, only this time in component-crowded spaces, but instead we were led up clanging metal steps to a floor furnished with leather sofas – Molinari green – big TV screens, tables with Prosecco, juice and finger food, while, through sliding glass doors that led onto a balcony, we were offered a prime view of the start and could peer down on to the pits.

Dolores had to shout because of the noise through the open doors: 'When are we going to get this key?'

I put my finger to my lips and leaned forward to speak into her ear. 'That's for Niki to decide.' I pointed at one of many TVs. Niki was sat half-way out of his car in the paddock talking to members of the Molinari team. 'I somehow doubt he's going to have time before the race.'

'So what are we doing here now, then?'

I handed her a glass of fizz. 'Just try and enjoy the experience. People pay huge amounts of money for this.'

Occupying the nearest sofa were a group of older men who looked as if they hung out with Silvio Berlusconi, but whose hair implants and Botox couldn't disguise the square shoulders of farmers. They toasted much younger wives or girlfriends with Viagra-like vigour.

Stood around the tables or along the balcony, a smattering of local celebrities mingled with various generations of *Bologna bene*, who I doubted took much interest in the race, but who habitually materialised at occasions like this.

We went onto the balcony. Here the noise was almost unbearable, then I realised most of the people were wearing earplugs. I spotted a tray by the entrance and picked up a couple of packets, thrusting one into Dolores' hand. They worked well enough, and we were able lean over and view the activity below. Things appeared to be getting serious and I watched Niki put his helmet on and slide back into the car. Flanked by engineers, he drove it to his place on the grid. Eighth. Three behind Molinari's Number One, Moyen, but from what I had learned about F1, still respectable. There were another dozen cars behind him and anything could happen between now and the finish, sixty-three laps later.

The other 'VIPs' drifted out to join us, pressing around the balcony as the race was about to begin, that ominous sky only seeming to add to the tension as the cars revved on the grid.

A wallop of rubber and petrol fumes rose together with the mechanical snarl. Five semaphore lights suspended in a bank above the track began to turn red. One – after another – after another – until finally, even with the earplugs, the sound became almost unbearable.

The lights went out.

The cars leapt off the grid, jostling for position even as the drivers wrestled with the inconceivable torque of a Formula One engine, and roared up the track.

Almost immediately there was confusion towards the rear. Cars wobbling as if they were caught in a wave of heat, then one was off the track, another sat sideways. In the unexpected quiet, I heard an 'Ooh', and the press of bodies lessened. Many of the spectators had rushed inside to follow the race on the big screen. I turned to Dolores, but she had gone too.

After watching the car on the track right itself, chasing after the others like the straggler in a murmuration of starlings, I headed inside. Dolores was stood, Prosecco flute in hand, gawping up at the race on one of the TVs. I was about to join her when a woman said in American English:

'Having fun?'

I turned around. 'Oh,' I said. 'Shit.'

'Well,' said Anna Bloom. 'I see you've lost none of that famous British charm.'

'I . . . Oh.' I lamely held out my hand.

'You mean you don't want to kiss mine?' She looked

amused. I hadn't seen Anna since we had, more or less, kissed goodbye a year or so earlier in her hotel lobby. I glanced warily around – we were receiving a few sly glances from the assorted 'VIPs', but no one wanted to blow their cool by actually approaching the film star, yet. 'Don't be a bozo,' Anna grabbed me. 'We're in Italy, aren't we?' She kissed me on both cheeks. 'I hope we're not blowing your cover,' she said in a stage whisper.

'We?' I asked.

'It's Dan, right?' Mason Kane gave my hand a firm shake. Every bit as renowned as Anna, he must have been older than me – I could remember seeing him in some independent films as a student until he turned action hero in various sci-fi and gangster franchises – but his long dark hair showed not a speck of grey. 'Anna told me you two had a pretty wild time of it when she was shooting Indigo's passion project in Bologna.'

Anna's marine blue eyes were giving nothing away. 'We had some pretty hairy moments,' I said. 'To be honest, it's thanks to her I'm talking to you today.'

Mason nodded respectfully. 'That doesn't surprise me at all. I, for one, wouldn't cross her. *Wooh* – Anna Bloom is armed and dangerous!'

'Although, strictly speaking, not here,' she said. 'In Italy, I mean.'

'But you've got your "torch", I presume?' I said.

She patted her no doubt impossibly expensive handbag. 'You never know when the lights are going to go out, hon.'

'If you'll excuse me, my dear.' Mason waved at a man I vaguely recognised.

Anna smiled at me fondly. 'You do seem to make a habit of bumping into your exes, Daniel Leicester.'

'You mean you and me? We were never . . .'

She glowered. *'And who's fault is that?'*

'You're the one that buggered off.'

'I had a movie to make,' she said defensively. 'And I *am* a movie star.'

'There's the rub. You're much better off with Mason. Seems like a nice guy.'

'Mason *is* nice, but we're not a couple. We're actually shooting together in Berlin but he's a complete car nut so had them halt filming so he could come here, and I said what the hell am I going to do, and he said come along, so here I am. We're heading back tonight.'

'Tiring.'

'Life is tiring, hon. Anyway – what the hell are you doing here? When he said we'd be flying into Bologna, I did think of giving the race a rain check and calling in on you and your lovely, lovely family but then I thought . . . well, anyway, here we are. How is everyone?'

I told her. 'Rose was pretty crushed by your sudden departure,' I pointed out. 'And of course, I was quite upset, too.'

'And I was pissed *at you* for not responding to my calls.'

'I was working.' Anna shook her head.

'Not all the time, buster. And Rose, yeah, I felt bad, but I messaged her on Insta to say how much fun we'd had and to come visit and all.'

'She never mentioned it to me.' Anna shrugged. 'So,' I said, 'are you see—'

'I'm not *really* blowing your cover though, am I?'

I considered it. 'Not really, no. Although we are working . . .'

'*We?*'

I nodded at Dolores, who was still enrapt by the race. 'My
colleague and I. But no one has any reason to suspect us of
anything, as far as I know, regardless of how much attention
you might draw. And in any case,' I said. 'I suspect the public
only have eyes for you.'

Mason came over with the man, who I finally recognised
as a three-time Formula One world champion. 'Sorry to
interrupt,' said Mason. 'But the only reason I could even get
Patrik to talk to me was if I introduced him to *Ms* Anna
Bloom.'

The Belgian took her hand and kissed it. Anna's eyes
drifted towards mine, absent their usual whimsy. We might
have shared a moment of regret for what could have been,
but then Anna was smiling through the introductions and I
was beating a retreat, while the crowd, as crowds tend to do
around Ms Anna Bloom, closed.

'What's up?' asked Dolores.

'Hm. Nothing.'

'I saw you talking to your old flame.'

'Anna is *not* my old flame.'

'Anyway, Niki's pitting.'

I looked up at the TV. The sound was on but only intermittently audible through the thunder of the passing machines.
There were subtitles, however, typed contemporaneously as
the drivers communicated with the paddock.

'Wets, *blue*.'

'We discussed this, Niki,' replied Jeremy. 'Forecasts are for a light shower, over.'

'Conditions changing rapidly, over.'

'No sign of that here, over.'

'I'm coming in on next circuit, have them ready, over.'

'Niki . . .' The connection was lost, or had been dropped.

'Blues, man, that's pretty heavy.' Mason was standing beside me. 'The heaviest tyres, in fact.' He gazed out. 'Those clouds are looking damn ominous, though, maybe Niki's right.'

'What's the implication?' I asked. 'I get they're for the rain, but does it make a big difference on the dry?'

Mason Kane looked at me in wonderment. 'You're clearly no race fan.'

'Busted, although I'm growing to like it.'

'*Massive* drag,' he said. 'Niki's currently up to fifth, good job – you know this generation of Molinaris have righted the up-lift but they're still a bit ponderous compared to the top three, and the new McLaren . . . Anyway, every millisecond counts, especially on the straight, and wets, even greens, they're for light rain, slow you down. With blues, you may as well be driving a tractor. Oh, here he comes . . .'

Mason took my arm and led me out to the balcony, the crowd parting reverentially around us. We peered down. Niki shot into the pit and the mechanics were waiting with the tyres. Even I could see the massive treads and blue rims. In a scream of metal and a swampy smell from the old tyres, the change was made and Niki was roaring off again.

Jeremy and Massimiliano stood at the rear of the pit watching him go. While Jeremy wore a look of vague disappointment, Massimiliano appeared enraged, prodding a finger in his son-in-law's face as they turned to go back inside.

Mason put an arm around my shoulders and shouted. 'Things aren't looking too peachy in *casa* Molinari, eh?'

'Why do you think Jeremy let him change?'

'Our boy Jeremy's a canny cove.' He said the last part in the Mockney that had been widely ridiculed when he had played a Bond villain. 'Niki's good, but he's not great. Jeremy'll claim he's got to trust the drivers. Either way, I think he's pretty cool if Niki fucks up. There's plenty of young blood to choose from, and Jeremy wants to lead a team of winners.'

'So does Molinari senior, as I understand. Then why keep Niki on the team, if he's not the best of the best?'

Mason frowned. 'Blood's thicker than water?'

'That doesn't sound like Max Molinari to me.'

Mason tapped his nose. 'People are strange, *fucked up*! Didn't Anna tell you that's the secret to acting? Civilians think – wow, it's so tough being an actor, having to, like, pretend to be all these different people. On the contrary – sure, it's damn hard to *fake normal*. I mean – what's normal? But no one is. Everyone's got a tiny bit of crazy, so you don't play the normal, you play the crazy.' Mason gave me a penetrating stare, as if locating my own crazy. 'What I'm saying, dude, is to be human is to be inconsistent.'

'So it would be consistent of results-driven Max Molinari to be inconsistent when it comes to his son.'

'That's right, *mite*.' We were back to the Bond villain. 'Life's nothing but a gamble.'

I glanced back up at the screen. 'Between wet and dry tyres.'

'Something like that. There – you see?'

There was a spot of rain on the camera lens. Then another, another. Chatter came from various drivers and their teams discussing tyre changes. Some kept going, others dropped into the pits, switching to wets, although green intermediates instead of the heavier duty blues, as per the forecasts. Meanwhile Niki, who had dropped back to seventh, began to ponderously move back up the field.

Then it happened. The downpour. Frankly, I didn't know why everyone was so surprised. I had lived in the area long enough to know the weather could change in a heartbeat and this was a place of extremes. Forty-degree summers and sub-zero winters. Cloudless days and then, whoosh, tropical rainstorms, and I guessed someone like Niki, who for all his shortcomings was as competitive as his father, must have smelled it coming.

It was chaos on the track as the cars on dries pitted and the ones on greens wavered by calculating whether it would pass or putting off the moment to switch to blues while the rain drilled on and on. It was falling so hard the crowd on the stands, who were already for the most part decked out in waterproofs, dashed for cover. Lightning bleached the room. Thunder battered the stand. If it were possible, the rain appeared to become even more insistent.

'They have to stop the race,' I said.

'Are you kidding?' said Mason. 'And look at our boy.'

I couldn't see it on the screen, but it was clear enough on the leader board. Niki Molinari was in third place. And it was then I had – well I wouldn't call it a premonition, more a hunch. I walked over to the balcony.

'You're not going out in that?' said Mason.

I wasn't, but from where I was standing, I could just about make out that first bend I'd seen Niki contemplating when I'd joined him along the pits.

A pair of cars whooshed past, closely followed by a third – Niki Molinari, scything through the water and sending the handful of spectators still stood on the stand running.

'They need to slow down,' I heard Mason say behind me.

It was close to the point where I'd seen those first cars come off at the beginning of the race, although now through the curtain of rain together with the sea grey of the track and con-crete sky, it seemed as if the cars were hurtling towards a wall.

'Too fast,' Mason muttered.

The cars seemed to shimmer as the leading cars took the chicane. Only something happened and they spiralled aside, fortunately in opposite directions, one being stopped by external barriers, the other ending up facing the wrong way by the side of the track. Between them, the dark green levi-athan of Molinari's number two glided through the chicane and disappeared around that bend.

'Well, dammit,' shouted Mason, his face full of childish delight, 'that's our boy!'

He dragged me back inside to look at the big screen. Niki Molinari's car was front and centre, sweeping down the middle of the track, number one in the leader table. The shot cut back to the cars of Vestappen and Leclerc caught by the chicane. Vestappen was standing a little distance from his Red Bull, front end crumpled. He pulled off his helmet and flung it on the ground. Leclerc was still, apparently, trying to get his car started, while the remainder of the field began to zip past.

'How long do you reckon this rain's going to hold up?' asked Mason.

'Could be another hour, could be another minute,' I said.

'Dammit,' he giggled. 'I'd put a ten on him to gain fourth. Good odds too. But hell, to see him win – it'd be worth it.'

'Why Molinari?' I asked.

Mason looked at me askance. 'Weeelll,' he said. 'The free car might have something to do with it.'

'You're their sort of "brand ambassador"?'

'I sort of am, Dan,' he grinned. 'It's a dirty job, but somebody's got to do it.' He glanced back up at the screen and winced.

'What?'

'Like you were saying – somebody seems to have turned off the tap.'

'And what does that mean?'

'Our boy has a calculation to make – does he remain on his blues? Does he switch to greens? The tyres of the others are fresher, that gives them an edge – his must be pretty . . . knackered do you Brits say? I love that word. Frankly, I can't see them lasting the length, and the McLaren, which is currently way back but is the faster car, is on greens. Dare Niki risk a pit? *Hello* . . .'

'Box for tyre change.' It was Jeremy's voice. 'I repeat, Box for tyre change, over.'

'Received,' said Niki, 'and rejected. I'm going to stick with these.'

'Niki,' said Jeremy. 'It's time to change to greens. We can get a podium from this, over.'

'Affirmative,' said Niki. 'Gonna stay as I am, out.'

'Ooh,' said Mason. 'That must hurt. Jesus, can you imagine what the fuck they are saying down there? You know what? I think we should take a look.'

'We can't just go down to the paddock,' I said. 'We're not allowed.'

'Man,' Mason placed both hands on my shoulders. 'You're with Mason fucking Kane, and whatever Mason wants, Mason gets. Come on.'

With Mason's arm around my shoulder, I was led out of the VIP lounge, past Dolores, who shot me a questioning look, and down those metal stairs. He grinned at the woman at the door who smiled obligingly back and stood aside.

The activity I had glimpsed as we had come in had been replaced by a crowd gathered around a bank of computer monitors to the side of the pit, while more engineers sat not unlike the crowd upstairs, but on plastic fold-up chairs, gawping at the race on TV monitors. The atmosphere was thick with the humidity of rain and track water, the gaseous whiff of hot, spent rubber, sweat and testosterone. It felt more like a boxing ring than an F1 paddock.

We joined the crowd gathered around the screens arguing extravagantly in Italian.

'What are they saying?' asked Mason.

'What everyone else is – what the hell is he doing? Will he make it? What a dumb fuck he is for not following instructions. They're saying the team's going to lose. What does that mean?'

'When Jeremy was talking about podium, he didn't mean a win,' said Mason. 'For the team a sure third place podium is better than nothing. And it's the Constructors that really matters to them.'

'The what?'

'The Constructors championship – what a team win is all about. It comes back to the roots of F1 – a glorified car showroom. It's not about the drivers – with Enzo,' Mason noted my blank look, '*Ferrari*. It never was. He didn't give a shit about the drivers, or only in so much as they won – even when they died, and a hell of a lot of them did in the early days – he barely shed a tear. First of all it was about the racing cars, *constructing* the best, the fastest. But a close second to that came the status it gave the cars that really brought the cash in, that made it all possible – the ones on the forecourt. Now maybe it's a little bit different, but in their heart of hearts, the real bragging rights for this lot is the Constructors'.'

'The consensus seems to be Niki doesn't stand a chance in making it to first.'

'And the consensus may be right.' Mason pointed. 'Look.'

On the TV monitor, the McLaren had crept up the remaining eight cars on the track to third, and there were still six laps to go.

'And see – the pack is now just two seconds behind Niki. The guy's pretty fucked. Even if he wanted to pit, it would be too late now, he'd be back where he began, eighth spot. Look.' He nodded at Max Molinari and Jeremy, bent over their computer screen. Massimiliano was swearing at the screen as if he was screaming in his son's face, while Jeremy was wearing a petulant pout. He straightened up and looked resignedly about. He spotted Mason and his face lit up. He arched his eyebrows as if to say – what can you do?

Mason grinned and shook his head.

'You're a friend of Jeremy's?' I asked.

'We're acquainted.' He looked back up at the screen.

'It's funny, but I've never seen him look quite so relaxed.'

'Calm under pressure. Before motor racing, he was a captain in the British military. Iraq, Afghanistan. I bet he's been in worse fixes.'

'You like him?'

'Sure, and mucho respect, man, seen him in action. F1, I mean – Dubai, Kuala Lumpa, Sydney, Austin, Monaco – he's a pain in the ass with the team, but he sure knows what he's doing. Off the circuit, he's a pretty chill dude, a bit like you. Not a star fucker, I mean.' He looked at me askance. 'Not that I'm saying you don't fuck stars.' He frowned. 'You're not poking into *his* business, are you?'

I laughed. 'I'd be going about it pretty brazenly if I was.'

'That's what I figured. Oh, *hello.*'

The McLaren was on the Alta curve when it made its move around the Williams – for a moment the two cars appeared tied along the stretch, but then, turbo sparks flying, the McLaren took the lead and dove into the Rivazza bend ahead of its rival. By now Niki was rounding the Bassa and nearing our stand, but with another three circuits to go and the McLaren just a second behind, and the rest of the pack a second behind him, it was looking bleak for Niki Molinari.

'You're friends with Niki, too?'

Mason gazed at me as if across a distance. 'Sure, we're pals,' he said. 'Though we hardly know each other. But we know *of* each other, if you get what I'm saying? Hey – you see that?' Mason pointed at the TV. The McLaren was bearing down on Niki, but that was nothing new. 'There, another.' Now I spotted it – a splodge on the camera lens. Another.

They were rounding Tamburello and the McLaren was clearly going to try and pass Niki, but just as they hit the curve, Niki swung wide, blocking its first thrust, then returning to the middle as it tried to come through. As they hit the straight, Niki clearly gave it all he'd got, sparks flying behind both cars as they raced to Tosa.

The entire room was on its feet behind Niki, screaming instructions and entreaties. By some miracle, Niki managed to edge it ahead around the final curve, the camera lens at the bend beginning to blur with the rain.

'Come on come on come on,' muttered Mason.

Then on Piratella – disaster. Almost without warning, the McLaren nipped ahead of Niki to power passed him. There was a collective 'Oh.'

'Bastard!' I heard Jeremy shout.

'Come on Niki,' someone shouted. 'Ni-ki, Ni-ki . . .' The chant rose as the rain began to fall more strongly – you could see it from inside the paddock, that same rain pounding down again outside, the steamy atmosphere of the tropics returning to the pit. I felt the moisture on my face, sweat roll down my back.

Niki was on the McLaren's tail at Acque Minerale, Alta, Rivazza . . . the rest of the pack crowding behind him. At least now he didn't have to worry about being out-paced – it was the McLaren that was slowing the traffic with its 'greens'. But the McLaren, as Mason had pointed out, was also the superior car. True, Niki's tyres could bestow milliseconds, even seconds of advantage, but so could the superior engine and aerodynamics of the McLaren.

The battle on those final two circuits would enter F1 lore.

As the commentator declared at the beginning of the final circuit: 'It's tyres versus torque today and all to play for right up to the chequered flag.'

Throughout the second from last lap, the McLaren had blocked Niki with seeming ease. Watching on the screen, I couldn't see how he could possibly pass the leader on those bends, and when it came to the straights, the McLaren's length lead was enough to make it to the next bend.

'And doesn't this,' said the commentator, 'make F1 the greatest sport on earth?'

The team roared as the cars shot past the pit.

They were reaching that bend, Tamburello. We strained to make out their position through the camera angle – straight on, the lens as opaque as swimming goggles, a pair of green and orange hammerheads were battling it out for first place. The shot switched to the drone above, which was clearly struggling to keep airborne in the renewed downpour, but it was clear – they were neck and neck and only one could make it first through the chicane.

'Oh Jesus,' said Mason. 'Oh Christ.'

This was how Niki had forced his way ahead in the first place – knocking the leaders out – but now he had the pack piling the pressure on him.

I thought of what he had said – would he have bounced Fabrizio off the track, even if it had risked his life? Yes, he would have, and I couldn't see him blinking now.

Only he did.

A collective 'oh!' went up as Niki fell back just enough to let the McLaren through. Jeremy's voice audible in the disappointed silence: *'Niki, Niki, Niki.'*

The McLaren shot towards Tosa with Niki barely half a length behind, but despite his best efforts, it somehow managed to keep ahead.

'The kid's done well,' reasoned Mason. 'They may say he choked at Tamburello but it means he put tactics ahead of sheer instinct. Number two on the podium's not nothing – guess he may be maturing, finally. Should please his old man.'

We watched the cars play the same cat and mouse, while the pack fought it out among themselves, Moyen for Molinari in fifth place. Then it was back to the front runners, the McLaren now comfortably fending the Molinari off as they rounded Acque Minerale – 'It seems the torque has it,' said the commentator – and along the straight towards Curva Gresini.

The shot switched back to the pack where Moyen had nipped around a pair of cars to grab third, although he was too far behind Niki to catch him.

But when it returned to the straight approaching the final bend, the shot was different – now a green hammerhead was in the lead.

'Gresini!' The commentator yelped. 'He took him at Gresini!'

As Niki rounded Rivazza in real time we saw the replay in a box – the McLaren went a little wide, possibly anticipating his pursuer, and Nikki zipped through on the inside like a ripple through the rain.

In the paddock, it was like a goal had been scored. It was like we were behind the goal. It was like we were behind the goal for the winning penalty at a World Cup. We were jumping, screaming, hugging deliriously. I don't think anyone actually watched Niki take the final, short straight and get waved through by the chequered flag. Correction – I may have glimpsed Jeremy, his back to me, hands on hips, looking up at the TV and shaking his head in wonder.

We surged as one across the bay to the wall separating the pit from the track as he cruised past, waving. The loudspeakers broadcast direct from his cockpit: 'I'd like to dedicate this to my friend Fabri, whose spirit was with me in the car today.'

Of course, from my perspective, things hadn't gone exactly to plan. I was pretty sure Niki hadn't expected to win or even make podium when he had invited us, and I frankly doubted we would have a chance to meet now as the first three cars pulled up and their drivers were whisked away for a weight check and the official ceremony, Mason and I heading back upstairs to watch it take place, but in the delirium of victory, that seemed a minor concern.

'You boys have a good time?' asked Anna.

'It was pretty damn exhilarating,' replied Mason. 'Our man won the day! Come on, Anna, you must have got a kick out of it.'

'Everyone did – even your girl over there,' she said, meaning Dolores. 'Are you going to introduce us?'

'*My colleague.*' I called her over.

'Hello,' said Dolores in accented English, her face still flushed from the excitement. 'You're Rose's friend.'

'Oh, yeah,' said Anna. 'That's me – *Rose's friend.*'

'Does she know you're here?'

'They flew in for the race,' I said gravely. 'They head back this evening.' I braced for a reaction from the eco-warrior, but came there none. 'And this is . . .'

'I know – hi.' Dolores held out her hand to Mason, her colour deepening. 'I like your films. I mean some of them. I've seen them. Some, I mean. The early ones. They were great.'

'Just the early ones?' said Mason.

'Well, I've seen others, too, of course. They're good, too.'

Mason wrinkled his nose. 'No, you're right. The early ones *were* better. But they didn't pay. You want to know a secret?' He leant closer. 'The only reason anyone still watches the old, good ones is because I'm famous for the new bad ones. That,' he winked, 'is precisely why I keep doing them.'

'Me too,' said Anna.

Dolores laughed nervously. I could tell she wasn't entirely sure they were kidding, and to be fair they were actors and English was her second language. Still, I surveyed her with something approaching amusement myself – I had never seen Dolores Pugliese look so ill at ease.

'Sure,' said Anna. 'Like the one we're doing now in Germany. I mean what's *that* about? Have you *any* idea, Mase?'

'*Oh my God I'm glad it's not just you.* No idea! I began to read the script but skipped to the end. I'm just learning a page a day, my dear, a page a day!'

'Then what happens at the end?' she asked.

'*You mean you haven't read it either?*'

Anna made a short intake of breath as if she had been found out, and they dissolved into laughter. Dolores grew a deep crimson but tried to look as if she was in on the joke. Mason glanced over her head.

'Ahah!' The drivers were gathering on the podium. Even

though the VIP balcony was already packed, the crowd parted to allow us through. I looked along the front of the balcony – Bologna royalty, mostly, captivated by Niki's big moment. All except one. It was one of the older men I'd seen when we first arrived, his deep tanned, anvil-shaped head, topped by a cap of flattened black hair, bent over his phone where thick thumbs tapped away. I glanced down at the paddock, expecting to find it empty – as far as I could see, the whole team was gathered behind a low fence near the podium – but a white-haired man was stood watching like we were.

Max Molinari reached into his pocket and pulled out his mobile. He went inside. When I looked back up, the other man had also disappeared. Money, I thought. Money talking.

Upon the top of the podium, Niki Molinari was beaming with joy. The other two drivers, including his team mate in third place, looked genuinely pleased for him. Niki was a popular guy on the circuit, and both of the younger drivers probably understood he presented no serious threat to their careers, that this was Niki's first, and almost certainly last, Grand Prix victory.

The cup. The champagne. Niki rushing into the arms of his team, Jeremy front and centre looking just as delighted as the rest. More champagne. A dripping, grinning Niki interviewed trackside.

'It was a controversial decision, to go with the wets so early,' said the heavily accented Italian journalist in English. 'The team disagreed.'

'This is my circuit,' said Niki. 'My land. I could feel the rain in my bones.'

'And in the end they went with your choice.'

'In the end, I'm the one driving the car.'

'And at the Tamburello, when you made way for the McLaren, a lot of us thought you had lost it.'

'Naturally, I would have liked to have been ahead, but I wasn't, and I knew I would win anyway.'

'*You knew?* How could you be so sure?'

'The rain was coming down. I knew I would get him in the end.'

'But you only had one lap.'

'It was a gamble,' Niki said, suddenly sombre. 'But I'm a gambling man, and this time I felt the odds were in my favour.'

'You felt it, like you felt the rain.'

'I did.'

'One last thing – you dedicated your win to "Fabri" . . .'

'Fabrizio Chiesa, my old team mate who died a few years ago. The greatest natural driver I've seen, second to none.' He held the cup up to the camera. 'This is for you, Fabri.'

'Come on,' said Mason. 'Let's go back down.'

We had just reached the bottom of the stairs when Max Molinari emerged from the rear of the paddock, the outline of his belly bulging from the team jumpsuit, a black holdall slung over his shoulder. He had plainly spotted me too, and was about to march past but then realised who I was with.

'Ah, Mason.' His stony expression splintered into a smile. 'Thank you so much for coming. You enjoyed the race?'

'Enjoyed it?' said Mason. 'Never mind me, Signor Molinari, you must be over the moon.'

Max Molinari seemed to take time to register what Mason meant, so I translated 'over the moon' into Italian: 'Delighted.'

'Oh yes. Very happy. A one and three. A very good result.'

'And your boy, too – Niki.'

'Ah yes,' he nodded vaguely. 'My boy. Niki. Yes . . .' His words petered out.

'You're not staying for the celebration?'

'Ah, no. Sadly I must rush. There is an emergency, at the house.'

'Nothing bad, I hope?'

'No, no,' Max assured him. 'Not too bad, but,' he sighed. 'I must go, nonetheless.'

'We're going to congratulate him,' said Mason. 'If you don't mind?'

'No, you boys go ahead. Enjoy!'

As we entered the paddock, Niki was being carried across the pits on the team's shoulders wearing that same puppyish look of delight. Another magnum of bubbly was handed up to him and duly sprayed, the bottle being passed around as they let him down to begin some serious partying. Someone spotted Mason and a cheer went up, the actor launching himself into the crowd and throwing his arms around Niki. I looked on, wearing a pretty soppy grin myself. Across the room, I spotted Jeremy with Molinari's Number One, apparently both congratulating and commiserating with him. Beside them, the sole woman in the paddock – Bianca, an untouched flute of champagne in hand – looked on with a sour expression, as if considering all the cleaning up.

Then Niki was stood in front of me, dripping with sweat or champagne, Mason looming behind him. 'Come on,' he said. 'I really need to take a shit.'

I followed them out of the paddock to a trailer where Niki

unzipped his jumpsuit as soon as he got inside. He stepped out of it naked save for a pair of briefs and socks, a rubbery odour rising from the discarded clothes, and headed straight to the far door, slamming it behind him. Almost immediately an enormous groan reverberated from inside, followed by unambiguous toilet noises.

'He really wasn't kidding about the shit part,' said Mason. 'I used to do the same, especially on stage, but that was mainly beforehand. Some actors throw up, mine came out the other way. It's biological, dude. It reminds us we're animals, not gods.'

'I rarely feel like a god.'

'Well, with respect, you've never accepted an Oscar or won a Grand Prix.'

'Touché.'

Mason shrugged. 'Sorry, but I mean , , ,'

'I know what you mean, Mason Kane.'

'My real name's Clementine Schwarzkopf.'

'It's not.'

'Nah.' Mason smiled. 'It is actually Mason Kane. My folks were California types, it's where I was conceived, in the South of France. Mason is actually "Maison", see? They dropped the "I" to make it less complicated, for which I am eternally grateful.'

A flushing sound, a window opening, a tap turned.

Niki emerged with just a towel around his midriff. He closed the door firmly behind him.

'Don't even think about going in there.' He padded over to the fridge, took out a litre bottle of mineral water and glugged half of it down. He slumped onto the sofa, flung back his head and closed his eyes.

'Aaaaaaah, *fuck*.'

'Fuck, man,' said Mason. 'You did it. You fucking did it.'

'I fucking did it,' Niki whispered. He opened his eyes as if waking from a dream. 'Did he see it?'

'Who?' I asked.

'Dad.'

'Sure. He was watching it from the paddock.'

'He saw it all?'

'He certainly did.'

'Saw me win?'

Mason and I nodded.

'I didn't see him.'

We looked at each other. 'He was coming out as we came in,' I said. 'Some kind of emergency at home.'

'Really? What kind of emergency?'

'He said it was nothing to worry about.'

Niki confusedly shook his head. 'Was it an emergency or not?'

'I couldn't say . . .'

'But *he saw the race*, you say?'

'Sure.'

'But how do you know if you were upstairs?'

'We were up and down. We were down in the paddock when you crossed the finish line but went up to watch the ceremony. Your father was definitely there with the team watching you win.' I thought back to that moment. I couldn't remember actually seeing Max, only Jeremy, but wasn't going to mention it.

'Because he wasn't at the podium.'

'Dude,' said Mason. 'He saw it, all right?' Niki nodded

slowly, then covered his face with his hands, drawing deep breaths between his fingers. 'Are you okay, man?'

'Sure,' said Niki, still speaking from behind his hands. 'At least they can say Niki Molinari won a Grand Prix.'

'They certainly can.'

'They can't take that away from me.'

'Never,' said Mason. 'You're in the history books, dude. And what a race!'

'It was worth it.'

'It sure was, man. All those years . . .'

'Whatever happens.' Niki withdrew his hands. 'Behind you,' he said to me. 'Beneath that first teeny cup.'

There was a line of trophies of ascending size atop a black TV cabinet. 'I got that for coming second in the Emilia Romagna under-14s carting finals. After Fabrizio Chiesa, of course.' I lifted it up. Beneath it, a USB stick. 'Use it wisely, padawan.'

'Hold on.' Mason turned to me. 'It's *Niki* you're here for? Damn it, of course! What have you been up to this time, you dog?' Niki's grin widened. 'Man, you gotta be careful. It was bad enough in my day, but with these phones everywhere your cock's gonna go global quicker than you can say TikTok.' He turned to me. 'He's been a bad boy?'

My eyes locked with Niki's. 'So he would have you believe.'

Chapter 15

The uncanny still of the hospital room. Its bare beige walls, TV running on silent. The hush of the linoleum corridor, despite the come and go of nurses. We barely notice hospitals until we are in one, when we soon come to realise that they, not we, are the still point around which the world revolves – the birth and death and stations in between. Hence those beige walls, that cultivated quiet; the high-set thermostat calculated to promote an almost soporific calm lest we are gripped by existential panic. It therefore came as no surprise to find Alba gently snoring as I arrived for my 'shift'.

She blinked, wondering where she was, then fingered the knitting on her lap and remembered.

'Is it that time?'

'Six,' I said. 'You probably needed the rest – I hear Little Lucia's keeping you both up.' I looked at the Comandante, his eyes closed but strangely un-asleep as only someone unconscious can seem.

Alba said: 'No change.'

'No change is good at this point. He needs to heal.'

'I suppose so, but it would be good to see him open his eyes. Just to know, you know?'

'I know.'

I was on the six to ten, which suited me as it gave me time to wind down and consider the events of the day, and I could always catch up with something to watch on my iPad. I tended to avoid reading at this time of night in case I fell asleep. Now the Comandante was supposedly out of danger, the hospital discouraged night stays, although they didn't tend to actually kick anyone out, and I didn't fancy waking up here at two in the morning.

I waited until Alba had taken her leave before beginning to recount the events of the day to Giovanni. The doctors had said his medications meant he was basically asleep, but knowing the Comandante as I did, I wasn't convinced, and I knew that if it was me lying there all day and night, I would be awfully bored.

'So, we picked up the key from Niki and I've given it to Jacopo. This should provide us with what electronic information we can get hold of this late in the day. Do I think Jeremy had something to do with Fabrizio's death? He had the motive, his apparently malicious behaviour towards Fabrizio's son is another pointer, and today I discovered he is ex-UK military who's seen action, so I suspect he had both the means and the bottle. Will we be able to uncover evidence? That's another matter. And, of course, just because he could have done it, doesn't mean he actually did. We will see what the key reveals.'

The Comandante's lips seemed to move. I leaned close. It was hard to tell. I put my ear to them, but nothing.

The old boy was in need of a shave and his hair was out of place. I smoothed it to the side and took his hand, hoping it might respond.

Dry. Rubbery. Warm. But again, nothing.

'This is not the end,' I said. 'This can't be, Comandante. You're going to get better and break my balls for years to come. Italian men don't die, they just grow older and smaller until they disappear, so you've got many years in you yet, just you see.'

There was activity outside.

A bustle of medical staff in hospital blues and whites entered the room, entirely ignoring me. I pushed back the chair as a nurse changed the Comandante's drip. A doctor came to read the charts at the end of the bed while another pair loitered by the door in the low lighting, seemingly discussing another patient. One of them – lean and shaven-headed – seemed familiar, but I was still struggling to place him after they had bustled away. It was only when I had fired up the iPad that the resemblance to Francesco Chiesa, Fabrizio's older brother, struck me.

Resemblance, yes, Chiesa – no. More like his younger athletic brother. Only that brother was no longer with us, at least in the flesh.

I swung the Alfa around the bend into Via Mirasole and opened the automatic gates. The lights came on in the courtyard, which I crept along in first gear. The TV was on in Alba and Claudio's *soggiorno*, tuned to *Occhio Pubblico*, or *Public Eye*, a true crime news programme. I had had some dealings with them myself in the past, but I didn't want to dwell on that.

I reached for the other fob and the garage doors began to rise. I swung the car around to face them. The headlights shone into a bare garage.

I sat there, engine running, gazing at the empty space where the Punto was supposed to be. But how was that possible? I looked into the rear-view mirror at the closed front gates. We had the most sophisticated security system on the market and frankly, unless you were actually going to scale the walls, which were lined with alarm sensors, and open the gates from the inside, there was no way you would be able to get in.

I wondered if Claudio had needed the car. I supposed he could have gone up to the house and borrowed the keys, but if that was the case, why could I see the back of his tangled black mop above the sofa, his thick legs stretched out beside Alba's? And didn't they have a car themselves? Nevertheless, I was about to get out to check, when my phone rang.

'Rose?'

'Dad.'

'Is everything all right?'

'Not really.'

'What's happened?' I had to catch my breath. 'Are you okay? I mean physically okay.'

'Yeah,' she said glumly. 'Fine.'

'Are you in danger?'

'Er, no . . .' I swear it was only then, focusing on the empty garage, it occurred to me.

'Rose,' I said. 'Do *you* have the car?' Silence. 'Rose?'

A long sigh. 'Yeah.'

I drew a deep breath. *Careful*, Lucia whispered in my ear. *Careful.*

'Have you had an accident?' I croaked. Silence. 'Rose?'

'Sort of.'

'But you're okay?'

'Yeah, I'm okay.'

'Are you with anyone?' Silence.

'Yeah.'

'Are they okay? What I mean is – was anyone hurt?'

'Well not really, although Stefi's a bit sick.' There were whispers in the background. 'No, she's okay, honestly.'

'And the car?' I was beginning to form a picture, and it was not a very pretty one.

'Dad. *I'm sorry.*'

Silence on my part.

'*Dad?*'

'Where are you?'

I turned around and headed back out of the gates, up Via Paglietta then onto the Viale. I followed the ring road until I took a turning that would lead me to the hills and the narrow, winding roads where apparently Rose had totalled the Punto. I hadn't asked her for any further information – I felt this was quite enough to be getting on with – and comforted myself that the important thing was that she and everyone else, whoever they were, apart apparently for her best friend Stefania, was okay. It was only a car, I told myself, and a cheap fourth-hand one we used for snooping around Bologna. I had been planning to give Rose use of it once she had passed her test, but now – well, that was out the window. If she wanted a car, she would have to pay for one herself.

The country road loomed tunnel-like in the headlights, moths flickering like confetti. A rabbit raced across my path, and I slowed right down to make sure it was alone – *Watership*

Down had plainly scarred me for life – until I came to a queue of traffic backed up along the lane. They were mostly Fiat Unos or Minis, the kind of cars rich kids were gifted for their eighteenth or twenty-first, and I immediately got it – I was approaching the site of a party. Forget nightclubs – most young Bolognese spent the warm months at raves in the hills out of the sight or interest of the police. They were notorious for drug abuse, rape, and even murder. Not that this put the kids off – that was the kind of thing Mum and Dad worried about. What worried them was what everyone else was doing.

Cars were parked along either side of the verge. Through the trees I could see flickering torch and phone lights. I wound down the window. The boom of Italian rap, the inky aroma of marijuana. I shouldn't be here, I thought. I shouldn't have to see this – I had spent the last few years conscientiously avoiding taking too intrusive an interest in my daughter's private life. I had wanted to foster a climate of trust between us – I gave her the freedom to do as she pleased because I trusted her to act responsibly. I didn't want to be the parent she set herself against and as a consequence did something stupid in rebellion.

And how's that working out for you? asked Lucia, who I suspected for all her right-on views, would have been precisely such a parent.

I followed the road until the cars and kids ran out and I was dipping back down towards Bologna. I began to wonder if I had gone too far and overshot, when I saw it – the boxy outline set at an angle to the road. My headlights picked out the tarnished blue rear of the Punto. Rose held up her hands, her skin bleached chalk white. Charcoal smears for eyes, blood red for lips. She was all in black, as had become her wont.

Another black-clad figure came to stand beside her, looking somewhat gormless, I thought, his eyes goggling in the headlights beneath a nest of curly hair. I didn't like the look of him. And then I spotted Stefania. Ah, sweet Stefania, who I had known since she was a toddler, and who, although I didn't exactly see as a good influence on my daughter, I regarded as at least relatively normal – Stefania wanted to study law at university and one day become a judge – being supported by another boy as if she was a wounded soldier.

Oh God. I pulled up the car behind the Punto and kept the headlights on.

'Dad.' Rose approached. I ignored her and went to check Stefania, now being propped against the rear of the Punto, which I rapidly discerned had been driven into a ditch. It was clear that if the boy, a man, quite frankly, or at least a university student perhaps three to five years Stefania's senior, let go, she would flop to the ground. The youth looked at me as if to say – *hey, what can you do?* I suppressed an urge to punch him.

I brushed Stefania's long damp hair away from her face. Heard Rose behind me.

'She threw up,' she explained. 'But that was before we crashed. In fact, that was *why* we crashed. She was vomiting and I panicked.'

'Stefania?' I lifted up her head. I was surprised to find sparkling eyes and a weak smile.

'Signor Leicester.' She giggled. 'Have you come to rescue us?'

'You're drunk, Stefania,' I said. She nodded affably. 'Have

you taken anything else?' She solemnly shook her head, then stopped. 'Well, one puff.'

'It was just weed,' said Rose quickly. She added: 'We were trying to get back before you got home.'

'Excuse me,' I said to the guy. I took hold of Stefania. 'Rose, help me with her other side.' Together, we supported her back to my car and sat her on a back seat.

'Do you think you're going to vomit again, Stefania?'

'I don't think so, Signor Leicester.'

'She's done a lot already,' said Rose. 'I don't think there's any left.'

'Oh,' I said, speaking from experience, 'there's always more.'

I went back to take a look at the Punto, shining my phone's light around the front. I could see the bonnet had concertinaed upwards. They couldn't have been going fast, but fast enough. I had also read about fatal car crashes happening up here, more often than not involving kids precisely like these. My blood ran cold.

'All right.' I stood back. 'Open the car up and make sure you've got all your things. None of you leave anything that might identify you.'

They did as they were told. The gormless one, who I had to admit would have been rather good-looking in a boyband sort of way were it not for the thick round glasses which must have magnified his eyes when I had first spotted them, came to stand beside me.

'How about you?' I asked.

'I didn't leave anything,' he said. He added: 'I'm very sorry about this, Signor Leicester.'

'Do I know you?'

'Antonio.' He held out his hand. I considered it. I shook it. We watched Rose recover her and Stefania's handbags from the car.

'And how do you know Rose and Stefania?' I asked.

'You see,' he said, even as Rose was mouthing *no*, 'I'm Rose's boyfriend.'

'I do see.' I looked at Rose. 'How old are you?'

'Nineteen. I was at Minghetti, but now I'm at the uni—'

'And you drive, do you?' Antonio shook his head. 'And your friend?'

'Marco?' The kid heard his name and waved.

'Yes, that dunderhead. Does he?'

'Er . . . no.'

'So, you think it's a good idea to take your seventeen-year-old learner . . . girlfriend, who legally is not permitted to be in the car with anyone but her father, and especially not with anyone else who does not possess a licence, to an illegal rave party in the hills?'

'*Dad.*'

'Signor Leicester, it wasn't like . . .'

Headlights rounded the bend. I was quite prepared for it to be the Carabinieri and for the jig to be up, but it was just another small car full of wide-eyed teenagers.

'Come on,' I said to Rose. We returned to the Alfa. Stefania was lying across the back seats. I checked to make sure she was just asleep.

'I'll get in the back with her,' said Rose. 'Come on, Toni.'

I held up my hand. 'Yes, you get in the back and look after your friend, Rose, but I'm not taking them.'

'*Dad.*'

The boys stood looking at me but didn't say a word. 'You guys just follow the road down,' I said. 'I'm sure you can work it out.'

'*Dad.* We can't just leave them! There's plenty of space in the car!'

'Try not to get hit on the way,' I told them. 'I recommend keeping your phone lights on.' I turned back towards the car.

'*Dad.* You can't do this!'

'*In*, Rose.'

She crossed her arms. 'I'm not leaving without them.'

'So, you want me to deliver your sick friend to her parents like this? I was going to suggest she stayed at ours to sleep it off, but if you prefer . . .'

'My God, you're a bastard!'

'Just get in, Rose.'

She looked between me and the boys. The curly haired one, Antonio, her 'boyfriend', said glumly: 'Go, Rose. We'll be fine.'

'*But it's dark, and Bologna's miles away.*'

'We'll be fine, won't we, Marco?' Marco looked less fine, but shrugged.

'I'm so sorry,' said Rose. 'I'm so sorry about this.'

'Really, don't worry.' Antonio glanced at me. 'We'll talk tomorrow.'

Rose gave him a hug and kissed him firmly on the lips. Although I looked on laconically enough, a part of me may have died in that moment. In any case, the kid had the grace to break it off and let her go.

'I'm sorry about this, Signor Leicester,' he said. 'About calling you out, the car, everything.'

'Take care getting home,' I said. *'Rose.'*

With another desperate hug, and the darkest of scowls in my direction, my daughter got in the back of the car.

I pulled the Alfa out, past the two boys stood forlornly by the side of the road, Rose pressed her hands flat against the window mouthing goodbye. Verily, I thought, Shakespeare would have to pen a new tragedy.

'Bastard.' I heard from the back.

'I'm sorry, Dad,' I responded. 'For taking the car without your permission, driving it illegally with a pair of guys I hadn't introduced you to, crashing it into a ditch, and,' I sniffed, 'allowing my best friend to get so drunk she was sick. She hasn't again, has she?'

'She's fine.'

'Check her mouth and make sure she's still breathing.'

'She's fine, aren't you, Stefi?' There was a grunt. 'See?'

'So I don't need to take her to the hospital?'

'No. God. Why must you always over-react?'

'It's not you that will have to answer to Cristina and Rocco if she chokes to death on her own vomit.'

'She's not going to choke to death . . . *God.'*

We continued along country lanes that began to grow amber in the light from the approaching city. 'Make sure she messages them, if she's still conscious, when we get her home.'

'It's going to take ages for them to walk back.' Sullenly: 'They could get killed.'

'Now who's over-reacting? It will do them good.'

'Do them good? How could it *possibly* do them good?'

'It's a boy thing, you wouldn't understand.'

'Great. Back to the usual sexist tropes. If it had been the other way around, would you have left us?'

'If you had been called "Robert", I probably would have.'

'Because I was male, but because I'm a "defenceless female" . . .'

'Precisely.'

'Toni could have looked after me.'

'Clearly not, otherwise I wouldn't have had to come out and collect you.'

A call came over the hands free. Claudio, sounding groggy. 'Dan. What's up?'

'There's been an accident with the Punto. No one's hurt, but the car's front-ended into a ditch in the hills. Could you get your guy who works for the comune to do a detour and pick it up tomorrow morning before the cops find it? Hundred, cash.'

'Sure. Just ping me the coordinates.'

We arrived at the Viale. In the rear-view, I saw Rose furiously tapping away at her phone. I could guess who to. 'Don't worry,' I said. 'Honestly, they'll be laughing about it in a few days.' She shot me a venomous glance. Stefania began to prop herself up, rubbing her eyes and looking decidedly queasy. It was only now, albeit ready to slam on the breaks and pull over the moment Stefi decided to throw up again, that I really began to think: *boyfriend*? *Stolen car*? *Crash*?

It was as if I had been living unknowingly above a fault line.

These things came out of the blue, of course they did, but still. What had happened to my little girl? I felt the precipitous acceleration of time as surely as Niki Molinari had hit turbo, even as I slowed to pull in to the Faidate Residence.

Claudio came out of the house, wincing as Rose and I helped Stefania out. 'She's . . .' I lifted an imaginary bottle to my lips. 'Ah. Anyway, it's all fixed with Mauro. Where do you want the Punto?'

I told him I would send him the address of the garage – it was possible the car might be salvageable but I didn't want to pay more than I had bought it for, which wasn't much – and followed Rose, supporting Stefania, upstairs. 'When you've got her changed into a pair of your pyjamas,' I said to her, 'let me know – I want to place her in the recovery position.'

'*Esagerazione,*' replied Rose.

'Meanwhile, I'll get a bottle of water – which she should drink from – and a bucket, unless you want your bedroom to smell of vomit?'

Rose steered her inside and closed the door. I got the bucket and bottle of water and left it outside. From inside my daughter's room I could hear the sluggish boom of 'come-down' music, along with fractured conversation. Stefi, it seemed, was beginning to return to life, and the two were replaying the 'trauma' of the night, voices raised in a disbelief that I suspected had something to do with my refusal to play taxi to their boyfriends.

Well, as long as they couldn't access any more booze, I would leave them to it. I went onto the balcony.

Our solitary silver elm appeared to have leafed almost overnight and was now the dominant presence in the court-yard, overhanging most of the grassed area and matching the height of *La Residenza*. We really should have had it cut back in the autumn, but that had been dominated by renovations. Now it would darken our apartment and Alba's house below.

Rose would be able to climb onto one of its branches from her window and sneak out like an American teenager in a romcom, although we had clearly moved beyond that point. The tree shimmered as if to say: you will appreciate my shade when it turns hot, and it had a point, it was an oasis during the summer months.

I gazed across the city. The russet roof tiles that rippled down to the bulk of the church of San Petronio might have been ferrous dunes around a crusader fort. Summer was officially distant, but you could feel it coming.

I longed for a cigarette. No, I longed for the company of the Comandante smoking up here beside me in the only place that it was permitted in our apartment, his elbows resting upon the age-smoothed grooves of the stone balcony.

Would he have behaved differently or better than me? Did he have similar experiences with Lucia? I put that out of my mind. I didn't want to think about her now. I reached for my own phone and went onto the WhatsApp group devoted solely to my daughter. It was a select club, with only myself, Alba and, albeit she was not family, Dolores. It had once included my former girlfriend, Stella, but she had now left the room.

These days I mainly asked them about present ideas for Christmas, birthday, etc, although we had been more active during Rose's adolescence, when I had basically farmed out the women's stuff to them. Now I wrote:

'Did you know Rose had a boyfriend?'

Despite the lights being out downstairs, Alba replied almost instantaneously: 'Ooh, you've met Toni? Isn't he a nice boy!'

That was it – this family had driven me to drink. I stepped back into the kitchen and poured myself a large glass of Scotch.

The following morning, I left relatively early for the office. Usually, the girls would have had to be at school even earlier, but they had 'revision time' before their exams, which probably explained why they had gone partying. As I cleaned my teeth, I examined my ageing face in the mirror, which I felt like I was meeting almost for the first time.

That phrase came to me again – *these things come out of the blue.*

Of course they did.

I'd felt so proud seeing Rose in the hospital corridor commanding the attention of the doctor. The next thing, I was picking her up after she had stolen and trashed my car. Proud and disappointed in as many days. Grist to the parental mill, I supposed, but this was about more than Rose being a child. You could try and fix a kid, or at least hope they might repair themself. This was about her becoming her own person, growing up to be as inherently inconsistent as the rest of us, to make her own mistakes – a lifetime of mistakes – and sooner or later I wouldn't be able to set things straight.

I took another long look at that ageing face, and splashed it with cold water.

Dropping into the bar on Marconi for my usual pre-work caffeine hit, I bumped into Jacopo and Celeste having breakfast.

'I suppose you're going to tell me you know all about Rose's boyfriend as well.'

Jacopo took a bite out of his cornetto. Celeste sheepishly stirred her cappuccino.

'You *both* did?'

'Was that what it was all about last night?' asked Jacopo. 'I looked out – you had two with you. The other was Stefania?'

'Drunk as a skunk. I couldn't present her to her parents like that. Rose had taken – and crashed – the car.' Jacopo winced. 'What can you tell me about this "Antonio"?'

'He seems all right. I've only met him the once, waiting for her outside the school. I'm sorry, Dan – she begged me not to tell.'

'Alba knew,' I said. 'And had met him, apparently.'

'Well, Alba's like her mother,' Celeste said matter-of-factly. I looked at her, vaguely offended by the bald truth of this statement. All these revelations were giving me a headache, or maybe it was just the whisky from the night before. I sipped my coffee, which I had neglected to sweeten. Very well, bitter suited my mood.

'And when was she going to introduce us, I wonder.'

'Probably wanted to put it off as long as possible,' said Celeste. 'God knows I never wanted any of my boyfriends to meet the old man.'

Jacopo nodded. 'I haven't met her old man.'

'But he lives in Naples,' I said. 'Is there anything else you can tell me about this boy?'

'Alba told me he was a medical student,' said Jacopo. 'First year.'

'No wonder your cousin liked him,' I said. 'She's always wanted a doctor in the family. Well,' I consoled myself. 'It won't last.' The pair looked at each other, then back at me.

'She's seventeen,' I added. 'Are either of you with your first love?'

'That's a funny way to look at it, Dan,' said Jacopo, who just because he had had a bossy Neapolitan girlfriend for a few months seemed to consider himself an authority on relationships.

'I'm supposed to welcome a kid who encouraged his younger girlfriend to take the car without permission and drive it to an illegal rave?'

Celeste snorted. 'Do you think Rose is so easily manipulated?' She turned to Jacopo: 'My bet is it was all her idea.'

'Now you're the expert on my daughter? You barely know her.'

'Doesn't sound to me as if you do,' Celeste snapped back.

'Hey!'

Jacopo laid a calming hand on my shoulder as the bar looked on.

This wasn't Naples, where raised voices were presumably commonplace, but neither was it Surrey, and conversation soon returned to normal. Celeste sipped her coffee and skimmed through her phone as if we had been discussing the weather.

'Anyway,' said Jacopo, 'the important thing is they were okay.'

'Looks like the car's a write-off. Nothing else to take her out in. That's her driving lessons up the creak.'

'I only spotted you because I was in the studio going through that memory stick Niki gave you.'

'Oh? So did you find the smoking gun? Or can we finally put the ghost of Signor Giorgio Chiesa's grudge to rest?'

Jacopo made a face. 'I began by checking the month either side of Fabrizio's crash, otherwise I would have been there forever.'

'I get that.'

'So, there was nothing in Jeremy Frost's calendar or emails to suggest anything untoward. And the deleted stuff, spam, all that, had long since disappeared. But I did find something in the archive. Namely, his messages – he probably didn't even realise, but because it was a company phone it automatically backed them up onto the server.'

'And?'

'Two weeks before the crash there's a message from a Bianca. Do you know who that is?'

'The track manager.'

'Saying "We need to talk." Just that. But obviously, that was fishy enough, so I did a search on their messages, and you know what I came up with?'

'They're having a fling,' Celeste butted in.

'They might be,' said Jacopo. 'I'd have to go through everything, but more to the point,' he held up his own phone, 'I came up with this.'

A photo of Fabrizio and Niki's sister Agnese Molinari sat in the corner of a bar not unlike the one we were in today, all white seats and tables, hands clasped together, bodies close.

Another – now they were kissing. Fabrizio was reaching out to stroke her cheek. More kissing. Then similar scenes in a restaurant. Finally, the pair arriving separately at one of those featureless, box-like hotels on the periphery of Bologna used by sales people. A photo of the register – a room in Fabrizio's name. Finally, a forwarded message.

'To pass to the client. Let me know if further field or desk work required. *Cordiali saluti*, Boris Malprese.'

'Bloody Sherlock,' I hissed.

'I'm guessing he didn't mention this when you met,' said Jacopo.

'No, he bloody didn't.' I thought about it. 'But why wouldn't he?'

'Client confidentiality?' said Jacopo.

'Isn't that just an excuse?' asked Celeste.

'He must have known about this when Giorgio Chiesa came to him,' I said, 'but apparently didn't say anything. He didn't tell me, obviously, and I'm presuming he didn't mention it to the cops.'

'Does he think Jeremy could have been involved in Fabrizio's death?' asked Jacopo.

'Or was he worried about being associated with the incident itself? On the surface he was only doing his job, but we all cut legal corners, and it's possible he could be prosecuted as an accessory.'

'If he didn't organise the hit in the first place,' said Celeste, without looking up from her phone.

Jacopo and I looked at each other. 'Are there any further messages like this?' I asked. Jacopo shook his head. 'What does that tell us?'

'If they discussed it further, they did so offline.'

'Bloody Sherlock.' I got back up.

'Where are you going?'

'Casalecchio.'

Chapter 16

The *commesse* were in the process of raising the shutters in the shopping centre as I arrived.

I walked the length of the mall and turned the out-of-the-way corner where Basil Rathbone was pensively smoking his calabash pipe.

Although I was surprised by the extent of Boris's duplicity, I had plainly been right not to trust him. They could set it as a section of my future Italian citizenship exam, I thought – perhaps a multiple-choice with various scenarios involving a cast of characters who may or may not be trustworthy. Yet regardless of their apparent rectitude, it would be a trick designed to weed out the foreigner, because a true Italian would know that the only people you could really trust were your family and the local butcher.

And not always your family.

The door to Sherlock's was locked, and I couldn't see anything through the frosted glass. I wasn't entirely surprised Boris was absent – he was a one-man-band, after all – but I also had the impression that he hadn't gone far. The door was pulled to, but gave, as if he had popped out for breakfast, and

I headed over to Ugo's, a rather legendary patisserie out here in the sticks. There was no sign of him there, so after a coffee and cannoli (well, it *was* Ugo's) I moseyed back in the hope I would find him returned, but the door remained locked. I called him but it went straight to the answer machine; sent a WhatsApp, but he still hadn't read it after a quarter of an hour. Something wasn't right.

I wouldn't have stood a chance of actually picking the lock with the dentistry-type tools I carried in my wrap, but the door was on the catch, which to anyone with a passing understanding meant it might as well be open.

I removed a plastic strip a little larger and more flexible than a credit card and, checking no one was watching, shoved it into the slot. There was a click and I was in.

Sherlock's office was not large – meant for a shop, it was perhaps the smallest unit in the mall, which also explained why it was around a corner, as if they had managed to squeeze just one more in. It must have suited Boris because it was accessible to shoppers, but not so visible they would feel self-conscious entering. And what did he need space for? It was just him behind a desk and a filing cabinet. There wasn't even a loo.

The client would sit on the other side of the desk, pouring their heart out within reach of the strategically positioned box of tissues while, I imagined, Boris would lean forward or back on his red leather upholstered swivel chair contemplating their tale of woe, or more likely how much he could bill them for.

Directly behind and above his desk was his certificate of incorporation, and on either side a photo of him – in uniform and another in plain clothes at the Questura. The rest of the wall space was occupied by framed black-and-white movie stills featuring the great celluloid detectives like Humphrey Bogart, George Raft, and of course Basil Rathbone, possibly intended to provide the housewives of Casalecchio with the impression that when they were consulting Boris Malprese they were also buying into the mystique of the legendary PI, and not just trying to catch their calloused-handed husband at it with the neighbour.

I peered beneath the desk. There was a rectangular patch where the computer tower had been, leads from the monitor and keyboard hanging forlornly through a hole above. I went over to the filing cabinet and gave it a tug, half expecting it to be locked, but the drawer opened easily, and was empty. I slammed it closed and tried the others – the same. There was nothing in the litter bin. Someone had been thorough.

I took in the rest of the office, although there wasn't much to see. It was only now that I remembered to put on my latex gloves – better late than never – and lifted up every picture to check behind. Nothing.

All right, no point loitering.

I waited until I was sure there was no one outside, and left the office, closing the door behind me.

I walked back through the shopping centre, buzzing Alba, who was working at home, and asking her to find Boris's home address.

'When do you need it?' she asked with the sound of Little Lucia sobbing in the background.

'Right away.' A huff and the line went dead.

I returned to Ugo's, took another coffee and positioned myself so I was facing the door.

First of all – was this nothing? Had Boris for some reason simply decided to clear out? Stay one step ahead of his creditors? It wouldn't exactly surprise me, but if he had done so, wouldn't he have taken the certificate at least? His old work photos? Or was it one of those husbands he had caught in the act, who had wanted revenge, or to get hold of the evidence?

It did seem rather coincidental, however. There was not just his involvement in our investigation, but his prior one on Jeremy's behalf. As far as I knew, Jeremy was completely unaware we were looking into him – unless Boris had decided to seek him out and tip him off.

I could feel myself sliding down a familiar rabbit hole and hopped smartly out. At this stage, speculation wasn't particularly helpful. Instead, my thoughts drifted back to Rose and her new boyfriend. I presumed the boys had made it home safely or I wouldn't have heard the end of it. And being boys, I doubted very much they would have taken it personally.

This Antonio. I guess I would have to make an effort not to hate him. On paper, he seemed a reasonable catch – not too old, a medical student, all the rest. I had to admit that perhaps Celeste and Alba might be reasonable judges of character, never mind Rose. Yet all the women in my life missed a simple point, something the Comandante would have immediately grasped – men know what men are like. No matter what a 'sweet boy' Antonio might be, he was still essentially a cretin being led by his cock, and would continue that way until he reached around twenty-five, when he would (hopefully) have begun to achieve sufficient maturity to be treated more seriously. All fathers understood that until then it was essentially women dating boys.

Actually, I thought, Dolores, might know what I meant. I checked the 'family' WhatsApp. There was still nothing from her. I called, but her phone went through to the answering service. What was it with everyone today? I sent her a direct message.

An incoming call – Alba.

'Via del' Gomito, 43,' she said, Little Lucia moaning 'Mamma' in the background.

Via del' Gomito, 43 was a modest apartment building outside the walls in San Donato. A middle-aged woman answered the door of a flat on the third floor. She turned out to be the former Signora Malprese. The apartment behind her smelled of boiled spinach.

'Sure, it's his "official" address,' she said. 'I still get his tax bills, which is convenient as I can see how much he's declaring – but that's it, he went to live with his tart.'

'And where can I find her?'

'Ahah – that I can't tell you, but it's not where you'll actually find him, anyway. She had the wit to kick him out too, I heard, when she discovered she wasn't the only one on his "list".'

'He gets around a bit, then. So where *will* I find him?'

'Why should I tell you?' Her grey eyes hardened with the rest of her face. I presented her with a €50 note.

'To be honest, you'll be doing yourself a favour,' I said. 'If you want him to keep up the payments.'

She plucked it out of my fingers. 'It's really the perfect place for him,' she said. 'Among the whores.'

She wasn't kidding. Boris was now apparently living in a

motor home in a car park in a former industrial estate near the airport. Officially, the car park was for use by legitimate campervan owners. In reality, it was mostly a base for the working girls lining the feeder roads to the *autostrada* who used the vans to 'entertain' their clients. When they weren't being employed for business, they would park them here.

There was a tap, portable toilets, and a nearby food and drinks dispenser. Compared to the Africans living in tents next to a tributary of the river Reno, where they washed their clothes and flung their waste, I suppose the car park was a step up, but it certainly took the romance out of campervanning.

There were only three vans in the car park when I arrived. A pair of young women with long black hair were sat outside. One in a red tracksuit had her feet upon the thighs of the other in grey sweatpants and a white T-shirt, who was painting her nails while the first smoked. Red glared at me as if I was a would-be client interrupting her downtime which, as a middle-aged man in an SUV, I supposed I might well have been.

There was a similarly dilapidated van nearby with grimy gold curtains closed across the windows, while some distance apart from these, stood one which looked as if it might actually have been purchased recently, albeit second or third hand.

'The Italian man,' I said to the women. 'There?' The smoking one considered me with undisguised contempt. She spoke to the other in a language that sounded like Albanian, who replied without looking up. Fair enough. I nodded politely and walked over to the van. The windows had their shutters down.

I knocked on the door.

'Hello?' No answer. 'Boris. *Sherlock*. Open up, we need to talk.' I banged more forcefully. The door fell open.

I leaned in. It looked as if the van had been picked up by a tornado and set down half a mile later. Broken crockery littered the kitchen surface and floor, while the diner table was broken upon its wooden column and leaning against the seating. Papers littered the linoleum like crazy paving. At the end of the van was an empty, unmade bed, I could just about believe may have been that way before whatever happened, happened. But there was definitely no Sherlock.

This time I reached for my gloves first. I stepped inside and raised the shutters. Spots of blood sprinkled the papers as if someone had been whacked around the mouth or nose. I picked some of them up – a demand from the Region for an income assessment to calculate university tuition fees for one of his kids, a selection of bills from the ex. Could he have decided to stage his disappearance and start again somewhere else? I wouldn't put it past him – blood splatter and all – but I would shelve that thought for the time being and take it for what it appeared to be. Test the most likely hypothesis first. Occam and all that, eh, Comandante?

I stepped over the other papers and opened the small cabinet at the foot of the bed. I couldn't believe this was all that Boris possessed – he had to have a lock-up somewhere simply to keep more than a change of clothes – but he certainly hadn't taken the office stuff home with him.

At the base of the cabinet lay a tactical knife. Razor-sharp and unsheathed, it would make short work of anyone who came within arms-reach.

If something *had* happened, it had taken place lightning fast and Boris hadn't had time to get to it.

I laid the knife back down, stepped carefully towards the exit and closed the door behind me. I walked back over to the women.

'Do you speak Italian? English?'

'What you want?' asked Red in Italian. She was older and fast-food plump. Otherwise, she might have been the other one's twin.

'What happened to the Italian man?'

An exchange in Albanian.

'Hundred each.'

'Fifty.' I pulled out two notes.

'Hundred.'

'Fifty, or I go.'

'Fine, you go.'

I pocketed the notes and turned towards the car.

'I no see,' she said. 'But she tells me – there was big banging two nights backward. She sees men take him.'

'Was he alive, on his feet? Or were they carrying him?'

'Sorry?'

'The Italian man – alive or dead?'

Another exchange. Back and forth. 'No, he walk. Not happy, but live.'

'And these men, what did they look like?'

'Italian men. One young, one old.'

'Did she get a look at what kind of car they put him in.'

She shook her head.

'Thank you, ladies.' I gave each a note. As I walked away, the smoker called:

'He come back? He good money.' I shrugged. 'We have van?'

I opened my car door. 'If you want the van, you might have to ask his wife,' I called. 'At least one of them.'

I drove the Alfa out of the car park and turned back towards the centre, but didn't go far – I wanted time to think. I pulled in at a nearby McDonalds and sat facing the traffic.

I thought back to Boris's camper. They had entered fast and grabbed him before he could get to the cabinet. A couple of blows to pacify him, then a quick-step march out. He can't have been expecting it, otherwise he would have probably kept the knife closer.

The professionalism appeared to rule out some angry husband.

Possibly. Maybe.

My phone buzzed. I pulled it out, but it was just a news alert.

I checked my WhatsApp. Dolores still hadn't opened my message. I gave her another call. No answer.

I called Celeste in the office, but no one had seen her.

I watched the traffic zip past.

Dolores sat at the bar by the stadium, that smile playing at the corners of her mouth.

Her all-too-easy acquiescence to my wishes: *'It can wait.'*

I flicked to my phone's gallery, gazed at the photo of Speedy, Giorgio Chiesa, and, it transpired, Dolores' 'Uncle Gigi'.

A little girl stood watching as her parents go up in smoke.

'What an idiot,' I said out-loud. I was referring to myself, you understand.

I called Celeste back.

'Do you still have a spare key for Dolores' apartment?'

'Sure.'

'Meet me outside. Don't ring. Don't go in.'

'But why wouldn't I ring, maybe she's sick . . .'

'Do as I say, Celeste. This one time.'

The most *fricchettone* streets of Bologna are Mascarella and Pratello. Mascarella is adjacent to the student area. Here you will find the bullet holes where student Francesco Lorusso, whose name is graffitied across the city's walls, was shot dead by a Carabiniere in the 1970s. But it is beneath the timber porticoes of Pratello old causes and their ageing campaigners really live on. It was here Red Brigade idol Sante Notarnicola ran a pub following his release from gaol, and also where the Liberation Day festival traditionally takes place, the street crowded with stalls promoting obscure and hopeless causes. It was also here Paolo Solitudine, an old anarchist found floating dead in the canals running beneath Bologna lived, and his apartment that one Dolores Pugliese came to inherit.

Celeste and Jacopo were waiting in the narrow pedestrianised street that ran between the terracotta and yoke yellow porticoes, looking up for signs of life. Both had their phones out, which was fair, I suppose – I didn't say they couldn't try calling her.

'What's going on Dan?' asked Jacopo.

'I'm worried about her,' I replied vaguely.

'Why?'

'She hasn't been answering. Maybe it's nothing but . . . something's going on.'

'What?'

I expelled an irritated sigh: 'Let's check if she's at home first.'

Like so many Bologna facades, Dolores' address wasn't giving much away. A graffiti-riddled door beneath a dark portico, an intercom with half a dozen buttons.

I rang the bell. As expected, there was no answer. Celeste handed me the keys and I opened up. Dolores' building was more modest than most: just a couple of ground-floor flats and a set of stairs winding upwards. We followed it to the first floor.

Since I had last been here, she had replaced the battered old wooden front door with a proper, iron-framed *porta blindata*, or security door. I considered the key, but decided to ring again. The bell resounded through the apartment. Not difficult, it was barely fifty metres square – living room/ kitchen, bedroom, bathroom. I tried again. Nothing. I considered putting my gloves on, but thought better of it – if anything had happened to Dolores, leaving evidence would be the last of my worries.

I unlocked the door and it swung open. The apartment appeared undisturbed – what I would expect from Dolores – an uncluttered narrow hallway, a neat and tidy *soggiorno*, a cream futon sofa set upon the white-painted floorboards that ran throughout the apartment. No TV but an old-style valve radio that I remembered had once belonged to Solitudine, shelves and shelves lined with old books, many of which I guessed had also been his.

The bedroom was dominated by an old black-iron four poster. The bed was an untidy mess of white duvet and pillows, a red knitted throw splashed like a puddle of blood upon the faded white floor. I hesitated. I couldn't help but see the dildo-shaped blue bottle of lubricant stood proudly upon her bedside table beside a nest of open condom wrappers.

Hung upon the poster beside it was a Molinari cap.

'Looks like someone's been having fun,' said Celeste. She went over and examined the cap. 'Dee's a funny one – she must have got this from that race you went to. Or,' she put it on. It looked ridiculous perched atop her crown of curly hair. 'One of the drivers? I never thought she would be into that sort of thing. Hippies seemed more her type.'

'You checked the bathroom?'

'Yeah.' She placed the hat back on the pole.

I left the bedroom, embarrassed. A small part of me hoped she *had* been snatched, just to excuse the intrusion.

I went over to the kitchen part of the living room, which looked down onto Pratello, and opened the cupboard door beneath the sink.

The biological rubbish wasn't much help, the recyclable however – a plastic holder which, the card separated into the paper bin told me, had contained four spools of black tape. Another, a Stanley Knife. I dug deeper and pulled out the flattened, rectangular box of a telescopic truncheon.

'What are you so worried about?' asked Celeste.

'Doesn't this worry you?' I held up the box.

'She probably bought it for self-defence.'

'Why would she need this, and pepper spray?'

'She bought pepper spray?' Celeste shrugged. 'Me too, sometimes.'

'But a baton?'

'I admit, that might be overkill. So where is she?'

'You tell me.'

'Maybe she's gone off with this guy.'

'On a work day?'

'Well, you know Dolores.' I considered that Molinari cap. Not as much as I thought, apparently. 'Has something else happened?' asked Celeste. 'Is that why she's bought this stuff? Is that why you're worried?'

'Keep trying her,' I said. 'If she responds, let me know. Better still, tell her to call me.'

'Where are you going?'

'I've got another idea.'

Chapter 17

'How can I help you, young man?' Speedy sat back in the battered armchair, crossing his long arms and legs Mantis-like, although judging from his daughter's vibes behind the computer screen, it was the female of the species who represented the greater threat.

'You haven't had one of my colleagues come to visit you?' I asked. Speedy looked puzzled.

'No, I don't think so. No one from Faidate's come here have they, Suze?'

A smoke signal rose behind the screen. 'No.'

He frowned. 'Why would they?'

I glanced up at the photo of the three men. 'Just trying to avoid us duplicating our work. We've almost closed the case.'

'I expect the kids will be happy,' Speedy said. 'Be able to get on with their lives.'

'Quite.' I pulled out a notebook and asked him again about the background to Chiesa's request. 'You mentioned you tried to convince him not to?'

'Of course.'

'It's only that the older son, Francesco, was sceptical . . .'

'Him? He's a doctor, isn't he? Some bigwig. The pair of them went into the professions, and Giorgio was so proud!'

'Really? According to them, he only had eyes for Fabrizio.'

'What did they know? What do kids ever know?'

Cue a disgruntled 'Ha!' from behind the screen.

I made a point of looking at the photo. 'This was taken at Da Vito, right? Your treat, I think you said.'

'Yeah, Giorgio had helped me with an injection system.'

'The other guy's one of your mechanics?'

'Carlo? No. He's a parts man – can source you the right part for any car, providing you give him the time, if you know what I mean.' He winked.

'Funny you should say that,' I said. 'I couldn't believe it – my daughter, who's learning to drive, took the car out without my permission to go to one of those illegal raves . . .'

'Oh mio dio. . .'

'Worse – she calls me at midnight. She's crashed!'

'Was she all right?'

'Thank god. But the car had front-ended into a ditch. I managed to get it pulled out, but it's a fifteen-year-old Punto and the garage is telling me it would be salvageable but they can't get a particular part.'

'Then Carlo would be your guy! He's got a yard out in Stadio – he strips them down and stores the parts before selling the hulks for scrap. I'll give you the—'

'Get out of here!' We looked around. 'Go on.' Speedy's daughter was standing up. 'Scram. Dad's gone on enough. We don't want any more to do with you.'

'I'm sorry,' I said. 'I'm really not sure what you're talking about.'

'Go.' She pointed to the door.

'Susanna,' said Speedy. 'I'm just trying to help the guy out, and send some business Carlo's way.'

At that moment his daughter truly looked as if she might bite off his head.

'I'm sorry if I've somehow offended you, signora . . .' I said.

'*Can it*. Now. Please. Go.' She began to usher me towards the exit.

'I'm sorry about this,' called Speedy over her shoulder. 'Carlo's—'

'*Basta*.'

'Like I said, signora,' I continued. 'I'm sorry if I offended you. I just wanted to wrap things up.'

'Right.'

'And it was kind of your dad to mention Carlo . . .'

'Hm.'

I paused by the open gate as Speedy watched from the office doorway looking genuinely bemused.

'Your father doesn't seem to think he's got anything to hide,' I said. 'Why do you?'

Susanna Bonnacini made a mean smile. 'If dad was as quick up here,' she tapped her head, 'as he was behind the wheel, he wouldn't have spent so long behind bars. Now.' She gave me a sharp but firm shove. 'Fuck off.'

Despite a couple of false starts, with the help of Google Maps it didn't take me very long to locate Ricambi Auto Rossi in a street off Via Saragozza.

It seemed a little out of place in what was a rather established old-style housing estate not unlike Cirenaica, but things were different back then. The walled yard might once have housed a printing press or ceramics factory. Now it was an auto parts business.

Because of the sheer weight of homeowners' parked cars, I had been obliged to leave mine in another road, but Dolores Pugliese had not faced the same challenge on her bicycle, which had apparently now been repaired, and was attached by a pair of thick chains to a lamppost outside.

Facing me as I entered the yard was a single-storey, red-brick building. There were two garages, one open to display hundreds of oily bits of old car. Next to these was some kind of workshop with its shutter down, and an office, blinds drawn.

I rang the office bell. No answer.

I really wasn't having much luck today.

I tried again. Even if Susanna had called to warn 'Rossi', I was pretty sure it would have been too late – Dolores would have got here beforehand. Had he managed to get the better of her? I considered the pepper spray, tape, knife.

Baton.

Boris hadn't had much luck against whoever had grabbed him. I doubted Uncle Gigi, AKA 'Carlo Rossi', would have stood greater odds against Dolores. Perhaps less – he would have opened the door to a skinny young woman who could be quite the actor when she wanted. Would he have recognised her? Highly unlikely given the passage of time, and even if he had, not before he had been sprayed in the face by the force of a thousand chilli peppers.

But you never know.

I rang again.

Banged on the door.

'All right,' I called. 'Either it's Uncle Gigi in there with Dolores, or vice versa. In any case, if you don't let me in, I'm calling the police.'

I glanced over my shoulder. If it was Gigi, I was unarmed. No Mace or baton for me. I got ready to run for it if he came at me with a knife. A gun, probably not, unless I wanted to get shot in the back.

I banged again. 'Last chance,' I shouted.

Finally, the door opened – Dolores, looking as if she hadn't slept for a week. I pushed past her.

'Jesus Christ, Dolores.'

It was dirty, strip-light bright in there. It smelled of oil and rubber and the sweet-sourness of something animal, which had plainly excreted from the man knelt in front of me, arms out-stretched, his wrists cuffed to the scissor-like poles of the car lift, the mud-encrusted undercarriage of an old Land Rover looming above him.

He looked wildly at me, trying to speak, but was gagged by a BDSM rubber ball strapped across his mouth. I admit my first thought was to wonder where Dolores had got it. My next – this was a disaster.

'Release him immediately.'

'It's him, Dan. He knows it, I know it.'

'We'll call the Carabinieri, Alessandro. He'll fix everything for us.'

'He won't admit it though.' Dolores said glumly. She picked up the baton from the scarred wooden work bench and weighed it in her hand.

'You've been using that?'

Dolores sighed. 'No.' Then she gave him a fierce look.

'Not yet.' The man swivelled between her and me, trying to talk, but only saliva drizzled down his chin.

'What precisely was your plan, once you'd got him like this?'

'For him to tell me what happened. Who was behind it.'

'Which is the job of the police.'

'The police . . .' She waved the baton like a wand. 'They'll go through the system. He'll get a lawyer. Even if they can pin anything on him, they might use him to turn informant. You know the Pentito law? So long as they cough up all they know, they're out in no time.'

'And *your* plan was?'

'Justice.'

'And this is "justice", is it? Give me that water.' I took the litre bottle on the bench and crouched beside the man. 'Don't cry out,' I said. 'I'm on your side.' He nodded insistently. I reached behind him and undid the buckle.

The ball came out with a sloppy plop. He drew in the air and I helped him drink. Once he had taken another series of breaths, he began to yell for help.

I cuffed him hard around the face. I think the blow surprised us both.

I took his slippery jaw in my hand. *'Don't.'*

'She's crazy,' he whispered. 'I was just doing my job and she sprays me and here I am.'

'Here you are.' I let go. 'Who are you?'

'Carlo. Carlo *Rossi.* Like it says on the sign.'

'He's lying.'

'She keeps saying that,' he boggled. 'As if she thinks I'm someone else. I've no idea what she's talking about. Please help me, signore. I'm just an ordinary man, an innocent man. This is a case of mistaken identity!'

'And why I should believe you, instead of my "crazy" colleague?'

'Look at my wallet! My ID!'

I went over to the denim jacket, pulled out his wallet, checked the identity card.

'Looks genuine,' I said to Dolores.

'Anything can be faked.'

I went through the rest – a few credit and membership cards, euro notes. Nothing that gave him away.

'Anyone can make a mistake,' I told her. 'Mistaken identity.'

'That's what I've been trying to tell her!' the man wailed.

If that really was the case, I thought, then we were in even deeper shit.

'That was how he did it,' Dolores pointed beneath the Land Rover. 'Fitted the bomb. He was a mechanic. That was how I found him once I'd seen the photo, by going around all the places.'

'It adds up,' I admitted. 'I'm here thanks to Speedy.'

The man's eyes lit up. 'You know Speedy? Then he'll tell you . . .'

I crouched back down in front of him. 'He'll tell us whatever you told him, friend. How long have you worked with Vladimir Bonnacini?'

'We go way back – must be twenty years. Please – I really need to go to the toilet.'

'Twenty years ago,' said Dolores. 'That's when he did it.'

'You have to admit,' I said to the man. 'You're not Bolognese. That's definitely a Naples accent.'

'So? There are millions of people from Naples, thousands of them in Bologna. Hey! Maybe that's why your young lady has mistaken me. Because there are similarities.'

'It's a possibility,' I said to Dolores.

'*It's him.*'

'I'll tell you what.' I straightened up and picked up his jacket, plucked out a phone. 'Your mum and dad. Brothers, sisters. Tell me your code and I'll give them a call.'

He sorrowfully waggled his head. 'They're dead.'

'Who?'

'My parents.'

'Brothers, sisters?'

'*I'm an only child.*'

'Not many Neapolitan kids are only children,' I said to Dolores.

'I was,' she admitted.

'You were, but I guess that wasn't the plan.'

'Probably not.'

'All right,' I turned back to him. 'Aunts? Uncles?' He shook his head. 'Cousins? Come on! You're telling me you haven't got any cousins? Even Dolores has cousins. There's no Italian in the world without cousins.'

'What can I say?' Sweat dripped off his face. 'I've got them, but I fell out with them.'

'Now might be a good time to make up,' spat Dolores.

'You're not making this very easy for me,' I said. 'How about you just give me the code so I can find something else that might help you?'

'*Please*,' he said. 'I really do need a piss.'

'I could probably just use a fingerprint.' He squeezed his

hands into fists.

'You're really not helping yourself.' I turned to Dolores. 'Have you looked around?'

'I've not really had a chance, Dan,' she said testily. 'Why?'

'Keep an eye on him. If he yells again, spray him.'

'I've used it up.'

'What? All of it?' She nodded. I gave the man a sympathetic look. 'If you shout again,' I took the baton from Dolores. 'I'll knock your fucking teeth out.'

'Please,' he pleaded. 'It'll be better for all of us if you just release me – we can forget this ever happened.'

I hesitated, glancing at Dolores. 'How about we *do* call the police? It can be discreet. Our contacts can clear this up if what you're saying is true.'

He bowed his head, sweat and snot dripping onto the floor. 'All right. I can't pretend I've been a good boy, so of course I don't want the cops sniffing about. But it's not like she says. I've got no idea who she is, I've never planted a bomb for Christ sakes.'

'You mean your work with Speedy, dodgy stuff like that.'

He tried to wipe his face on the shoulder of his denim shirt. 'Speedy. Yeah. Cars, that sort of thing.'

'Which would explain why Susanna didn't want to pass on the details. You've got a friend there – *ben piazzata*. Well-connected.'

'Susanna, she's a good girl.'

'Anyway,' I placed the baton on the bench. 'Keep schtum if you want to hold on to your teeth.'

'But I need to piss . . .'

'Go ahead. It stinks enough in here already.'

I went through to the office, which could have come from the same brochure as the Bonnacini's – oily carpet tiles, battered desk, tired and grubby upholstery. It was hardly the ladies' salon I'd initially had him down for.

I slipped on the gloves and took a look through his filing cabinet, but everything seemed legit – receipts for machines, engine parts, tax stuff – then his desk drawer. Nothing incriminating in the top one, but in the one below, a Glock 9mm in its carbon carry case. Unloaded. At the back of the drawer – two boxes of bullets. I brought the case into the workshop.

'Dangerous profession, mechanic?'

'Hobby,' he said. 'I belong to a gun club. I've got a licence.'

'I'm sure your licence would say something about keeping it locked up. Where's the gun cabinet?'

'At home. It's legal to carry it to and from the shooting range.'

'Which is what it was doing in your desk drawer.'

'That's right. Look, please . . .' I went back into the office and was about to put the gun back when I noticed something odd about the carpet. The half dozen tiles between the side of the desk to the wall appeared new.

I took a paperknife and slipped it under one. It flipped easily up. They were all just resting there.

Beneath them – a trap door.

Chapter 18

I loaded the Glock and snapped back the slide so there was one in the chamber.

Crouched by the door and gently lifted the hatch, pointing the pistol into darkness.

Cold, clayey air rose to greet me.

Wooden stairs led down.

I fished out my phone and switched on the light. Gun and phone pressed before me, I made my way down.

There was a light switch at the base of the stairs. It blinked on to reveal a large *cantina* with a terracotta-tiled floor. White-washed walls were lined with grey, rust-flecked filing cabinets, loose stacks of papers piled on top. It didn't look like they had been touched in years – the cabinets had a patina of ingrained dust, cobwebs criss-crossing the drawers. The papers were compressed with damp and mould. At the far end of the room an iron door was bolted closed, as if it was a fridge or cold store.

I pulled open one of the drawers. There had been little effort at filing, it was the same inside as on top – stacks of papers in brown or green folders, or simply loose. I picked one up: lots of technical writing I couldn't make sense of.

I closed that drawer and opened the one below – same story. I lifted out a batch and brought it to a large picnic table in the middle of the room. The top folder was bulging with oversize papers which I opened wide – blueprints of some kind of machine prototypes. Visible at the bottom right-hand corner of both – *Giorgio Chiesa, Ing.*

I took a photo.

At the far end of the table was some kind of counting machine. On the floor beneath it, stacks of cardboard boxes sealed with brown tape.

I lifted one onto the table and ran a key down the tape. Cash, lots of it – hundred, fifty, twenty-euro notes – sprung out. I checked the others – same story.

I considered that bolted door again.

I wasn't sure if it was a good or bad thing it was locked from this side.

There were four heavy-duty bolts, two at the side and one each at the top and bottom. That was an awful lot of bolts for a fridge or cold store.

With a growing sense of dread, I moved towards it.

I drew back the bottom bolt, then reached for the top.

I noticed a light switch by the side, flicked it, half expecting to be plunged into darkness. Nothing.

It was for inside.

I withdrew the final bolt. Levelling the pistol, I pulled the door open.

The room wasn't airtight. It couldn't be, otherwise nothing could live in there and there was – or had been – something alive, judging from the sour stink of sweat and urine.

A bare bulb cast a dim pall. Like the rest of the *cantina*, the floor was tiled, but the walls and ceiling were mottled with the cardboard innards of eggboxes – the crudest form of soundproofing. A tarnished wheeled table stood by the door, littered with an assortment of steel implements you might buy in a job lot from an old-fashioned dental studio. Most appeared unused, but some were smeared cherry red.

There was a stripped-down car engine in the middle of the room, and some kind of form was behind it. I looked down the sight of the gun. The barrel was trembling.

'You're alive?'

Boris Malprese emerged around the engine. He was barefoot in a blood-stained blue sweatshirt and jeans, his face swollen, with the green-tinged pallor of a toad. He rattled like Marley's ghost.

He croaked: 'Please.'

I had spotted a key by the counting machine. I came back and opened the padlock. His hands fell to the floor, his handcuffed wrists were raw.

'Get me out of here.'

I helped him to his feet. His legs appeared to have been spared, and after a false start I was able to support him across the room and slowly up the stairs.

Dolores was stood there as we emerged.

Boris slumped in the chair behind the desk.

'What the hell, Dan?'

'I think we can safely say you've got your man. There are boxes of cash down there, too. And the blueprints that were stolen from Giorgio Chiesa.'

'Water,' gasped Boris. Dolores went and got the bottle. He

glugged it down.

'But what are you doing here?' I asked. 'Why did they grab you in the first place? Was it to do with your work for Jeremy Frost?'

Boris shook his head. 'Gambling. I'd always suspected there was something going on – it's a gambling ring.'

'You mean those numbers I passed to you? Are you saying Giorgio Chiesa and Fabrizio were involved?'

He shook his head. 'The opposite – they'd noticed something was not right. But that's just the half of it – the gambling's only a means to an end, what it's really all about is laundering mob cash.' He shook his head. 'This is the tip of a much bigger operation.' He shuddered. 'We've got to get out of here.'

We helped Boris through to the workshop. Uncle Gigi's eyes widened even as I felt Boris's sinews thicken.

Before I knew it, Boris had grabbed hold of the baton and swiped Gigi across the forehead. Gigi's head lolled back like a drunk's. Boris got in another blow before I could stop him. Gigi whelped like a beaten dog while Boris dropped to his knees, coughing.

'*Release me.*' Gigi whined: 'I think he broke my collarbone.'

Dolores went over. I thought she might be about to undo the cuffs but she stood in front of him with her arms crossed.

'Uncle Gigi,' she said. 'Who told you to do it?'

He blinked up at her. 'Please,' he said. 'Dolores . . .'

'So, you know my name.'

'I . . . I heard him saying.'

'Why did you do it? Who ordered you?'

'*Please*,' he gasped. 'The pain. My arm. Just the left one.'

She gave it a prod. He screeched.

'*Dolores*,' I said.

'Tell me.' Gigi looked wildly around.

'Then you'll release me?'

'We'll think about it,' I said.

'You won't beat me?' He eyed Boris, picking himself up to slump against the bench. I shook my head.

He looked pleadingly up at Dolores. 'I'm sorry, darling.' Sweat dropped off the tip of his nose, his forehead was blossoming with what would become a mighty bruise. 'It was an order. And when you get an order from them, you don't have a choice.'

'Who ordered it?'

'My *capo*. Pietro. Pietro Solana. But he's dead now.'

'*Why?*'

'I don't know, only – that they had to get rid of her.'

Dolores stumbled backwards.

'*Her?*'

'Your mother, my cousin. Look, I'm so sorry. I've thought about it every day—'

'*Her?* Not my father? He was the one investigating the gangs.'

He shook his head. 'I don't know anything about that, only what I was told. It was definitely her.'

'But Mamma was just a clerk, she did their expenses.'

I exchanged a glance with Boris. 'Book keeping.' He nodded. 'You said she was an accountant, Dolores.'

'Yes, but . . .'

I stepped forward. 'And that's what this is all about, isn't it, Gigi? Money laundering, washing money for the mob.' I frowned. 'And somehow fixing races. But how's that possible? It's a business in the international spotlight. It's not, I don't know, garbage collection.'

There was a buzz at the door.

We froze. The first syllables of a yell from the man on the floor, then the *whop* of a baton passing my ear.

A sickening *crunch* as it connected with Gigi's face.

Dolores grabbed a clump of Gigi's hair and pulled it back, forcing the gag into his mouth through a mess of blood and saliva, as Boris hung onto the car lift to keep upright.

'Carlo!' Another buzz. Banging on the door. I stepped quietly into the office, squinting through a gap in the blinds. It was the anvil-headed bloke I had seen at the circuit accompanied by a younger one with jet black hair, the fringe cut straight across his forehead, and dark, restless eyes. He had the kind of thuggish beauty you might admire while he strangled you.

More bangs. 'Where the fuck are you?' His companion pulled out his phone. There was a buzzing from the workshop and Boris came into the office holding the phone up. SALVO, it said. Thank God it was on silent.

A huge thump. 'Son-of-a-*bitch*.' They began to back away. There was a white SUV parked at the entrance to the yard. They got in it and drove off.

A choking sound.

I went back into the workshop. Gigi's eyes were wide with terror, blood drooling down his chin.

'Release the gag,' I shouted.

Dolores, who had been grasping the strap behind him, let

go. Gigi jerked forward, blood and broken teeth splattering onto the floor. He jolted back, emitting an agonised moan.

'Unlock his hand.'

Dolores looked at me questioningly. *'Do it.'*

Gigi gasped as his arm dropped. He began to sob.

'What did they want?' I demanded. 'Why were they here?'

Gigi was panting through his smashed-up mouth. 'Get me out of here,' he begged. 'Hospital.'

'What did they want you for?'

'Please . . .' He spat out more blood.

'Tell me, and I'll help.'

He glanced at Dolores and Boris.

'Don't worry about them,' I said.

He tried to lift his arm, blenched. 'Punishment. Niki.'

'They're going to punish Niki Molinari? What for?'

'Winning. Disaster. Cost them.'

'But what's that got to do with Niki?'

'Owes them. Thousands from cards.'

'There's your answer,' said Boris. 'That's how they fix them.'

'Does what they say,' continued Gigi. 'Can't fix the leaders but can fix him. And he fixes the middle. . . order.' He gave me a desperate look. *'Please.'*

'Which is how they make their cash,' said Boris. 'Typical mob – skim their income from the middle so no one notices. Under the radar. But "mid rank" Niki winning – well, that's a big hit for them.'

'Whatever happens.' I thought of Niki's comment in the trailer.

'But what had Dolores's mum to do with any of that that?' I asked.

Gigi shook his head. 'I was just a soldier, don't know. But after, someone said she'd begun to get close to the northern connection.'

'Their business here, you mean?'

'Don't know, I just . . .' He gasped and swung back on the left handcuff. He began to fight for breath.

'Dolores,' I said. 'Let him go.'

'It could be a trick.'

Boris picked the baton back up.

Go on, I mouthed. Dolores unlocked and Gigi collapsed onto the floor. Scrunching up his left arm with a gasp and raising a hand to his throat.

He let out a strangled cry.

'She's right,' said Boris warily. 'He could be faking it.'

Gigi's face contorted as if someone had indeed tightened a cord around his throat. He tried to sit up but didn't make it; he began to writhe on the floor.

Dolores swivelled around. 'I think he's really sick. We'd better call an ambulance.' I looked at Boris, who responded with an almost imperceptible shake of the head. 'What?' She drew out her phone, but I took it from her hand. She looked at me aghast: *'I have to call.'*

On the floor in front of us, Gigi turned sheet-white, began to gasp like a landed fish.

'Dan,' she said. 'Give it back! *We need to call an ambulance.'*

'We can't. I'm sorry.'

'What do you mean we can't? He's dying!'

'Trust me, Dolores.'

She stared at me wild-eyed, then made for the door.

I caught her.

'Let me go! Let me the fuck go!'

She struggled hard. Tried to twist away as she had learned in the self-defence classes – elbow me in the guts, draw her heal down my leg and stamp on my foot, but I had attended the same classes, and managed to hold her still.

'I'm sorry, Dolores. I'm sorry.'

Chapter 19

I let her go when it was over.

Dolores straddled him, massaged his chest. 'Uncle Gigi, come on!'

'He's gone, Dolores.'

'*He can't be.*' She looked up at me, tears streaming down her face. 'He killed my family!' She began to pound him. '*Mummy,*' she moaned between low sobs. '*Daddy.*'

Finally, she shifted off him to crawl across the floor and prop herself against the wall. She raised her knees and covered her face with her hands.

I joined Boris on the other side of the car lift.

We had apparently had the same idea. I tested its sturdiness. 'Pretty new,' I said. I pointed to the locking mechanisms on either side. 'It would be difficult to fake a collapse.'

'I did one of these before. An industrial injury claim, I mean. Nothing near as nasty, but it was the car that fell off the ramp, not the ramp that collapsed.'

'That would probably work better,' I agreed. 'And explain the injuries.'

'Stuck under there,' said Boris. 'He suffered a heart attack.'

'Are you feeling better?' I asked. 'You look pretty rough, yourself.'

'Feel worse.' He lifted his sweatshirt. Among the inevitable yellow and black bruises, there were jagged raspberry strips.

'*God.*' I looked at the corpse. 'Did he—'

'Nah. Just looked on, grinning like a demented cunt. The old one did the peeling – craft knife and pencil.' He lowered the sweatshirt, very gently. 'To wrap the skin around, see. Then he'd let the young one have a go, like it was bloody on-the-job training.' He shrugged. 'I'm sorry about losing it. I think the bastards were only keeping me alive because they were having fun.'

'You told them about us?'

'I hadn't.' He shook his head. 'Yet. Despite everything, I wanted to hold something back for when they got bored and decided to put a bullet in my skull.'

'We're agreed, however, that you owe us one.'

'More than one,' said Boris.

'And really, this is your mess to clear up. If you hadn't . . .'

'I get it – if I hadn't beaten the shit out of him, he would still be alive. And where would that have left *you*? You're better off this way, but you know that.'

I glanced at the body. 'I know that.'

We turned to the car ramp. 'Then what do you reckon? We lower this down enough and . . .' He made a pushing gesture, and took a sharp intake of breath.

'Sore?' With that swollen face his smile was more a sneer.

'Better to feel something,' he nodded at Gigi, 'than nothing at all.'

***

I crouched beside Dolores.

'Hey,' I said.

She nodded at Gigi. 'You let him die.'

'He was dying,' I said. 'I just didn't stop it.'

She wiped away the tears and snot. 'He was a bad man.'

'And it was better he couldn't identify us, all things considered.'

'To the mob, you mean?' I nodded. 'Do you think he could have told us more, though? What about this northern connection?'

'I don't think he was very high up the food chain. They moved him to Bologna to keep him out of the way, look after their base. But he was mainly a petty criminal, doing jobs for the likes of Molinari and pinching supercars with Speedy. He might pick up stuff he needed to know, but my guess is he had given us about as much as he was going to.'

'Mum and Dad wouldn't have wanted it this way – they would have wanted to see him turned in.'

'Most of all, they would have wanted you to be safe. And look at what you've achieved. You've completed what you mother began. I'm sure she would be very proud.'

Dolores's eyes drifted above my head. She looked down at me, and nodded.

I suggested Dolores go outside and load her bike into my car while Boris and I attended to other business.

Because of the blood, there was no point moving the corpse to the other end of the lift, better to place it facing upwards beneath the front of the Land Rover.

It took a little time to position it correctly, rolling Gigi back and forth upon the trolley he used for working beneath cars before we thought we had got it right. We would only have one chance, after all.

We lowered the lift as much as we dared.

I reached into the car and gently released the handbrake. We eased the Land Rover towards the edge of the lift, before giving it a hefty shove.

It toppled across Gigi's head and shoulders in a thud of old metal, a cloud of dry mud.

We stepped back, waving the dust away. As the old Land Rover yawned and rattled on top of Uncle Gigi, I had to admit, we hadn't done a bad job.

'There may be some debate as to what actually killed him,' I said. 'Trauma, shock, heart attack . . .'

'But not some pissed off PI with a baton,' said Boris.

I glanced at the workbench. 'We'll have to make sure to remember to take everything.' I passed him the Glock. 'Put this back in his drawer. Just so we're clear what you'll tell the police – you were able to pick the padlock . . .'

'With the pick you're going to give me that I had conveniently secreted upon my person.'

'And they had left the cell door open . . .'

'Because they're idiots.'

'Which was how you were able to make your escape, only to find Gigi, or Carlo here, pinned beneath the car in what appears to have been a terrible accident.'

'They're not going to believe any of this, you know.'

'And they're not going to care, because they will have discovered a secret mob hideout with thousands of euros in cash and goodness knows what else in those cabinets.'

'True, although they *will* guess someone else was involved. My former colleagues are *not* actually idiots. Well, not all of them.'

'And . . . ?'

'I won't say a thing, because I owe you one.'

'Rather more than one, as you said. And publicly they'll put it all down to great police work, so as far as the mob is concerned . . .'

'The cops discovered me themselves, thanks to their outstanding investigative work. I don't think they'll need much encouragement to feed that to the press.' He squeezed my elbow. 'Have I said "thanks"?'

'You haven't, but you're welcome.'

Boris looked around. 'Don't worry about any of this, Dan. You're not the only one with friends in high places.'

When I arrived back at the car, I found Dolores sat in the driver's seat staring straight ahead.

'It's done?'

'It's done.'

'What now?'

'We'd better call Niki Molinari and warn him.' I looked at her expectantly.

'What?'

'Didn't he give you his number?'

She sighed. 'If you want *me* to call him, then you'd better give me back my phone.'

Chapter 20

'I thought you were a bit keen.' Niki Molinari smiled like the cat who'd got the cream.

We were sat around a fancy metal table in the garden at the rear of his *palazzo*, although by garden I mean a hectare of sculpted parkland with its own copse, grotto, and water feature, green with lily pads. These old *palazzi* were not only built with security in mind but, providing you were rich enough, the facilities to sit out a siege in relative comfort. Lockdown can't have been much of a trial at Palazzo dei Cieci.

'To be honest,' Dolores said breezily, 'I didn't expect to ever see you again.' This wiped the smile off his face. 'Nothing personal. I mean, the sex was all right, but you're not really my type.'

Niki raised his eyebrows along with the corners of his mouth. 'Well,' he said, 'as long as the sex was all right. I am here to serve.'

'Oh, you could definitely do more of that, like all men. If you really want service, you're better off with a woman.'

Niki and I both shifted uncomfortably. 'Anyway,' I said. 'Now we've got that out of the way, you've got a big problem.'

'Is that why you told me not to leave the house?'

'Right. And frankly, I'm surprised they haven't already tried to get to you.'

'Who do you mean?' He waggled his head, but those flaring nostrils gave him away.

'Your mob friends you owe the cash to. They're coming to punish you, apparently.'

His smiled like a kid caught red-handed at the pantry door.

'This place is practically Fort Knox,' he replied nonchalantly. 'Two gates, CCTV and a *portiere.*'

'But you can't stay here forever,' I said. 'I admire your cool, but in your place, I'd be a little more concerned.'

'I won a Grand Prix, man. They can't take that away from me.' Despite the smile, his voice broke: 'They can *never* take that away from me.'

'You were supposed to lose, of course.'

He slammed a fist on the table.

'I damn well wasn't meant to win!'

'Tell me,' I said. 'How it works, exactly.'

He glanced at Dolores, but had apparently already written her off as a future prospect.

'Bets on the position, that sort of thing. I can usually deliver. I mean – I'm a *damn good driver.*'

'And if you can't make the required position?'

He gazed after an emerald-blue dragonfly dancing across the surface of the lilypond. 'Let's say I'm a little more accident prone than the others. And it depends who I happen to clip on my way into the barriers . . .' He shook his head. 'Look, it's nothing new – they were fixing races all the way back to Tripoli in the thirties.'

'That doesn't make it okay.'

'I get that,' he said flatly.

'So what happened this time? What made you change course, so to speak?'

Niki shrugged. 'Fabri, maybe? Your snooping brought up a lot of ghosts.' He grinned. 'That day, it was like he was with me in the cockpit, I couldn't let him down. And it was our home turf – I could *smell* the rain, I *knew* how to win.'

'But it meant shafting the mob.'

He sighed, then gave me a shrewd look. 'You know what? They can suck it up. You say they're going to punish me? Oh yeah? How? Beat me up? I can take a beating. Break my hands? My legs? That would be like shooting your cash cow. I've got another race in a fornight. Nah.' He shook his head. 'Fuck 'em.'

'They're going to react, however,' I said. 'And these are serious people we're talking about. You don't want to mess with them.'

'What would hurt you?' asked Dolores.

'Apart from your brush-off, you mean?'

'A good question,' I said. 'Who are you close to?' I glanced at Dolores. 'Girlfriend? Ex-girlfriend?'

'I've plenty,' he said. 'Of both. Obviously, I wouldn't want to see anyone harmed, but—'

'Family?'

'Dad? The bastard didn't even hang around to congratulate me, and they're hardly going to touch the head of Molinari.'

'How about your sister?' I asked.

'Sis? She . . .' He lurched forward. 'But they wouldn't do anything to harm the boy, would they? Fabri's kid?'

Chapter 21

'You know where she lives, then?' Niki asked from the back.

'It's also Jeremy's place, right? The guy you and Agnese fingered for Fabrizio's death?' I steered us through the city traffic. 'It might have been helpful if you had happened to mention the involvement of the mob.'

'That had nothing to do with it,' said Niki. 'Fabrizio didn't gamble. Fucking was his problem. In particular, fucking my sister.'

'And you don't think your friends might have used that for leverage?'

'I wouldn't have said it was their style, and he would never have thrown a race, not Fabri. Especially not for a woman.'

'Not even for your sister?'

'*Especially* not for my sister. Fabri would have lived the rest of his life as a monk if it would have meant a millisecond's advantage. Which reminds me – did you get anything out of those files I gave you?'

I thought of the photos of Fabrizio and Agnese. Boris's job for Jeremy. 'We're still looking into it,' I said.

We drove through neat San Lazzaro, out, alongside the

vineyard. The gate to the property was open, the silver Vernice in the driveway.

Agnese came running down the steps as we pulled up. Before we had even gotten out of the car, she had her hands on the bonnet, that beautiful face like the mask in a Greek tragedy.

She grabbed Niki by the collar as soon as he was out.

'He's gone!' She held him so hard I thought she might throttle him. 'Gone!'

'What happened?'

'As soon as you called, I went looking for Michele. I thought he was in his room, but he wasn't. So I went around the house, then outside. The girls were with the alpacas. I asked them if they had seen Michele, and they said yes, some men had come down the driveway. They said they worked for Jeremy and had been asked to take Michele to see him at work and he had gone with them. Of course, I called Jeremy straight away . . .' She began to sob.

'Where did it happen?' By now the two little girls had materialised and were in tears around their mother's skirt.

I crouched beside them. 'What kind of car were the men in?'

'A big white one.'

'And where did it stop?' She pointed near the beginning of the driveway.

I ran over. I could clearly see tyre marks in the gravel. On the grass nearby was an envelope, an alpaca grazing precariously close. It looked on incuriously as I retrieved it.

The envelope was addressed in blue ballpoint capitals to: NIKI. I wasn't going to wait on ceremony. Following the family inside, I opened it.

NO POLICE. BEHAVE AND HE WILL BE
RETURNED AT END OF SEASON.

The family was stood in a spacious modern kitchen. Kids
wailing, mother raving at Niki. I forced the note into Niki's
hand.

I looked on as he read it, frankly lost for words.

What a mess.

The sound of a car skidding to a halt. Jeremy rushing
into the kitchen, wild-faced. Shouting in English to his wife:
'Where is he? Where is he?'

'Gone! He's gone!'

He turned to me. 'What happened?'

'He's been kidnapped.'

'What? Why? How?'

'Niki can tell you more. He's got the note.'

'Note?' Now he was on Niki. 'What happened? What
note?' Niki passed him the paper. *'What the fuck?'* Jeremy
roared. 'What does that even mean?' Niki explained.

The girls were now clinging to Jeremy's jacket. I signalled
to Dolores. We stepped out of the kitchen.

'Can I leave you here?'

'You're kidding.'

'It would be good to have someone on the spot.'

'And you?'

'I'll be in touch.'

Chapter 22

The phone was picked up after three rings.

'I didn't expect to hear from you so soon,' said Boris.

'You're certainly sounding better. What's the status?'

'The "status" is I'm sat in the Questura first aid centre while they work out what to do with me.'

'And you've told them . . .'

'What we discussed.'

'And they've responded . . .'

'As I predicted.'

'So, it's fair to say the site is now crawling with cops.'

'I imagine so. What is it, Dan?'

'A hunch.'

'About?'

'If they were going to snatch someone, they would probably take them to where you were held, right?'

'It had . . . the amenities, if that's what you mean. Although it might have got a little crowded.'

Unlikely, I thought. You'd be rolling around in a car trunk by now with that bullet rattling around your skull. 'So they would need somewhere else to go in a hurry.'

'I guess. Now what's this about? Have they snatched Niki?'

'What would you say if I was able to point you in their direction?'

'I would say "thank you". I'm sure my former colleagues would be very grateful.'

'Grateful enough to keep our names out of it?'

'I'm sure it wouldn't be a problem.'

'Then keep an eye on your phone,' I said. 'They might need to act fast.'

'Are you going to give me a clue?'

'Like I said, for now it's just a hunch.'

The car sat nav informed me it was pretty much a straight run – just fourteen minutes through the flat countryside.

I was pulling onto the main road when my rear-view was darkened by the bulk of Jeremy's SUV. Its headlights flashed like stun grenades. I guessed he wasn't asking me to make way.

I pulled up. As I got out, he was already stood there, as stony faced as a soldier at a checkpoint.

'What are you doing?'

'Following up a hunch.'

'About what?'

'Where they might have taken him.'

'And where would that be?'

'Your father-in-law's.'

The mask cracked. He spluttered: *'What?'*

'Like I said – just a hunch. If I was you, I would go back and comfort your wife. Let me deal with this.'

'And why *the fuck* would you think Max is involved?'

'I think he was in contact with one of the people who took Michele.'

'What? When?'

'At Imola. The Grand Prix.'

Jeremy turned his back on me and raised hands to hips as if he was confronting the old man there and then. He twisted to face me: 'Hang on. How do you even know what Michele's kidnapper looks like? You weren't there when it happened.'

I needed to think about this. 'I was on his trail. That's why we were at your place, why we warned your wife, but we arrived too late.'

I watched Jeremy process this information as efficiently as he might the implications of a burst tyre on race day. 'All right,' he said. 'And now you think they've taken him to Max's. But why there? Surely, they've got somewhere better?'

'That's been closed to them. I'm guessing this could be a fallback before they sort something else out.'

'So we need to get there ASAP,' he said.

'I do,' I said. 'I'll let you know as soon as I get there and we—'

'Bugger that.' He ran back to his car.

The fourteen minutes to Palazzo Molinari-Pepoli seemed way too few with Jeremy Frost's SUV glued to my rear like the worst kind of boy racer, and my options running down with every kilometre. I was no stranger to risk, but I liked to be its arbiter. Jeremy felt like one wild card too many.

I slowed right down as I rumbled along the track beside the canal leading to the *palazzo*. I flashed my lights to give

Jeremy a warning, and we stopped about twenty metres from the entrance.

We made our way to the gates, crouching by a gap between the fence and a tree.

'They've got pretty good security,' he said. 'Most of it CCTV affixed to the main house, but it depends if anyone is monitoring it.'

'Possibly more likely now than ever,' I said. 'And look.' There was a white SUV parked beside a pair of Molinaris. 'That's them.'

'You're sure?'

'I am.' I pulled out my phone.

'What are you doing?'

'Giving the address to the police.'

'Wait, they said "no police".'

'Don't they always?'

'Please.' His hand covered my phone.

'Isn't that what you would want, Jeremy? We've caught them, and we haven't got long.'

Jeremy Frost shook his head. 'If the police get involved, what happens? Possibly a standoff. Negotiations. Even a firefight. Michele could get hurt.'

'They're the experts.'

'Expertise is sometimes over-rated,' he observed. 'You can train people to the limit, but in the end, they're still human, and make human errors.'

'Then what do you propose?'

'Paying them.' I looked into his credulous eyes, remembered the guy was completely out of the loop.

'It's got nothing to do with that. I mean, why do you think

Max Molinari—'

'Whatever.' He didn't have time for details. 'Give them whatever the hell it is they want. Trade Michele for myself, if need be.' He stood up and began marching back to his car.

'Jeremy,' I called. 'It's not so simple!'

He opened the car door and began to climb in. 'They don't know that I know. I'll just be dropping in on the family. And that's what it's all about here, isn't it?' he added bitterly. 'Family?'

Jeremy steered his car up the bank and around mine, stopping at the gate. He leaned out of the window and tapped in a security code. The doors opened and his car rumbled down the track towards the *palazzo*, a black cloak of crows rising behind him.

Damn it.

Before the gates shut fully, I nipped through. They clunked closed behind me.

I considered the *palazzo*, looming ahead like a fortress behind those trees, then moved away from the road and strode diagonally across the field towards the fence, keeping an eye on Jeremy parking beside the white SUV. He headed around the main building, presumably making a beeline to the Molinari home.

He was a confident bastard, sure enough, but no amount of swagger was going to swing this one. I looked at my message again.

I pressed send.

Chapter 23

I had made my way warily along the side of the field to where the cars were parked, picking my way through the cypress so I had a view of both the main building and the one at the rear where the Molinari lived. Set amid curated gardens, the scene appeared as tranquil as ever. The flowerbeds were blooming, insects buzzing. But somewhere in one of these buildings was Michele, and between him and me and Jeremy, a pair of rather tasty *mafiosi*.

I dashed across an exposed stretch of grass and crouched behind a statue – a blank-eyed Diana. I had a clear view of the rear house now.

I guessed the key meeting points would be either in the dining room at the rear of the Molinari home, or the *soggiorno*, which greeted you as you entered from the front.

They could have stashed the kid almost anywhere in the main building, but my bet was they would want to keep him close to the family for the time being. This was their fallback plan – the mobsters hadn't got things straight themselves yet, so they would want to talk it through with Max.

I wasn't sure what Jeremy's idea was, but he was no fool.

I doubted he was about to go blundering in. My guess was he intended to act innocent, scout it out. And if that didn't work, try and strike a deal. But he had got the wrong end of the stick – this wasn't the kind of deal you could strike. When you were playing the mob's game, they set the rules. And Niki had broken them.

Yet there still had to be a certain fluidity: pieces were in movement, and with movement came possibility. It was growing warmer every day. In England it might be summer, in Italy it was just warming up, and along with the villa's shutters, the side windows were open to usher in the scent of bluebells, roses and crocuses.

This part of the house was elevated like the front, but there were a couple of metal garden chairs in the shade of the building. I carried one over, and stood on its back to pull myself into a room.

An office, it seemed. Certainly, there was the glass-topped table with a computer and swivel chair, which I pushed aside as I clambered in. But it was more than that – if I had been struck by the absence of memorabilia when I first visited the house, here it all was.

The desk faced a floor-to-ceiling trophy cabinet filled with gold and silver. At its centre dozens of medals hung from their ribbons, in front – a large silver-framed colour photograph of Max Molinari shaking hands with Niki Lauda in front of an early Molinari F1 automobile.

The other walls were filled with colour and black-and-white photos memorialising Molinari super- and racing cars, victorious drivers, and Max himself together with local and international celebrities. Upon a shelf running above the door and continuing along the wall that ran behind his desk were lined drivers' helmets, their gleaming visors down.

The door was closed but as I pressed my ear to it, I could hear the murmur of conversation. Jeremy talking loudly. Too loudly, perhaps. I could just make out a response from another man, presumably Max. I doubted the mobsters, if they were present, spoke English.

I opened the door a crack.

'I couldn't bloody believe it,' Jeremy was saying. 'He certainly made me look a fool. What do you think of his chances at Brands Hatch?' I heard Max Molinari's non-committal mumble. 'You know I've been Niki's loudest critic,' Jeremy ploughed on, 'but hands up, I've got to admit I may have got it wrong . . .'

I heard someone coming along the corridor and stepped back from the door. By her perfume I knew her – Aurora Molinari, Max's wife.

Another mumble, and Max was following her down the corridor towards the dining room.

So that was how it was – they had Jeremy at the front and the gangsters in the rear. Only, their Neapolitan friends would surely be growing restless.

Then I heard someone else in the corridor – Jeremy, hesitant, hyper-alert.

I swung the door open and he jolted back against a table. A flower-filled Chinese vase rocked menacingly. He grabbed hold of it with both hands.

'Keep them occupied,' I whispered, indicating I would check upstairs. Jeremy nodded.

'I was thinking, Max,' I heard him boom as he clomped

down the corridor, 'we really should celebrate your boy. Do you have any Prosecco in the fridge? Oh, hello! I didn't realise you had guests . . .'

I left the room and climbed the stone staircase. Confronted by a pair of corridors on either side of the landing, I figured the rear of the house would be a slightly better bet.

I trod softly upon the parquet. The first door was slightly ajar. I pushed it further – a blue-tiled bathroom.

The door opposite was closed – I pressed my ear against it. Nothing. It was a gamble, of course it was, but I gently eased the handle down.

A guest bedroom, I presumed. Bed made. Shutters closed but windows open. It was gloomy and cool and there was no sign of Michele.

A communicating door by an old wardrobe. I paused again. My ear against the wood created its own hushed chamber.

I tried the handle but it was locked.

Checking the corridor again, I made for the room. There was no point hesitating now – I opened the door.

Nothing – another guest bedroom, twice the size as the first with an ensuite bathroom.

It was the same story across the corridor. Room upon empty room. I could see why they hadn't bothered completing the main building – there was more than enough space here.

I had begun to cross the landing at the top of the stairs when I heard steps below.

I plunged into the first room along.

And found myself face-to-face with Aurora Molinari.

Chapter 24

Max's wife spun around to face me. Sat at the dressing table, her puffed features betrayed plastic shock, but her eyes seemed truthful, and these were full of tears.

She didn't look like she was going to scream, but I raised a finger to my lips.

'He's not here,' she hissed, gripping the table. 'He's downstairs.'

I opened the door a fraction. It could be true: the footsteps hadn't ascended.

I looked back into those eyes.

'Go,' she hissed. *'Get him out of here.'*

I hesitated, then opened the door all the way. I stepped back onto the landing and glanced along the unchecked corridor.

'Go,' I heard behind me.

I began my descent.

The singing was not like anything Italian I had heard, more like some Middle Eastern lament, the woman's ululating voice slinking up the stairwell to coil around me. Beautiful, sad, seductive. I could not make out a word she was saying, but might easily have stood entranced in the gloom if urgency hadn't pressed me on.

I opened the basement door.

The song echoed around the darkened garage.

'*E nonna nonna nonna nunnarella . . .*'

Floating over the smooth, flat shapes of the parked cars.

'*O lupo s'ha magnata'a pecurella . . .*'

Suspended around me even as new notes followed.

'*E pecurella mia comme faciste . . .*'

Flickering with the candle light in that far corner.

'*Quanne mmocc'a lu lupo te vediste?*'

Throwing shadows of sheep and wolves against the wall.

The old housekeeper, Maria-Rosa, was dressed in her habitual black with her grey hair tied tightly back. She was sat upon a cane chair among those Nazi murals, doing her knitting, while behind her the Lamborghini slouched menacingly in the gloom.

A candle was set upon a small alcove built inside the wall, its quivering flame seeming to give the soldiers life, as if they really were marching back to the front. Upon a cot beside her, Michele lay asleep, his thumb in his mouth. His duvet was patterned with vintage automobiles.

Without looking up, Maria-Rosa said: 'I used to take Niki here every birthday, and when he had done particularly well at school. It was his treat to sleep among "his soldiers" as he called them. Even during the winter! He didn't seem to care, although I don't mind telling you, I did. During the summer we even used to host sleepovers with his cousins, until one of the spoiled brats made a scene about them being

Germans or some such and that was the end of that. They're just paintings, just soldiers. They kill. They die. They're the lucky ones: too young to know the pain of living.

'*e pecurella mia comme farraie . . .*' She slipped effortlessly from words to song. '*Quanne mmocc'a lu lupo te vedarraie?*

I said: 'And now Michele is down here. He must be very tired to be sleeping this time of the day.'

'Oh, you know kids – they're running around one moment, dead beat the next.'

A sound from above. I froze, waiting to hear steps descending, but nothing. Only the click-clack of the woman's needles, her gentle, mesmerising hum.

'Well, I'm afraid they've now decided to move him upstairs,' I said. 'His *nonna* wants him to enjoy the lovely spring air.'

The woman finally looked up. Even at her advanced age, she could have modelled – her crinkled olive skin clung to high cheekbones and a refined nose that had assuredly never been touched by a surgeon's knife. Her black eyes shone. She might never have been young – it was as if she had come out this way, fully-formed.

'She said that, did she? Well, she might have mentioned it before I brought my knitting down.'

She began to place her things into a string bag while I stepped around her.

'In the meantime,' I said. 'She also asked you to pack up. She really doesn't want him down here, she says it's too unhealthy.'

'What does she know?' The old woman muttered. 'She never looked after the children. She was always more interested in the next party.'

I crouched beside Michele. My plan, such as it was, was to take the boy back upstairs then sneak out the front door. After that, we would make a dash for the car. Hopefully the old dear would take her time so no one would realise until we were gone.

I placed my hand on the boy's arm.

'Michele,' I said. He didn't rouse. I shook him gently. 'Come on, time to get up.' Nothing. I gave him a further shake then glimpsed a box of pharmaceuticals in the shadows by the bed.

So that was how it was.

It happened as I began to reach beneath him – pain jolting between my shoulder blades, jerking me upright as sure as a puppet on a string.

There again, in the kidneys.

I swivelled to face the source of the attack – the old woman's coal-black eyes bore into me as she thrust the scissors under my ribs.

I lashed out, catching her on the chin, and she spun backwards.

The handle of the scissors was slippery with my blood. My first instinct was to pull, but she was coming at me again, screeching. I threw another punch but she ducked under my arm.

We were face to face and I felt her claw at the metal inside me.

I'll never forget that flash of false teeth, her garlic breath as she managed to close her fingers around the handle, spitting some Neapolitan curse.

I brought my forehead cracking down on hers.

She dropped like a bag of bones.

Chapter 25

I was leaking, I was cramping, but decided not to pull the blade for fear of turning a stream into a flood.

I yanked back the duvet and launched the boy, still fully clothed, over my shoulder.

'*Zia?*'

Auntie. It wasn't Michele, it was a young man's voice from the stairwell. That beautiful thug, I was sure.

'Everything okay?'

There was yelling, shouting from above. Smashed crockery, glass. The scrape of furniture. The thud of a fight. Jeremy, buying time. But there was no way I would make it up the stairs now.

Shambling and grunting with the weight of the boy and the spike in my guts, I lumbered between the cars towards the far end of the basement.

A pistol crack above. Another.

I made it to the shutters, slammed my palm against the green button set into a concrete column.

The shutters grumbled to life. Sunlight seeped across the garage. But I didn't make for the outside. It was as much as I could do to heft the kid back between the ranks of low-slung sports cars.

Footsteps were coming down the stairs. I crouched beside an old bronze Jaguar.

'*Zia?*' The door slammed open, a string of curses. 'Auntie! What has he done to you?'

A cough, a Campanian curse: 'Just get him.'

'Son-of-a-bitch!'

I could hear the kid weaving between the cars towards the rising shutters. Watched him duck down and step onto the lawn. Beautiful, stupid thug. I pulled Michele further behind the Jaguar, and watched the mobster, clutching the pistol in his hand as if it was a toy, run first one way across the grass, then another.

This time he didn't come back.

I felt the adrenaline begin to drain away, the pain in my guts come on as if the old bird was twisting the blade. I felt tentatively around the wound. My shirt was heavy with blood, a syrupy puddle expanding around my knees. If I didn't get help soon, it would be over. I pulled out my phone. There was a reply from Boris.

THEY'RE COMING

But when? My blood-slippery fingers found the emergency number.

Discretion was no longer required. I called 112.

I was stabbed, I whispered. Bleeding badly. There were people with guns. Come. Please. Come quickly.

'We're coming, signor. Hold on.'

I scrolled to Rose's number. My thumb wavered between calling and writing. In the end I wrote:

You are everything to me and I have always wanted the best for you. You make me proud every day. There is nothing you have ever done that has made me love you less, and there is nothing you will ever do. Just being you is all I could hope for. You made my life complete.

My thumb wavered over 'send'.

The kid reappeared outside, marching furiously up and down, ranting – *son-of-a-bitch, I'll fuck you up. I'll fuck you up, you piece of shit...*

He stopped, spun to face the big house. With his back to me, he ran inside.

It was now or never – I emerged from behind the Jaguar but couldn't make it to my feet. Instead, I began to crawl towards the shutters, my blood drizzling onto the smooth concrete. I paused to gather my shirt around the root of the blade to stem the bleeding, but it was like squeezing a bloody sponge. I was wasting time. I shuffled forward.

I made it to the column. Crying out, I reached up to the red button.

Managed to press it on the second try. The shutter doors shuddered back to life and began to close.

I crumpled back against the grille of a silver Porsche, my legs splayed out in front of me. I knew I should try to crawl behind the vehicle for cover, but I'd had it.

I watched the kid re-emerge, march across the grass in my direction. I waited for him to spot me.

Instead, he gazed upwards, began to circle distractedly.

He raised his pistol and opened fire.

A rushing sound like a gust of wind. Was it inside my head or out? The pain had begun to loosen its grip, dissolve into a sugary-doze. The opposite of adrenaline. I was no fool, I knew what that meant, and struggled to keep my eyes open.

The kid had stopped shooting in the air. His gun had jammed and he was fiddling with the slide when he finally registered those leisurely-closing shutters, and me.

He cleared the breach, lifted the pistol. Strode towards me, barrel flashing.

A thump like a stone upon the shutter. The ring of another shot ricocheting off polished chrome.

A trio of eruptions, whining and shattering and smashing in a shower of glass and cement dust.

Darkness descending, and the kid too: on his knees, his front. A boot on his back, a gun barrel against his head, as the doors finally shuddered closed.

Chapter 26

The garage lights were on. A pair of cops in dark-blue fire-repellent uniforms and black balaclavas, clattering with body armour and with carbines strapped across their backs, had me on my back and were tearing my shirt away as others swarmed, yelling instructions.

A hiss as some powder-like substance was dumped on my wounds. I looked sideways to see Michele being carried away.

'Jeremy,' I said. 'Has anyone seen Jeremy?'

'Calm yourself,' said one of the cops. 'Stay calm.'

'An Englishman,' I said. 'He's the father.'

'Calm yourself.'

The shutters rising. Blood-red uniforms – an ambulance crew.

Further treatment on the spot, then a mix of police and medics lifting me onto a stretcher, carrying me out the front, around the big house and back up the path to the parking. Those crows circling like vultures. Don't leave me alone, I thought. Don't let them near me.

An armoured truck had blocked in the ambulance and they couldn't get me inside. I was set back down while a cop went running back to the house to look for whoever had the keys.

I watched as others were carried out. The first in a hurry, his face covered with a mask, a drip held in place by a medic as they ran towards the helicopter.

Jeremy.

Another at a calmer pace. The shape beneath the red blanket did not reach either end of the stretcher. Unmoving, its face covered. I thought first of the other mobster and tried to remember how large he had been.

Like most Italians, he had not been a big man, but he had been broad enough – an enforcer type with a low centre of gravity, but not slight enough to match that silhouette.

Not Max Molinari, either.

His wife? Could Aurora have thrust herself into the fray? I had heard two gunshots upstairs. Might knives also have been used?

They laid the stretcher down nearby.

It couldn't be Michele? Overdosed on the sleeping medicine they'd given him? Struck by a ricochet?

'Don't worry, Daniel,' said the ambulance woman. 'See – the cretin in the van is coming now.'

The helicopter rose in a cloud of lettuce leaves and crows. Dust billowed around us and the medic tried to shield me. But as the blanket blew away from the stretcher, I saw who was under there: Maria-Rosa, the old woman, a neat bullet hole where an eye had been, leaving the darkest, blackest pit.

Chapter 27

This being Italy, the hospital authorities thought they would be doing us a favour by placing me in the same room as my father-in-law, although I can't say I received the warmest of welcomes.

'What the hell happened to you?'

'I was attacked by an old woman.'

'It looks like it.' The orderlies helped me out of the wheelchair and onto the bed. I sat upright, facing him, as they fixed my drip to the frame. They propped up some pillows, I lifted my legs, and laid carefully down.

'Well,' I winced. 'At least you appear to be on the mend.' He harrumphed. 'I hope you weren't too disappointed to wake up on planet earth.'

'By the looks of you,' said the Comandante. 'It's fortunate I'm not bidding this world *adieu* just yet. Now are you going to tell me what's been going on?'

'And yet,' said Giovanni when I had finished. 'We appear to be no closer to resolving the commission that led you to this pretty pass.'

'You mean whether Fabrizio Chiesa was murdered? Despite the evidence that Jeremy knew about the affair, I've got nothing to suggest he had anything to do with his death. The evident love he has for Michele seems to scotch the suggestion that he wanted to send the boy away out of spite.

'And although it does appear that both Fabrizio and his father had begun to suspect something was going on with the races, I couldn't find anything that specifically pointed to him being murdered because of it . . .'

There was chat outside our room and a doctor sauntered in.

'Ah,' said Giovanni as the man picked up his chart. 'Doctor Chiesa, you remember my son-in-law, Daniel.'

The doctor glanced at the empty chair beside the Comandante's bed before he realised he meant the person lying in the bed beside him. The surprise was as much mine as his – the athletic medic I had noticed on my previous visit was indeed the tumescent table thumper I had met in Osteria Grande.

'It seems Faidate Investigations will soon be out of your hair,' continued the Comandante.

'That shouldn't be a problem.' He jovially smoothed his shaven head. 'But I hope you've left a little cash in the pot. As I was saying, not for me so much as sis. Those kids eat up money.'

'Even better than that,' said the Comandante. 'Daniel has informed me he has discovered your father's stolen blueprints – your family should be able to successfully lay claim to the invention currently patented to signor Molinari and be in line for a significant sum.'

The doctor shook his head in wonder. 'Then the old man will get his due after all.' He gazed upwards. 'It's just a shame he's not here to appreciate it.'

'The Lord moves in mysterious ways, Dottore Chiesa,' said the Comandante with the certainty of one who had had the occasion of recent acquaintance.

As soon as Chiesa left the room, the Comandante leaned across to me. 'Remind me again, Daniel, precisely what you found among young Fabrizio's belongings.'

Those hospital days came to feel like an epilogue. Jeremy had been brought in in an even worse condition than me – shot in the chest, the bullet had clipped a lung. Following a spell in ICU he had been placed in a room on his own.

Once I had got back on my feet, I set off in slippered feet, steering the drip carefully beside me, along the corridor to see him, but the police guard stationed outside informed me he wasn't accepting any visitors except his wife and family.

While I sat in the communal area regaining my strength, I noticed a familiar figure saunter past with a bunch of flowers. He came back empty handed a couple of minutes later.

'I thought you said you weren't a flowers kind of guy.'

Niki Molinari grinned. 'They were from the team.' He flopped down opposite me and stretched out. 'He still won't see me.'

'Can you blame him?'

'*I am* family, after all.'

'You think he really sees it that way?'

Niki fixed me with those ice-blue eyes. 'You English are funny.'

'I'd be pretty sore if my child was kidnapped as insurance against my uncle's gambling debts and I almost got killed in the process.'

'I owe him an apology,' he said solemnly.

'Has your father apologised to you?'

'Dad's stepped down,' he said with a remarkably straight face. 'As far as the police are concerned, it was just a kidnap attempt. Or at least until someone pointed out his stash of stolen cars in the garage.'

'Not me.'

'My bet is it was someone with a grievance. Someone he'd used his whole life to get what he wanted. Someone he knew was weak and could be manipulated by his "investors" to do what they needed.'

'He was the "northern connection".'

'What's that?'

'Someone who should be in gaol.'

Niki frowned. 'When did you last hear of a rich guy doing gaol time? In any case, he's no stranger to incarceration. You met Maria-Rosa, I believe.'

'A kind of golden cage.'

'Protecting their investment.'

'Then I guess you and your sister were not so different from Michele in that regard – hostages, so to speak. But you didn't realise what was going on?'

'Why would I? Maria-Rosa and her granddaughter were just "family retainers" as far as we were aware. It's not as if we were the only wealthy family with staff from down south. No – I managed to fuck up all by myself, or so I thought.'

'So what now? Will you continue to do their bidding?'

'Molinari is withdrawing from this year's Grands Prix following the trauma of recent events,' he recited as if he were reading a press release, 'and suspending its Formula One team indefinitely.

'Jeremy Frost is leaving and being touted to take over at McLaren when he has recovered from his injuries. He wants to return to the UK so he can be close to Michele's new school. Following the departure of Max Molinari, Molinari also have a new CEO.' He grinned.

'Congratulations.'

'I've got my trophy.'

'But what about Fabrizio? Do you think they tried to manipulate him? To get him to throw a race?'

'You know, I asked Dad the same question. He insisted no. He said that on the contrary, Fabri was special. My father managed to convince his friends from the south that Fabri would actually *win* championships. That way Molinari, and therefore they, could make even more money. In fact, it's probably to Fabri I owe my own career.'

'How so?'

And now I saw Niki's grin for what it had always truly been – a barely disguised grimace.

'I would be the sacrificial lamb.'

Chapter 28

I was discharged from hospital earlier than the Comandante but was still not in any shape to pick him up when his time came.

Rose sighed. 'God, this is *so much* easier.'

'Eyes. Road.'

'Did you know it's also got an automatic collision warning?'

'I can see why you think that might come in useful.'

She glanced at me.

'*Eyes . . .*'

'You're so funny.'

'It only hurts when I laugh.'

'Well,' she said dryly. 'You certainly have me in stitches.'

'*Brava.*'

Rose smiled. 'I admit, I've been waiting for that one.'

The car park at Maggiore was packed as usual, but I was impressed with the way she navigated the Alfa to find a space.

Rose instructed me to get out first, angling the car to block others from nipping in while she exited the driver's side to help me out. She slotted the SUV in in three goes.

'Impressive,' I said.

'Despite its size, it's so much more manoeuvrable.'

'You get what you pay for.'

'Are you really not going to spend €600 to get it fixed?' She meant the Punto.

'It's what I paid for it.'

'Look, I can contribute . . .'

'We'll see.' I was actually planning to buy something better, and safer, but I was in no hurry to tell her. I wanted to avoid being inundated by pictures of cute Fiat 500s and VW Beetles, which I definitely didn't plan to drive around town.

The Comandante was sat waiting outside the hospital as we arrived, a somewhat gangly, curly-headed youth with thick glasses beside him in a white 'doctor's' coat.

Antonio was volunteering as a porter at the hospital when he wasn't studying. I had to hand it to the lad – he was certainly showing commitment.

He helped Giovanni to his feet, and together the four of us moved slowly towards the car. As he helped the Comandante into the back seat, he said: 'Now remember, *Nonno*, if you need anything . . .'

'I will be sure to call a proper doctor, young man.' The kid's smooth cheeks reddened.

'Welcome to the family,' I said.

'I don't know,' Rose grumbled. 'We really should go straight home, that's what the doctor ordered.'

'Your boyfriend, you mean,' I said.

'The real ones. I'm sure they wouldn't approve.'

'I've been stuck inside that damn place too long,' said the Comandante from the back. 'I could do with some fresh air.'

After a short spell on the *autostrada*, we turned off and began to cross the hills. Rose steered around the curves with aplomb, giving mountain-bike riders a wide berth. I had almost begun to relax when she began to look wildly around.

'But isn't this . . .'

'That's right. Please keep your eyes on the road.'

As we passed at a snail's pace through Ca' Nês, Rose began to pull in at the spot where Fabrizio had come off the road.

'Keep going,' I said.

'But . . .'

'Just carry on.'

She glanced in the rear-view mirror. 'There's no flowers,' she said.

We descended to a valley of farmland, bathed gold and emerald green in the afternoon light.

'Daniel,' the Comandante said from the rear. With some discomfort, I turned to face him. 'I did wonder whether we should be worried.'

'About what, Giovanni?'

'Our employee and this "northern connection".'

I thought of Dolores, of holding her as she fought to get help; as she beat against the chest of her dead uncle. Would she go after Max Molinari?

'No,' I said. 'I think that's done.'

'She's got it out of her system?'

'In a manner of speaking, I think so, yes.'

The Comandante looked satisfied.

'Is everything all right with Dolores?' asked Rose. 'What? Well, it's not much of a leap – you've only got two employees.'

'More than that,' I said. 'There's Jacopo, Alba . . .'

'But they're *family*.'

I remembered Dolores's playful smile: *'One daughter's enough, eh?'*

'We could have meant Celeste,' I said.

'The only "northern connection" she's interested in,' said Rose tartly, 'is Uncle Jacopo.' She rounded the bend to the little town of Montegrigio wedged between an outcrop of rocky hills.

'We've arrived,' I said.

Chapter 29

Doctor Francesco Chiesa opened the front door looking, as ever these days, like the 'after' in a weight loss advertisement.

'It was good of you to travel all this way,' he said, 'but we would could have come to you.' He looked the Comandante and I up and down. 'Especially in your condition.'

'This signore *is* your doctor, isn't he?' said Rose.

'And as I was just saying,' said the Comandante. 'After being cooped up for so long, it is so nice to breathe some country air.'

'Please.' Francesco ushered us along the hallway. 'We're in the garden.'

The rear of the sister's small terraced house backed onto one of the *calanchi*, its elephant-hide cliff face glooming through a fringe of trees.

The patio was bordered by tulips and roses while jasmine flowed in fronds down the back of the house. The sun would soon descend behind the cliff, but for the time being only the canary yellow swings at the far end where the twins were playing was in its shade. The buzz of insects competed with the chatter of a nearby stream.

We took our seats and Fernanda arrived with coffee and a plate of chocolate-speckled biscuits.

My daughter was quick to pluck one up.

'If you like those,' said Francesco, 'you should have tried one of Fernanda's. She was quite the baker, once. Maybe you should take it up again,' he said to her, 'now the kids are getting bigger.'

His sister shrugged non-committedly.

I opened the report. Reading from the summary, I explained that we had conducted the investigation to our satisfaction, had found no reason to believe Fabrizio Chiesa had been murdered, and were content to allow the notary to consider the case closed.

We included our invoice, to be set against the Chiesa estate, which the siblings agreed was reasonable (in fact, all things considered, it was very reasonable). In turn, they explained that they had already initiated proceedings against Molinari Automobile SpA, and their lawyers were confident of a swift settlement, especially now that Massimiliano Molinari was being prosecuted for having cars stolen to order. The last thing the company needed was further scandal.

From the foot of the garden, the children called for their mother.

'Are we done?' she asked. The Comandante and I exchanged a glance.

'Surely,' he said.

'We can't thank you enough.'

We watched her go.

'The children,' said the Comandante. 'Young Fabrizio never saw his nephews.'

Francesco shook his head. 'Fabri died just under a year before they were born.'

'It was by invitro . . .' said the Comandante.

Now the doctor looked puzzled, 'So I understand.'

Rose looked at me questioningly. 'IVF,' I said quietly.

'A very common phenomenon,' the Comandante remarked. 'One sees many, how should one put it, older mothers with twins.'

The doctor nodded. 'It's true, they were trying for years.'

'And how are you feeling now, Doctor?' I asked.

'Me?'

'I must admit, I didn't recognise you when you first came to see the Comandante in hospital. You didn't look a bit like the first time we met in Osteria Grande. I honestly thought that, for a medical professional, you seemed quite unwell.'

Francesco unconsciously scratched the back of his neck. 'Ah, yes. I would have been puffed up. I'd eaten the wrong thing.'

'An allergic reaction,' said the Comandante.

'That's right. Well, if we're finished, I'd better get going.' He began to rise.

'You signed your father's death certificate,' said the Comandante.

He paused. 'What's that got to do with anything?'

'How did that come about?'

'I . . .' He looked between us. 'Fernanda was . . . tied up, so I said I would keep an eye on the old boy. I admit, I hadn't been in for a few days. When I finally got there, he was dead.'

'A heart attack,' said the Comandante.

'He was an old man. He had a history of heart disease.'

'Thereby avoiding the requirement to go to the coroner.'

'There was no need.'

The Comandante looked at me.

'Your father was severely allergic to sesame, wasn't he?'

Francesco frowned. 'And how would you know that?'

'Friends with access to medical records.'

'That's outrageous!'

The Comandante didn't blink: 'Shortly before his death, the late signor Chiesa was staying with your sister. According to a neighbour, he had been here for a week, but returned home after one of the boys . . .' He looked at me.

'Marco.'

'Marco was rushed to hospital with anaphylactic shock due to some food he had eaten that he had discovered in the garage.'

'You know what kids are like.' I glanced at Rose. 'Scavengers. They eat anything.'

'I'm *seventeen*,' said Rose, 'not seven.'

The doctor blanched. He cast his eyes down the garden at his sister and the children, raising a fist to his mouth as if trying to keep whatever he wanted to say inside.

'*Doctor*,' said the Comandante.

'Fabri's bag,' he said. 'The food was inside. Dad was raving about it afterwards. "The bag! The bag!" From what I could understand, Marco, together with a friend, had been digging around in the garage and come across it. Fabri must have forgotten it when he was working on the bike that evening, and all that time later the kids came across it tucked away somewhere and tried whatever was inside.'

'This bag,' I remembered the one I had come across among Fabrizio's' belongings. 'It was leather? Burgundy?'

He nodded. 'I didn't give it much thought, to be honest. I was more worried about my nephew in the hospital. I didn't put two and two together until . . . Well, a few days later, when I found him. Dad, I mean, in bed clasping Fabri's photo. He had consumed whatever vestiges had remained. It was more than enough, apparently.' He looked at us. 'I decided not to mention it so as not to upset Fernanda. It had been touch and go with Marco.'

'So presumably whatever your father and Marco consumed contained sesame. Does it have the same effect on you?' Francesco waggled his head.

'It prompts an allergic reaction, yes, but the severity skipped a generation – it's as bad with my nephews as it was with Dad. The symptoms are milder for me, as they were with Fabrizio.

'Shortly before we met that first time at the notary,' he continued, 'I had picked up a cake from my usual *pasticceria*, where I knew what was inside, but a new pastry chef had apparently changed the recipe. It hit me within minutes and whack, out with the Epipen.

'Fabrizio would have had a similar reaction, although I believe it usually took a little longer for the symptoms to develop. Within half an hour, or thereabouts. If he didn't get treatment, he would have a Crohn's-like reaction and could be in bed for a couple of days.'

'Your brother had a big race coming up the day before he died,' said the Comandante. 'The Italian Formula Two championship. If he had won, he would have almost certainly gone into the main Molinari team. And he was favourite. There would have been a great deal of money being wagered

on him. Not the same level as in Formula One, but perhaps
hundreds of thousands of euros. And while your brother
appears to have been beyond reproach . . .'

'At least of being corrupted to influence the outcome of
the race,' I said.

'There may have been other ways,' continued the
Comandante, 'to . . . influence him.'

'Regardless of whatever deal Max Molinari thought he
had struck with the mob.' I followed the Comandante's gaze
toward the swings.

Francesco leaned forward. 'Are you suggesting Fernanda
tried to persuade Fabrizio to throw the race?'

The Comandante shook his head. 'Persuade? No. You
mentioned your sister and her husband had tried for a long
time to have children, which apparently included rounds of
IVF. But you said they're not very well off?'

'There's not as much money in lawyering as you might
think,' he said. 'And her husband's a teacher. Each attempt
cost an arm and a leg.'

'She was approaching her forties by then, wasn't she?' I
said. 'Time was running out.'

'But what are you suggesting?'

'We know that your brother visited your sister earlier that
evening,' said the Comandante. 'Perhaps they shared a coffee
. . . and he ate some of her delicious biscuits?'

Rose's eyes widened.

Francesco gazed down at the plate. 'He loved them,' he
said tonelessly. 'I could imagine him scoffing them up and
slipping a couple in his bag for later.'

'Only on the way home,' continued the Comandante,

'perhaps the effect of the hidden ingredient was stronger than expected, or your brother was distracted at the wrong moment. In any case, there was a terrible accident.'

'*Jesus Christ*,' murmured Rose.

Francesco clutched his head with both hands. 'Dad must have realised,' he moaned. 'Found it in the bag and put two and two together . . . I'd thought it was guilt about his grandson but . . .' His voice broke. 'Soon after the boys were born and tests confirmed they reacted the same way, my sister kept repeating how she was being punished. For what? I said, it's just one of those things. But she kept going on about it being all her fault. At the time I thought she just meant the family genes but . . .'

'She poisoned him,' Rose said softly.

'It must have been how she could afford to keep trying,' said Francesco. 'And what tipped Dad over the edge. When he understood, he would never have been able to face her again, maybe not even his grandsons . . .'

'Leaving us to discover the truth,' I said.

'If Signor Chiesa considered the implications of his will at all,' remarked the Comandante. 'Which in his grief, I very much doubt.'

Francesco sat back, devastated.

'I'm sure your sister never meant it to happen,' I said. 'As you pointed out, Fabrizio's symptoms would have been nowhere near as severe, she would have only expected him to be out of action for a couple of days.'

Francesco looked at the Comandante. 'What are you going to do? Will you inform the authorities?'

'The case is closed,' said the Comandante. He pushed the report across the table.

The sun dipped behind the hill, shrouding the remainder of the garden with that lingering winter chill. We watched the children swing back and forth beneath the grey cliff.

'Higher,' they yelled. 'Higher.'

Acknowledgements

As luck would have it, when I began to research *Last Testament*, the Imola circuit was holding an open day, and visitors were free to wander around the paddocks while F1 cars roared along the track and pulled into the pits. This helped me get a proper feel for the atmosphere that one might otherwise only be able to capture from the stands, on television, or among the entourage of a celebrity like 'Mason Kane'. The *autodromo* also has days when the public can walk the track, so for F1 fans, I would recommend checking it out if you plan a pilgrimage to 'Motor Valley'.

Grazie mille to nephews Luigi and Simone Zicchino for accompanying me on my visit to the Ferrari Museum in Maranello (although I don't think it was a massive chore), and author Heleen Kist for providing myself and nephew Massimo the opportunity to visit the Ducati factory which, despite focusing on motorbikes, certainly added to my understanding of that world. Thanks also to Graham Evans for providing an insight into the world of the 'grease monkey'.

I would like to express my gratitude to my fellow authors in the D20 group for their support throughout the year, especially Victoria Dowd, Philippa East, Louise Hare, Charlotte Levin and Trevor Wood, who were kind enough to read my previous novel, *Italian Rules*, at proof stage. I would also like to say a huge thanks to *Death and Croissants* author Ian Moore for taking the trouble to read *Italian Rules*, and Harriet Tyce for her continuing support.

I am immensely grateful for the continued and enthusiastic counsel of Krystyna Green at Constable and my agent Bill Goodall. Thank you to ever-patient Amanda Keats for steering me through the production process, along with copy-editor Colin Murray, proofreader Rebecca Lee, and of course publicist Henry Lord for garnering those all-important reviews.

Finally, my wife Lea, who helps ensure my observations about Italy (as well as my spellings) are on the ball, and is my editor of first resort.

Tom Benjamin
Bologna, July 2023